GOLIATH

Also by Shawn Corridan and Gary Waid

GITMO

GOLIATH

A NOVEL

WITHDRAWN

SHAWN CORRIDAN AND **GARY WAID**

Oceanview Publishing

Longboat Key, Florida

ISBN 978-1-60809-215-4

Published in the United States of America by Oceanview Publishing
Longboat Key, Florida
www.oceanviewpub.com

10 9 8 7 6 5 4 3 2 1

PRINTED IN THE UNITED STATES OF AMERICA

To my lovely wife, Julie,
who continues to inspire me, always and forever.

—Shawn Corridan

To my wife, Patty,
who must have decided long ago to tolerate my idiosyncrasies.

And to my long-dead father, Tom Waid, twenty years
in the Navy, three Bronze Stars for actions in the Pacific.

—Gary Waid

GOLIATH

PART I

CHAPTER 1

THERE IS STILL much to think about. And always I am surprised. After three days at sea, no job could be so grand. I remember the last ship, with drunken Captain Markov and his stinking yellow cat. A pigsty. But this, this is stupendous. I am a child, with the king of the sea under me. I must not forget. At dinner this time I will say, "Yes, Captain, I am Mr. Fyodor Ivanov. This is my honor." And Bennkah, *a ship-to-end-all-ships, will be my home.*

Aside from the teak and the plush leather and the wealth of electronics, the actual design of the bridge deck was not that different from most modern supertankers. At such an early hour, LEDs from an array of equipment formed a muted, sterile ellipse of information in primary colors. The glow reached into the haze and hollowed Third Officer Ivanov's eyes and cheeks, turning him into a caricature of mariners down through history, seafarers doing their watches by the bells, minding the compass, steering the ship.

Yet in front of Ivanov, as might be expected, there was no binnacle-mounted ship's wheel, but a modern leather-wrapped steering wheel the size of a large dinner plate. It was a symbol, nothing more, moving in miniscule corrections, linked to hydraulics that responded to the instructions of the autopilot, a computerized fluxgate compass system that commanded the synchronized rudders to steer the ship. The system was never wrong. *Bennkah's* pilothouse was a cathedral of intricate yet simple design, sending and receiving signals to and from every nook and cranny of the ship and all the relevant points of earth, sea, and sky.

Ivanov, weeks ago when he was called up, had decided this was easy work. The on-duty helmsman of such a tanker as *Bennkah* need not touch the controls except to micro adjust or review data. Everything was automated, even the climate. The air inside was warm and comfortable. He had no thick wool coat, only a blue sailor's pullover and a watch cap that displayed the chevrons of his rank. So his job was to be vigilant, intent on the monitors. His eyes ignored the horizon and the icy slush on the windows in front of him. There was nothing to see outside anyway, except the muted, amber shapes of deck lights and a blue-black darkness beyond. And there was nothing to hear, either. The dull thrumming of giant turbines far below blocked out the whistle of the wind and the sounds of whirring wipers slinging ice into an invisible abyss of cold water and colder sky.

He was about to go off watch. His body was stiff from four hours of tedium, doing almost nothing in the face of such an automated marvel of Russian engineering. As far as he was concerned, there could not have ever been such a fantasy as this bridge. The only touch of reality was a child's toy perched on the dash—a plastic bobble head of President Vladimir Putin. The painted likeness was smiling, nodding almost imperceptibly, head going up and down, back and forth in the near-dark shadows.

Reality for Ivanov, then, was not a spaceship bridge deck, but a smiling Putin, nodding up and down, back and forth.

He watched the toy for a moment. Then he, too, rolled his head up and down, side to side, loosening his neck muscles. He'd smoked too many cigarettes, and his mouth tasted of harsh tobacco and too much coffee. He glanced to his left, where his captain, Mr. Nicholas

Borodin, stood, feet apart, eyes forward, hands clasped behind his back. The captain had emerged from his quarters only a few moments ago. Soon, at eight bells, he would take over. The big ship had been traversing the northwestern edge of the shelf known as the Aleutian Bank. They were approaching a course correction that, two hours from now, would take them well into the American side of the Bering Sea proper and then into the ice. It was early, yet the captain always took command in such situations.

The captain took command of every situation.

The captain is a prick, thought Ivanov, smiling to himself. *And a puzzle. But I will introduce myself at dinner this time. He will like me.*

Third Officer Fyodor Ivanov wasn't alone in his confusions about his captain. Borodin was an enigma—only fifty-six years old, but with a face ravaged by the fatigue of many long seasons at sea. He seemed tired beyond his years. And humorless to a fault. There was no joke telling or sharing a drink with Borodin. The man wore the cloak of command and exuded power and control with every breath. Like his life depended on it.

Maybe it did, thought Ivanov.

Of course, to be selected as captain of such a great ship, newly commissioned in Vladivostok, had to have been quite an honor. Ivanov could not fathom such a job, one that carried with it certain overwhelming responsibilities that would undo most men. He looked away. Just a few more minutes, he thought. Soon he could drag his tired body to bed.

* * *

In the smoky gloom Captain Nicholas Borodin frowned. Deep in thought, he ignored his junior officer. He also ignored the guttural whispers coming from the rear of the bridge in the section known as the Visitors Lounge, a carpeted arena where wealthy oilmen could watch the operations of such a boat and preen and display their plumage. They could crow at their investment prowess. They were part of the giant Russian oil machine.

Only two men occupied the club seats now, and neither one seemed overly qualified to crow except to each other. They weren't oilmen, they were experts—self-described tech men involved more in the workings of the ship than its cargo. Just arrived from the officers' quarters, they had taken coffee from the steward and were already lacing it with strong vodka in a Russian ceremony as old as the frozen tundra. They leaned their elbows on the varnished hardwood table and drank their Bolshevik coffee from white porcelain mugs. One of them, Chief Engineer Vitrov, a small, round, hairless man afflicted with a skin condition that reddened his face and coarsened his features, was trying to explain something to his companion. Vitrov had been assigned as escort and babysitter for the honored guest earlier that week, but it was a formality. They had known each other from their almost two-year association in Vladivostok.

"Look," the chief said, taking a large steel ball bearing from his shirt pocket and placing it on the table. It rolled in a slow circle, then made the Sign of the Cross as the ship moved through the sea with an ever so slight pitch and roll.

"Big ship. Good weather. Yes," he said, grinning.

The other man, younger and full-maned, laughed. He'd been the leader of the design team that had been responsible for creating *Bennkah*. He was a man used to subservience, even if it contained a bit of familiar jocularity. After all, he and the chief were working friends now. He wagged his head in appreciation. "Yes, Mr. Vitrov," he said. "*My* good ship. And *big*." He wore the Western-cut clothes of the Russian superrich.

Captain Borodin heard the exchange but chose to ignore it. He had more important things on his mind. The spitting rain and sleet had kept the seas down, although with such tonnage at his command, middling seas were a joke. His concerns were internal, not external. He scanned his monitors, checking for anomalies that might signal a problem.

Everything is normal. Everything is as it should be. Everything is accounted for.

He closed his eyes for a moment. If he were a God-fearing man, he might have prayed, but instead, he turned to his third officer and relieved him.

The ship's clock rang eight bells.

On the dash the bobble-head Vladimir Putin smiled at the captain. It nodded its painted head.

Back and forth, up and down.

Like the Sign of the Cross.

CHAPTER 2

Two hundred miles east, salvage tug Skeleton, *Dutch Harbor, Alaska*
NOVEMBER 26, 0830 AST

IN NOVEMBER, AND in these latitudes, the cyclical events of daylight and dark were skewed and meaningless. People woke up and traveled to work in the dark. In the late afternoon they went home in the dark. During the day a sun appeared that was often subdued and depressing and lasted for only a few hours. On the docks, the final week of November was a time for the end of things. A time for finishing up the year's work. A time for buttoning up, packing and sealing supplies and equipment in preparation for winter. Many boats were hauled and blocked in yards while others were left afloat to be winterized, engine fluids drained and replaced, hull heaters commissioned and tested. Mountains of fishing gear were carted away to be warehoused and worked on during the months-long cold weather to come. In late November, except for the few hours before and after the meridian, the gloom and the coming of the snow and ice became their life. Soon the season would grip them and would not let go until spring. It was the way things had always been in these latitudes and the way things would remain.

At this late dawn hour, under a phalanx of blue-white halogen lights on the western end of a dilapidated commercial wharf in Dutch Harbor, Alaska, a salvage operation was in progress. The hundred-foot steel salvager *Skeleton*, and its small and tired fifty-five-foot auxiliary, *Bones*, were extracting one of the local fishing trawlers from the rancid mud of the harbor. The early hour was a function of the tide tables more than anything else. A nine o'clock low tide meant an easier lift, which translated into less strain on the equipment.

This trawler was not one of the big crabbers from the *Deadliest Catch*. It had been many years since this fifty-year-old scow had enjoyed such similar care as its TV-star cousins—care that included regular maintenance schedules.

So the bedraggled forty-six-foot boat that had plied the waters of the Aleutians for all of its life was down on her luck, which was why she had succumbed to a lousy thru-hull fitting two nights ago. When the float switch on her bilge pump failed, she had taken only two hours to sink, settling into the silt of the bottom like a fat old hen squatting on her droppings.

A crowd had gathered to watch the operation, limed by *Skeleton's* halogen glare and back-lighted by a low northern sky featuring scudding belts of black clouds surrounding a bisected northeast sun so steeped in haze that a man could look right at the core and not shade his eyes. The water was also black and uninviting, a telltale of the winter to come, not the locale. During much of the year, Dutch Harbor was picture-postcard beautiful. And even now, if one were to look farther east between the dark hills of the near Aleutians, the mainland slopes of Alaska displayed themselves, blue-gray and indistinct except at their mountainous peaks, where early snow reflected the true value of the subarctic sun in all its glory.

On this date, at the end of the wharf, no muted colors or vaulted heights were appreciated. Down in the harbor, nothing at all seemed to be very glorious or clear. In the worn-but-serviceable wheelhouse of *Skeleton*, Captain Sonny Wade ignored the screeching of the hawsers and the rumbling of the pumps. He looked down at his wheel bench to the framed, water-stained photo of his ex-wife, Judy, the girl he'd loved since high school.

He remembered taking the picture as she stood at the bow of *Skeleton*, his new commission. It had been an earlier, happier time, when they both were excited about the project ahead. Back then the world was theirs to conquer together. No more Sonny working in faraway oceans for foreign companies, no more months away from home tending to other people's successes and failures, working his ass off for little reward. Back then, *Skeleton* and Dutch Harbor had been a lifeboat of sorts to Sonny.

And for that brief moment in time, Judy was still the anchor, the most beautiful person in his life. The picture said it all, even with a dab of paint on her chin and her soft bangs shadowing her eyes, smiling her patented, award-winning smile for the camera.

A hell of a woman.

Four years later she was gone, leaving many things unsaid, abandoning her failing, disgraced Sonny like a bad dream. The old photo was before the fall. It didn't show the disappointment, even horror, that later helped to cloud Judy's expression and put years on her face.

I understand, kiddo, he wanted to tell her. *Nobody in their right mind would have stuck around.* He squinted at the faded shot and tried not to blame her. He wondered where she was. Never a letter, never a call or an e-mail.

Not even to Mary.

Mary, their daughter, now fully grown, whip-smart, disdainful of her mother, doting to her dad. Mary, who stood by him as his beacon, hard and fast among the wreckage of Sonny's life. She was like an angel sometimes. Too damn stubborn, though, and forgiving of him. Her generosity was sure to come back and bite her. Yet even if he knew in his heart she was sacrificing her own happiness for him, he couldn't deny himself the indulgence. He was a frigate bird circling for scraps . . . or signaling a sort of elongated doom in the midst of the gale.

Even now, Mary was hard at work doing the float, out in the thick of things in her fatigued, neoprene diver suit and her hard hat, performing the job at hand, barking commands to the men.

Sonny tore his mind back to the present. He scanned his gauges, then examined the drama outside through scarred windows. He had to get his head in the game. Outside, bit by bit, the gray was giving way. He had a crew to lead, five guys who wanted a paycheck.

Sometimes, though, it wasn't easy. And every year got worse and worse.

From outside, Mary's voice rose above the din. She was shouting for another foot of lift.

Get your head on, Sonny told himself. *Do your job.*

Sonny crossed over to his starboard control station and took the reins. The ropes of vein and gristle in his forearms bunched and relaxed as he throttled the secondary hoist engine. With his elbow he hit the transmit toggle and raised his mouth to the intercom. "Manny," he said to his engineer behind the wheel of *Bones*, "gimme some room." Then he ordered Cowboy, his first mate, to unloose the reel dog and cable up. In three seconds the wire came tight. When *Bones* drew back on her spring lines, the sunken trawler began to rise.

CHAPTER 3

EVEN AT THIRTY-THREE meters long and twenty-six feet of beam, *Skeleton* listed a few degrees to port as she began to pull several tons of steel and mud and equipment off the bottom of the bay in Dutch Harbor. The small trawler hadn't responded to float bags or pontoons, so Sonny had ordered their four-inch trash pump out of winter mothballs and put his strongest man, an Eskimo named Stu, onto the controls. In the past, the discharge hose had tended to get away from the smaller guys. Not so with Stu.

Then he ordered an airline hooked up to one of the pneumatic ports. He commissioned another of the crew, Tick, dreadlocked and grinning, to don a mask and breather, take a swim, and work the hose down into the aft hold of the trawler. While Tick was busy underwater, Mary also went down into the boat and plugged the vents and thru-holes. Soon mud began to gush away in huge gouts. Air bubbles from *Skeleton's* compressor roiled the silt and aired up the trawler's compartments from the top down. Within an hour the combination began to work. The boat began to rock itself out of the mud, which shifted things around just enough so that cables could do the rest.

Now Mary stood in two inches of water on the trawler's pouring aft deck. She stood in her neoprene suit among twisted wires and toppled fishing gear, hanging onto the rigging with one hand and bending her knees with every surge of energy, as the salvage engines roared and the cables pinged and the steel groaned. She was a pro, tall and strong like her mother. And damn good-looking. She gave hand signals that told the winch handlers, Cowboy on *Skeleton*, and Second Mate O'Connell on the foredeck of *Bones*, what to do. They, in turn, executed the precise pulls of the two winches so that the boat would remain level as it rose up into the harsh glow of the lights.

Although Skeleton Salvage was forced to use older gear, the experienced crew made up for any shortfall. They'd been in the business for a while and worked together well. Sonny knew, though, that they were an odd group of guys. Some might call them misfits, almost a zoo sometimes, or a menagerie. Yet together they sensed the workings of the *Skeleton* as one.

There was Cowboy, wild and strong and quick thinking, a prodigy straight from the Alaskan oil fields.

And good-natured Stu, a native fisherman and strongman once fired by the Alaskan Professional Wrestling Commission for breaking both his opponent's arms in the ring.

The second mate was a self-described southern redneck named O'Connell, who had his Marine ticket and several years of offshore experience in the Gulf of Mexico.

And, of course, there was the lithe and agile Tick, a dreadlocked, white Rastaman nut job with dreams of Jamaica dancing in his head.

Manny kept the equipment working. He was a Mexican émigré and an engineer of the greasy-hands variety, who could take anything apart and make it work. Without Manny, the *Skeleton* would suffer mightily.

But there were always the detractors. Always the people who had to complicate things.

On the dock, among a cluster of idle fishermen—some white, some native—a drunken voice rose above the noise. It was directed at Sonny, who had stepped out onto the wheelhouse landing.

"Hey, Wade, you gonna stink up the place again?"

An empty gin bottle sailed out from the dock and splashed into the water beside the streaming trawler.

From another group of men on the wharf, another taunt shot out over the bay. "Yeah, Wade, what we need's some more fuckin' oil on the salt banks!"

Mary, enraged at the assault and at the desecration of a perfect lift operation, cast her eyes over the riffraff and glared up at her father. *Don't take this shit, Dad*, she seemed to say.

Sonny ignored her. He ignored the taunts and the jeering and the catcalls as he had for years. He stepped back into the wheelhouse and toggled the intercom. "Cowboy, Manny, O'Connell, gimme your readouts one at a time, hydraulic, heat, and oil."

There was more work to be done. Screw these people. Screw 'em all.

* * *

On the docks that morning a young man sat on his sea bag, apart from the others, and watched. He'd never seen a salvager work. He'd never seen any of it except in textbook pictures and diagrams. He marveled at the ease with which everything came together. He decided, at the first opportunity, to speak to the captain, the infamous man known as Sonny Wade.

CHAPTER 4

Великан

Somewhere north of the Aleutians

IN SPITE OF the confused seas, the bow of the great ship rose and fell no more than a dozen feet per cycle. Her roll could be measured in tiny fractions of the actual freeboard amidships, and concepts like *yaw* did not apply. In one of her wardrooms near the centerline of the behemoth there was a snooker table, installed at the behest of the team of naval architects, who insisted that their ship would accommodate the game of cushions and angles just fine. And in steady seas they had been right. Stability reigned and the ivory balls on the green felt rolled true.

The designers of a ship such as *Bennkah* knew that stability would be inherent in her ballasts and her gross weight. After all, she was the largest tanker ever built. The largest tanker to ever sail the seas, and nothing short of a modern military aircraft carrier was as powerful. Her diesel turbines and her generators created enough energy to power a small city.

Which was what *Bennkah* was. In every way possible. Her decks were as long as five football fields and almost as wide as the Rose Bowl. Six Goodyear blimps could land on such a deck. That is, they could land if it were not for the massive cranes that serviced the spaghetti of pipes and pump stations, which stood amid miles of pathways going in and around the transfer stations—all to accommodate holding tanks full of so much Siberian sweet crude, a delivery from *Bennkah* could conceivably influence oil prices around the globe.

Indeed, the ship was so large that motorized crew conveyances were the norm—deck engineers zipping this way and that in modified golf carts or scooters. Or sometimes on bicycles if they were pressed to get somewhere and nothing else was accessible. On a normal supertanker a crew of twenty-six plus the captain was enough. On *Bennkah*, because of the extremes in weight, size, and complexity, fifty-seven officers and men, all Russian, held station and participated in the watches.

* * *

At the visitors lounge station on the bridge deck, the chief and his designer guest had been enjoying each other's company for some hours now. Words were being exchanged and vodka had loosened the strings of propriety. After all, they had never been informal with one another. And now *Bennkah* was a reality and the shakedowns were over. Much of the pressure was off.

The chief squinted at his companion and dropped his head in feigned somnolence. He looked up. "This is boring me," he said. "I'd rather be with your wife." He smiled. "She has tight ass like little boy."

The designer snorted. "Maybe she is little boy, eh?" He took a sip of his spiked coffee. "Why are we south?"

"Our captain worries too much," said the chief. "He does not want to scratch the paint on his new ship. Soon we turn north and meet the ice."

"This boat will eat the ice."

"I will eat your little boy wife."

"Hah!"

* * *

Eight decks below, in the engine room, there was no quiet to be had. And on one of the raised, central, diamond-steel grids twenty-five feet over the shaft alleys, one of three generators, the main diesel monster that supplied power to most of the ship, was experiencing a small problem. At the bottom of the inspection plate for the central raw water pump, one drop of water appeared and dripped onto the deck. At the top of the same plate a spit of steam escaped into the noise and disappeared.

In the wheelhouse, on the dash, the plastic Vladimir Putin paused, then nodded his head.

CHAPTER 5

Dutch Harbor

GROWING UP ON the rocky, windswept plains of the Aleutian Islands had always seemed like a privilege to Sonny Wade. The stark light and salt smells were a part of him. He knew every pea-rock road and every modest house. He could identify each small church and hardware store and was a fixture along the wharf, where city blocks were divided up into muddy fish house yards, piled high with traps and gear and the fecund sights and sounds of the Aleutian Banks and the Bering Sea fishery. Until he was thirteen years old, Sonny knew no shoes except church brogans or calf-high rubber boots. Life for him was school, then work, then more work. His father had been a tireless provider for the pair. He was a man who understood the shortness of the seasons and the value of discipline.

Sonny's father had also been his hero—the best navigator that the boy had ever known. And even when later Sonny had attended the adjunct Merchant Marine Academy in Fairbanks, he never met the equal of his own dad when it came to reading the seas and the currents.

His father was also a teacher and a confidant. Sonny, as a single-parent kid growing up, had no greater friend than his own dad. Nor such a taskmaster.

In June, when the silvers were running and you could smell the ripe pungency over an undulant sea as slick as glass, the pair of them would fill their small fishing trawler time and again, racing the fleet back to the docks to get the best price, then racing back out to sea to set the lines again. And during the short smelt season they would come in at midnight, gunnels three inches from the water, so full of fish that a person would have to spring from winch to rail to stern cleat not to get mired in the swarming life on the deck. Shoveling tons and tons of smelt when you were dog-tired and your ears rang and your shoulders sagged with fatigue was the norm. No rest for the weary, though. And workdays ran together like water through a sieve.

Years later, when Sonny recalled those days, he remembered the ache in his limbs and the burning behind his eyes, and he wished for a time so innocent, so attuned to the seasons, and so infinite and lush and never ending. Yet there was always an ending. Adulthood and marriage and a child, a seaman's life and tugboat work that took him around the world and up and down rivers as diverse as the Amazon delta system and the Suez Canal and the entire length of navigable waters in the Mississippi basin.

Sonny sat in *Skeleton*'s wheelhouse. He put his calloused hands to either side of his hat brim, adjusting his hat as if it meant something. Only a moment ago he'd been punching buttons on his little hand calculator, figuring up the bill for the owner of the just-floated trawler, a local fisherman named Jimmy Reston. Now he was trying to steel himself for something he had never been good at—arguing with a customer and dealing with a disaster. Jimmy Reston had just produced a personal check made out to Sonny's Salvage & Rescue. The date was handwritten in. It was dated April 1, five months from now. "But I got some cash, too," Jimmy said. "A little, anyways."

Mary and the rest of the crew had all crowded into the wheelhouse to listen as they drank their coffee, trying to warm up. Jimmy had just offered a pittance and a plea for time. He wanted to renegotiate the contract they'd signed.

"C'mon, Jimmy," said Sonny. "What you're offering doesn't even cover my fuel bill. Much less crew pay. You know that."

"I got problems, Sonny," said Jimmy, pointing his chin toward his family on the dock. His face was shadowed and concave with want, his eyes hollowed, his lips pulled back.

Outside on the wharf, Jimmy's wife and kids were stuffed into the cab of an old Chevy pickup. The wind had come up and the temperature had dropped. The truck was swaying on its springs. The brood looked miserable. Jimmy's wife held a swaddled baby displaying its outrage, screaming. The shrill wails were so loud they escaped the confines of the cab and carried over the fifty feet of wharf, then across both decks to the group ensconced in *Skeleton's* wheelhouse. The display was probably genuine. Or the most outrageous exhibit Sonny could remember.

Mary exchanged looks with the rest of the crew. If she'd been raised differently, she'd have spit on the deck.

Jimmy dropped his eyes so that Sonny couldn't see them. He said, "Season's over, man. Now I gotta drain my Cat, take the heads off, hope like hell the gear's not shot." He shuffled his feet like a kid, ashamed. "Batteries'r gone, Sonny. Rig's busted up. Wife threatening to leave . . ."

Sonny sighed. *Crap,* he thought, and glanced at the top of Jimmy's head. He ran his eyes over the tableau. *This can't be happening.* His crew would never forgive him. His daughter would flat out explode.

On the dash, Sonny's ex-wife, Judy, smiled out from under her wispy bangs—a perfect paint-daubed face forever locked in time by the framed photo. *I know you, Sonny Wade. You're a fool.*

Sonny said, "So what can we do about the bill right now, Jimmy? Your insurance—"

"That's just it, Sonny. I ain't got insurance."

The room grew still. Jimmy looked around at the crew, then back to Sonny.

"It was canceled," he said, pulling a wad of cash out of his pocket. "All I got's this. Two thousand. 'Til next spring."

Sonny looked down at the pitiful handout. He took the money into his palm and it felt moist and soiled. Cowboy and Tick and O'Connell turned away. Stu put his big hand on Mary's shoulder. They'd all seen this before. It was typical, and they were almost used to it. The six of them had just pulled Jimmy's boat from the mire, from total ruination, a job worth ten grand easy, and now they were going to have to listen to another decision by Sonny, a decision as predictable as the tides. Cowboy raised up. He took a sip of his coffee as he watched Sonny staring out the window. He followed Sonny's gaze, squinting at the bedraggled pickup full of kids.

A minute went by. Sonny rubbed his nose and pulled his eyes away from the windows and back to Jimmy. He rolled his palm down and deposited the money back where it came from. "Keep it," he said.

"Sonny, I'm sorry, man—"

"Keep it."

"I don't know what to say . . ."

"Just say you'd do the same for me," said Sonny.

"In a heartbeat. You know that."

"Sure I do. Now git, before Janelle and the kids freeze to death."

Then Jimmy Reston started to cry. His hand reached out toward Sonny, then floated back to his pocket and shamefully replaced the money. What pride he had left was gone. He never looked at the pissed-off crew. It took him ten seconds to remove himself from *Skeleton*. In thirty seconds he was driving his family over the washboard apron and away.

And that's when the shouting started.

CHAPTER 6

THE ANGRIEST SENTENCE came from Cowboy, who was not shy about sharing his thoughts. He had never been able to handle the complicated circuitry that was supposed to control his emotions. He was a hothead, a bar fighter, a man unequipped for subtlety. Now, fuming, he'd suddenly felt he'd endured too much nonsense from Sonny for far too long. He said, "If you ain't the damnedest—the most stupidest—"

Sonny said, "Alright—"

"The most goddamndest—"

"Okay—"

But then O'Connell joined in, deciding to clarify things further to his boss. Sailors aren't intensely introspective, so he shouted something unintelligible that ended in, "—just plain stupid, Sonny. Jimmy lied about his insurance. He has a fucking *boat* now, that he didn't have three hours ago—"

"I know, I know—"

Mary screwed up her face like she smelled something bad when she said, "Dad? What in the name of—"

"Hey!" shouted Sonny. "It's done!"

Tick blinked and pulled his dreads over his face, turtle-like. He probably didn't want to be there. He wanted a spliff and a beer. He sat down hard on the cracked green vinyl bench at the aft bulkhead.

"Shit," he whispered. "I wonder what it's like in Montego Bay right now."

Stu rubbed his arms and his neck and picked at the trailing threads of his stained jacket.

The room grew quiet except for the sound of a cold rain that had begun and was sliding through, pattering on the steel walls, making the world even more miserable.

Sonny's voice, when it came, was subdued. "I don't wanna hear it." He pointed at the spot on the dock that had just been vacated. "We've all been there before."

There was a pause, too long.

"Yeah, Dad," said Mary, breaking the silence. She shook her head and leaned in close, her face only inches from Sonny's ear. Her voice cracked when she said, "Except we're there now."

"Really? I hadn't noticed," said Sonny, refusing to look at his daughter. He took two steps to the starboard door and un-dogged the porthole, allowing the cold, wet air in. The wheelhouse had grown stuffy. He put his face to the opening. His world was coming apart piece by piece, and he had just failed his crew again. And he knew they were right. He had a contract. He could put a lien on the trawler this afternoon. He could take the gear right now, today. He could put the men to work with torches and wrenches and do what salvagers around the world do, and he would have every right and the law was on his side.

Except that he'd grown up here and knew the fishermen and knew the life, and goddamnit, he couldn't just be a prick to someone who had his own set of troubles and was obviously scraping the bottom of the barrel. Winter was coming. It wasn't right.

"Dad," said Mary. "Are you listening?"

It was a long time before Sonny responded.

CHAPTER 7

Великан

ON ANY ULTRA-MODERN ship there were always anomalies that the design engineers insisted on because of issues related to the working environment. The corrosive nature of the sea demanded that certain time-tested types of equipment be used, no matter how antiquated. There were questions of maintenance. The easier a problem was to find, the easier it was to fix. And running a malfunctioning microchip to ground through miles of buried circuitry could take hours or even days.

So up on *Bennkah*'s bridge, on the back side of the wheel bench, an old-fashioned mercury switch made contact and an electrical servo came to life. In the blink of an eye it alerted one of the computer boards that there was a temperature problem with the main generator in the engine room. The board relayed the information to one of many monitors and told an alarm to sound. It was not a critical warning, but an alert. A problem to be solved. Responding to the beeper, Captain Nicholas Borodin reached out to the lock switch on the offending gauge and reset the sounding toggle. He sighed impatiently and motioned to Vitrov, still relaxing in the visitors lounge at the rear of the bridge. The chief nodded back to his captain, before he pulled his handset from his belt, typing in the code and pushing the button for the engine room.

Deep in the bowels of the ship, in a sound-protected, Lexan-windowed cubicle the size of an average living room, an assistant engineer named Mikel Brov, second in command in the engine room, picked up the phone.

The cubicle was an oasis of sorts, situated in the forward center section of a wide, long, beautifully engineered concentration of power. In two shaft alleys below the lower decks, huge diesels transferred thousands of torque pounds of horsepower to the main shafts, both made from a hardened bronze alloy especially milled for *Bennkah* to exacting dimensions that belied their girth. Overhead, a lacework of color-coded pipes competed with neat bundles of wiring and transfer boxes. Everywhere there were safety partitions and bulkheads and aluminum or diamond-steel brackets and braces. Circling each pit, polished brass rails prevented any oiler or seaman from actually touching the working hardware. Because the noise was deafening, a system of strobe lights had been installed—engine alarm strobes, pump alarm strobes, fire strobes or bilge strobes. Even a brilliant white light on the aft firewall alerting the crew of any rudder room problems. There were inescapable visual warnings of possible catastrophes, disasters that no one expected to ever see on such a modern ship. The entirety of the arena was a bit overwhelming, not only in size and complexity, but with respect to sensory overload.

When Second Engineer Mikel Brov picked up his bridge phone, he was watching through his windows as steam poured from a pump seal on the main generator. The raw water intake had malfunctioned. "*Da,*" he said into the phone.

He listened for a moment.

He spoke into the phone to his chief. "It is the sea suction again. I think we have polar bear stuck in the baffles."

When he heard no laughter, he decided that Vitrov was serious.

His smile evaporated. He spoke into the phone. "Some wiring will have to be replaced this time, sir. But I will send Uli to switch suctions. We have to get water to that block before we shut it down. Except, sir, there is other problems."

He listened for a minute.

"Ya," he said. "I have fuel line with thirty pounds vacuum. I am going to switch filters." He replaced the phone in its cradle. Then he put his ear protectors on and exited the control room.

On the bridge, Chief Engineer Vitrov stood up so fast he sent his chair tumbling to the carpet. He shouted into the phone. "Mikel, that is much pressure! Turn off lift pump first . . . Mikel . . ."

When he got no response he said, "Fuck!" Then he excused himself and left for the engine room. He passed through a rear exit and directly into a steel-walled plexus of corridors featuring hydraulic hatches not unlike the modern stainless steel elevator doors seen in big-city skyscrapers. He approached one and hit the trigger. The doors slid open to reveal a Lexan-encased tram car. He got in and said, "Engine room." The car sped aft, then began to descend, passing first the officers' quarters, then the pool deck, the gym, the dining room, past the seamen's deck, and into the bowels of the ship.

In the visitors lounge, the designer poured himself another shot of vodka and drank it down. He was alone at the table now, and he was more than slightly drunk.

Six paces away, Captain Borodin stood at the wheel. Another buzzer sounded. After resetting the offending monitor, the captain turned all the way around and studied the naval architect for the first time that morning. "Come look," he said. "Please."

When the man approached, the captain pointed out the displays, one after another, stopping at the offending heat and fuel monitors for the main generator. He was a powerfully built man, but shorter than his guest by two inches. He had to look up to meet the man's eyes. He said, "Remember, sir, this is not a shakedown. Now we are working. We are at eighty percent capacity, drawing eighty-three feet of water. We weigh seven-hundred-thousand tons."

The captain faced away and scanned the gauges again. "These—this little distraction—it is real. It is something. Not good. You will see."

As if to mock Borodin, another beeper began to sound. He examined the gauge, then shut it off. He turned to his guest. "Another glitch," he said. "The fire prevention system just went black."

"Mr. Borodin," said the designer, "you worry too much. Your engineer is first-rate. He will fix problem."

Borodin looked at the designer and started to reply. Nothing came out except a rush of air, his chest contracting with the weight of command. Then he put his hands into the pockets of his tunic and nodded, dismissing the drunken designer. He took a step to his left and began to check off his gauges, walking the length of the bridge. He cast his eyes forward through the series of window panes, down to the foredeck below. The wind and rain had grown worse. The men on watch were probably huddled in their respective duty stations, drinking coffee and seeing to the maintenance of machinery that was not exposed to the weather. The captain looked over the bows and scanned the gray seas ahead. His legs and feet were aching again, a result of the job and the tedium. He pressed his toes down into his shoes and curled the arches of his feet away from the soles to stop the tingling. He was again feeling the strain of standing watch. He pivoted on the ball of his right foot, reversed his course, and paced all the way to the starboard landing.

One day he would buy a pair of good shoes.

CHAPTER 8

As the tram car carrying Chief Engineer Vitrov went through the fire hatches and dropped into the engine decks proper, the very vocal, aggravated man was still trying to contact his Second, Mikel Brov. Ten seconds later he put his phone into his pocket and slipped his ear protectors on. The noise was deafening, rendering his handset useless. And Brov never wore his headgear because he said it got in his way. Vitrov strode down the main corridor and into the soundproofed control booth. *Where the hell is that idiot?*

The chief scolded himself. Usually he ran a tight ship. He knew that a ship, *any* ship, was only as good as its officers. And Second Engineer Brov had come from the best maritime school this side of the Urals. He'd had eight years of tanker experience and a Five-A rating. So surely he was following the proper procedures. After all, any second engineer, even the second on a third-rate oiler running beer or bratwurst or Black Sea Beluga caviar, knew that you couldn't fuck with valves that are under so much suction. The thing was simple: a hot engine means you power down, yet you can't *shut* down until the blocks cool. But the fuel lift pump had to be turned off before you switched the lines. No shutdown means no switching of filters under load. Period. Even the *idea* that his Second might not know that was disconcerting to say the least.

* * *

As the chief was striding down the corridor, he was thinking through all this. And Brov was at the main generator maintenance deck, following his color-coded fuel lines with eyes as myopic and tunneled as someone might expect from a man overworked, underpaid, and by now confused. In spite of his rating he was a man undertrained to deal with such complexities—complexities like what he'd just had to pore through for the past four hours—computer readouts including data sheets and return flowcharts and characteristic icons that demanded attention. He was at the moment squinting through a set of goggles that forced his eyes to remain focused ahead and not to the sides. He was only a few yards away from his chief oiler, Uli, who was trying to open the bypass wheel on the sea suction. The overhead wires were under attack by pressurized steam escaping from the blown seal. They were inundated with salt, and the entire area was enveloped in hot salt vapors so intense, that to keep one's hands on the machinery required fat, mitten-like gloves that reached up to the thick part of one's forearms. The generator was way too hot to shut down, so Uli was doing his job as best he knew how—easing the bypass open so as to allow raw water in at a trickle, not a gush. He was doing exactly what he should have been doing.

* * *

Brov, however, was not. And he couldn't see. His goggles were now so fogged that vision was impossible.

On a large diesel engine there are multiple filter systems that decontaminate the fuel on its way to the main, high-pressure injector pump or pumps that use what fuel they want and send the rest back through the return lines to the tanks. The whole feed system is a circuit not unlike that of the human body's circulatory system. One of the main components of this system is a lift pump, an electrically motivated assistant that helps deliver fuel from one or another of the reservoirs, then through the filters and into the engine. On *Bennkah*, the lift pump for the main generator was situated on the fuel line. There was a vacuum gauge to alert the engineer to any filter-clogging problems. If the secondary filter in use was switched to its redundant replacement, there were three operations to perform. Shut on, blowback, and clear. Then open the mate.

There was a warning placard on the diamond plate:

SHUT OFF LIFT PUMP BEFORE SHIFTING CANISTERS.

With thirty pounds of vacuum on the gauge, there was not just an excess of pressure on the lift pump side of the harness, but a dangerous excess. So when Brov stopped the line for no more than a second, the still-operating lift pump pushed hundreds of pressure pounds of fuel into the line and one-half of the set of canisters exploded.

In seconds, a one-inch diameter, high-pressure stream of fuel sprayed across the operations theater and across the steel deck where Uli was working, trying to ameliorate his own gush of scalding steam that was destroying the overhead wiring.

As happens in life, mistakes and failures tend to generate more of the same. At that moment, there was one elongated blue arc of flame from the overhead wire harness, and the battened union of sprayed, salted, and shorted-out wires gave way, dropping the electrical assembly to the fuel-washed deck, which ignited in an explosive rush.

That particular electrical assembly was independent of the generators and powered by batteries. It was an important feature, because it monitored the various safety shutoffs, and until the steam had attacked it, it alerted the various heat sensors that ran the fire-control system. It was a safety precaution, but poorly designed. And because the flaw wasn't discovered during *Bennkah's* shakedown cruises, the recent prolonged hot gush of salt steam had rendered the fire alarm system useless.

In one second a sheet of flames inundated the generator deck, the still-running diesel generator engine, the remaining overhead electrical assemblies to port and starboard, and the two men intent on their own singular operations. Neither Brov nor Uli had time to even scream.

In three seconds, more fuel lines began to melt.

In five seconds the gout of ignited fuel had migrated downwards to the main decks, across the gaps and over the huge main turbines that were doing their thing, turning the shafts that swung propellers as thick as buildings three stories high.

In five more seconds the conflagration was complete. As strobes went off impotently, there was no triggering of the automatic fire prevention system and no power in the control room that would normally trip the breakers and shut off the fuel supply. An intense liquid wall of flames poured vertically, down under the mains to attack the other sources of fuel, and across the decks to the various supply lines. There were a number of men at their stations on the walkways. Most of them had no time to react. One was able to make it to the door of the control room, then duck inside, temporarily putting off the inevitable. The mass of flames was so intense, it destroyed everything and everyone in its path. Chief Engineer Vitrov ran for his life back up the corridor, through the still-operating fire doors and into the tram station, where he found the auxiliary control panel and began throwing the switches in a vain attempt to shut down all the supply systems.

Then the rest of the main power grid failed and the lights went out, replaced by the soft red glow of low power emergency LEDs.

From what sounded like a tunnel of fog, Vitrov heard the secondary generators next door try to ramp up. Then he heard a series of explosions as their electrical windings fired up and reignited the purge of fuel.

The *Bennkah* was now an inferno.

CHAPTER 9

IN THE WHEELHOUSE, Captain Borodin felt the new vibrations of his ship and scanned his remotes. Some of the engine room gauges were normal. However, some of them were pegged at zero. And the fire prevention system was still out. He picked up his phone and pushed the button for Vitrov.

* * *

Chief Engineer Vitrov's handset rang, a shrill cadence designed to be audible over the sound of engines. A light began to blink. Vitrov was still running. His communicator went unanswered.

He had been unable to retrace his former path in the tram car—the red LED lights had been replaced by a subdued orange glow that signified battery power override, not enough to run automated trams. So he'd decided that the quickest way to get back to the bridge was to take the access corridor that ran between the tankage, up the middle of the ship. He would go down two levels, then forward. Amidships he could climb one of the exit ladders. It would be a lousy trip, but better than the alternative. He had to get somewhere unaffected by the emergency in order to send fire teams aft, to maybe flood the area and prevent a catastrophe. He was out of shape and half drunk and had to stop every minute to clutch his chest.

He stumbled to a stop and bent over at the waist. His head was spinning, his stomach in knots. Blood pounded in his ears. He couldn't faint. Not now. He had work to do. He leaned against one of many interior bulkheads, a wall of steel labeled *"No. 6 Storage."* It was a midships port tank that should have been containing several thousand barrels of crude. But the double-walled bulkhead was hot to the touch. Too hot, he thought. He jumped away. Six feet forward there was a small steel door two feet square. An inspection port that he'd never seen before. He opened it and peered inside. He took a moment to adjust his thinking. What he decided he was looking at was beyond anything he'd ever imagined. He put his phone to his ear and pushed the button at his chin.

"Borodin," the captain answered from the bridge deck.

Vitrov began to gasp. "I am on deck eight, at number six storage. I am looking through the window here. This strange little screen." He paused, held his chest. "Now I get it," he hissed. "Your agitation. The worrying over the gauges. The pacing—"

"Yes," said Borodin.

"You knew all along," said the chief.

* * *

Borodin heard a subdued buzzer sound to his left. He scanned his gauges one more time. A flashing light said *"Storage tank 6."* He turned his head and looked across at the naval architect, passed out on the long bench behind the visitor's lounge table. He returned his gaze to the bridge array and found one of the visual monitors above his station. It said *"Deck 8."* He flipped a switch and an image came to life on the screen. "Yes. I knew," he said.

"You will burn in hell for this," said the chief.

"Yes," said Borodin, watching the screen. "But unfortunately, Comrade—"

On deck 8 a thousand-degree wall of flame poured forth from the engine room seeking more oxygen. It was white and blue when it engulfed the chief engineer of *Bennkah*.

Nicholas Borodin finished his sentence into an empty phone. "—you will be there before me."

CHAPTER 10

Dutch Harbor

SONNY WADE WAS determined to maintain control of his temper. In the overheated atmosphere aboard *Skeleton*, he knew that to go off on his men or his daughter would be a mistake. He somehow had to convey a semblance of normality. He abandoned the bridge for a moment and retired to his living quarters situated below the wheelhouse. When he rejoined the group he was carrying a bottle of Cockspur rum in one hand and a sheaf of envelopes wrapped in a rubber band in the other. He dropped the bundle onto his cracked leather barber chair that had been the pilot seat in his father's boat. Then he began pouring shots into each coffee cup. He took his time. The silence grew.

Outside, the gray skies had continued to weep, a freezing rain that left icy puddles on the decks of *Bones* and *Skeleton* and added to the muddy tracks and work scars along the wharf. A few gulls sat atop the weathered pilings, forlorn and hungry. Across the road, under the eaves of an old clapboard building, there was a sign by a wooden door that said "Willy's." A slush-streaked picture window was decorated with neon that blinked on and off in blurred, irregular patterns of shadow and light. The images advertising beer, wine, billiards. A few men had gathered under the awning. They were waiting for the owner to open the bar.

Sonny stood in the silence of the wheelhouse and gazed out across the wharf. The wooden door across the street opened from the inside and the line of idle men disappeared into the gloom. "So," he said.

Mary set her spiked coffee down and snatched up the rum bottle and sipped from the uncapped neck. She needed a bigger jolt than her father had poured. She gasped and put a finger to her lips, looked at him, and spoke with a measure of forced control. "I can't believe we even took that job. That old trawler . . ." She pointed her chin down the docks in the general direction of the now-raised boat. "Jimmy'll be lucky to ever get her going." She shook her head. "You knew that, Dad."

Sonny pressed his lips into a line and glanced at the picture of his ex-wife. When he spoke, he appeared to be addressing her and not his crew. "What'd you want me to do," he asked, "let him and his family starve?"

O'Connell decided to answer. "Better his than ours."

Sonny directed his eyes at the second mate. "You didn't just say that, did you?"

O'Connell looked away.

Sonny picked up the pay envelopes and passed them out. He ran his eyes over the group and tried to ignore the unease that had invaded every blinking eye. "Guys, here's your money. But there's no more work until spring. We're two weeks 'til ice-up."

As one, the men looked down at their outstretched palms containing what was sure to be less than what they'd hoped for.

Manny, who'd been quiet up until now, squeezed his eyes shut and opened them. "You'll never make spring, Cap. No way," he said.

Tick said, "This totally sucks, man."

Cowboy raised the envelope to his nose and pretended to sniff, disgusted. "Serious, dude," he growled. "This shit's wearing thin." He grabbed the bottle from Mary's hand and took a long pull. He wiped his lips with the back of his calloused paw.

The normally silent Stu took a step toward Sonny. He was mad, which was out of character for him. "Keep your fucking money," he said, throwing the cash envelope down. "I'm out." He turned his back and went down the companionway stairs and past the wardroom. A moment later the galley door opened and shut. As he climbed over the rail and onto the dock, he shouted in Sonny's direction. "I should have stayed with Sharpe!"

When the rest of the crew began voicing their objections again, Sonny tuned them out. His head was splitting and his hands were tired from clenching and unclenching, and what could he say anyway? How could he frame a response that they hadn't already heard? If this was the end of the road for his crew then so be it, and there was nothing to promise and nothing to hold out as a sign of better things to come, and maybe next year would be better.

And maybe pigs fly.

Sonny turned his back on his daughter and on the rest of his men. He glanced at the photo of his wife, then he descended the gray iron steps of the companionway. He entered his stateroom and shut the door.

CHAPTER 11

Великан

Now, at this late hour, the only man left alive in the engine room was wearing a gas mask. He was the one crewman that survived the first rush of heat. He sat in one of the padded seats behind a massive, ergonomically curved console decorated with gauges and levers the use of which he could only guess at. This was his first time inside the Lexan-walled super control room. His name was Rupik and he was a Chechen from one of the Balkan states in the Ukraine. He was nobody—an oiler. A few short years ago he was milking goats. Later he did barge work on the Lena. He studied for a time, took some tests. Now he was going to die.

He couldn't close his eyes. He wanted to but he couldn't. In front of the Lexan window a charcoaled reef of burned bodies lay like so much meat, spattering and crackling, flaming up, puddling into the deck plates. *They're dead. One minute goes by, and everyone I work with is dead.* He began to sing a song. "Yo ho heave . . . ho . . ." He smiled to himself. *The Song of the Volga Boatmen.*

Boy, I am fucking hot.

He noticed that sometimes there was a clear patch out there. One of the blowers must still be working. When the smoke opened up enough he could watch the different chemical colors burn along the aft firewall, fingers of orange and green and purple reaching up into pockets of surviving wire or plumbing. Then there would be a flash and more explosions and fire, billows of heat, like the surface of the sun. Overpowering where he sat, too, but not so bad as the other side of the windows. No. Most of the equipment in the huge engine room was unrecognizable.

He watched the Lexan melt.

"Yo ho heave . . . ho . . ." *Song of the Volga Boatman.*

Then the Lexan caught fire and exploded inward, and he began to scream as the thick hot plastic wrapped him in flames. In a few seconds he was dead.

At the forward bulkhead, in the companionways, and in front of the worthless exits, which were now doorways to nowhere that had been warped then fractured by heat and explosive fuel burns, more bodies were piled up, beginning to melt, victims of the raging inferno. One level up the crew's quarters were in flames. Above that the gym and the theater and the kitchen had been fire-gutted and were no more. The entire working area, the aft end of the ship, had collapsed in on itself as the blaze took control of all the systems designed to run the massive operation.

In the now disabled wheelhouse Captain Borodin and his just-arrived bosun's mate began their emergency protocols. While the bosun manned the wheel, Borodin's right hand slammed down on first one, then another of the manual alarms. The naval architect woke with a start, scanning the wheelhouse, confused. Officers, disheveled and not fully awake yet, rushed into the bridge area, unsure of the situation, unable to comprehend the scope of the catastrophe. The ship's sirens, fueled pneumatically and designed to sound throughout the giant vessel, added to the cacophony.

"My ship is eating itself," said Captain Borodin under his breath. "Stand aside!" he shouted to the bosun.

One by one the digital gauges began to zero. Then the steering hydraulics began to lose pressure.

"Disengage the automatic steering!" he ordered, as step-by-step the ship began to lose any sort of correctable angle. When his rudders refused to respond, Borodin stepped away from the controls. He turned and glared at his drunken guest. He instructed the now-reeling design engineer to call the naval yard in Vladivostok and explain the situation.

"And, my friend," said Borodin, "if you would be so kind, ask your oil friends at *rosneft* to pray for us."

Then Borodin grabbed the radio handset. He began transmitting the obligatory Mayday over Channel 16. The young bosun tried to take the wheel again, but Borodin pushed him aside.

The man exchanged looks with his captain, then raced his eyes up and down the room at the frantic officers trying to access the emergency lockers that were holding international *epirb* units, or life-support access codes for the pod, or mobile communications equipment, fumbling with keys they had never used. Smoke was beginning to fill the room.

"We are on fire!" shouted the frightened bosun. "We have lost our rudders! We have no steerage!" He began to cry. "I will not jump. I cannot swim."

Sweat coated Borodin's face as he completed his Mayday. He replaced his handset, keyed the ship's intercom, and spoke again. His husky voice traveled the length and breadth of the great ship—in control, always in control. "Attention, officers and men, this is your captain. We have a code red. Code red. Hydraulics are not functional. Backups are not on line. The rudder room is unavailable at this time. The helm is no longer responding." He turned and faced the men in the wheelhouse as he finished his announcement. "Please note, the life pod is not on line. Take appropriate action now. We are less than one minute from grounding. All officers are to don their gear and report to stations. Out."

Under the turbulent seas, beneath the counter of the gigantic ship, the huge propellers were contained in a Russian version of power assistance technology called Kort Nozzles, huge water scoops designed to feed more water to the blades. With no pneumatics on line and only the forward momentum of the behemoth providing power, the shaft breaking system tripped its springs much like the breaks of a locomotive, and the props began to create drag as they were forced to slow.

The rudders were turned with hydraulics that were also non-functioning. They were now motionless, refusing to interfere as the ship ran aground at seventeen knots, gouging a huge trough into the muddy bottom.

Seventeen knots became sixteen then fifteen as the bow started to arc upwards.

At twelve knots the ship began to slew sideways at ten then twenty degrees, raking copious amounts of solids up, ripping the bow thrusters away, placing an incalculable torque on the running gear astern. When she reached twenty-two degrees, the ship began to heel. The stern thrusters were ripped away, then the Kort Nozzles imploded and the propeller shafts went unprotected. Twenty-four degrees off centerline and ten degrees of list caused the shaft bearings to give way and spun the rudders out of their quadrants, disintegrating any running gear that wasn't already chewed up. Water began seeking relief, pouring into the rents astern, swallowing the vestiges of rudder bearings and shaft housings.

The *Bennkah* had now become a ludicrous facsimile of its original intent and specifications.

At six knots, the towering pyre *Bennkah* completed her final degree of list and began to right herself. If the proper gauges had been working in the now-flaming wheelhouse, they would have registered almost thirty degrees of list, much too much for such a ship to endure, except she was loaded with crude oil and mired in mud, which stopped any immediate spillage of her precious cargo.

At two knots the billowing black smoke caught up with the fire. No place on the ship was spared. No one alive was able to respond. *Bennkah*, the over-700,000-ton monster of the seas, had tried its best to conform to a new shape dictated by inertia and mass, and even though huge gouts of water and mud poured into the rudder room, and fires raged throughout the upper and lower decks, even though the wheelhouse was a flaming wreck and all electrical and plumbing systems were eviscerated, the design of the great ship and her ballast saved her from breaking apart. And because of the internationally mandated double-walled construction of the tankage on such a monstrous ship, the flames could not reach the crude.

Her crew, however, did not fare so well. Most died immediately. A few minutes later, on the starboard observation deck, a captain, a designer, a bosun, and a quartet of officers scanned the horizon for the impossible—assistance from an unkind God. Some of them screamed and prayed, all succumbed. And somewhere by the bows sixteen men, most of them deckhands, the meat and bone remnants of what would be called the greatest maritime conflagration in history, threw themselves over the railings and into an arctic sea.

Days later the furrow on the ocean bottom would be mapped and measured at 2.4 miles long, so it was not surprising that the many corpses in the water took a while to find. They were pulled from the forty-degree seas each in his own time. One of the Coasties, an officer later reprimanded for speaking aloud in front of the press corps, called them "popsicles."

But at this time they were still swimmers, trying to escape the huge coffin that was *Bennkah*, now finally at full stop.

CHAPTER 12

Dutch Harbor

SONNY SAT IN his dad's old barber chair and gazed out the windows, slick with cold, slanting rain. Everyone but Mary had abandoned ship, all of them angry, all of them in the process of reprogramming their lives for the coming winter ice-up. Mary had removed her neoprene dive suit and showered and put on a pair of clean Levis and a sweater two sizes too big. She busied herself with the ledgers, sitting at the rear navigation table counting debts and obligations that couldn't be met. The quiet was oppressive, a heavy bolus of unspoken heartache.

Sonny pretended he didn't notice Mary's silence. He reached up, turned the radio on. He spun the dial to Channel 16, the Coast Guard channel, and adjusted the squelch and the volume so that it poured unintelligible white noise out into the ether at the lowest volume possible. *Skeleton's* electronics were not new, but they performed well. Her VHF antenna, called a "Fat Boy," was so sensitive the unit could pick up an occasional ship from as far away as Cold Bay. Sonny would listen for hours some days, never turning it off, just tuning it out when he was busy. "You never know what's in the cards," he would say.

Except now. He wasn't saying that now.

Mary finally tore her eyes from the books. The reading light had blinded her, so for a minute or two she pretended to look away into nothing while her eyes adjusted to the muted interior glow. Outside it was gray. Inside it was worse. She blinked, sighed. "Dad, what are we going to do? The guys are pretty pissed."

Sonny didn't respond.

"Dad . . ."

Finally he said, "Guys are always pissed. That's why they call 'em guys. They piss and moan, they dribble, shake their dicks at whatever's closest. They'll get over it."

"Not this time, they won't," whispered Mary.

"Meaning?"

"Meaning . . ." She sighed. ". . . Manny was right." She turned back to the ledger, put her finger on the crease between the pages. "We won't make it to next spring."

Sonny took a deep breath and lifted his feet off the footrest castings and stomped them on the deck. He stood in his self-imposed gloom and turned to face his daughter. Outside the rain had turned to full-on ice and the wind had come up. The noise of weather going through the rigging made him speak up. His voice cracked when he said, "What if we move some payments around? There's gotta be something—"

"No!" She paused. "I mean, no, Dad. We've tried everything—"

"—some way—"

"Dad! Listen! There is no way!" She rotated her body back to the table and lifted the ledger and pulled a sheaf of papers out from under it. She squinted into the near dark where her father stood. "This is a letter from Larry Johns' attorney. It's real. He wants his tugs back, like, yesterday."

Sonny reached up and flipped the VHF to full scan mode. It began scrolling through all the possible channels, looking for a voice in the ether of static.

"Dad, we're broke. We should have pulled the plug months ago. And every day we put it off, we go further in the hole. I know it, the crew knows it, everybody in Dutch Harbor knows it. But you."

There. It was out. The cold, hard truth. A long, weighty pause passed before Sonny finally said, "I know it."

Mary took a step toward her father. She put her free hand on his shoulder and rubbed the taut muscles, a tenderness only Mary or her mother had ever been allowed. The movement belied her next remark, whispered into the nape of Sonny's neck. "Then why, Dad," she said, "do you spend all day hovering over the radio scanner?"

In the silence that followed, the VHF automatically took itself out of scan mode and began to broadcast: "*Mayday*," it said. "*United States Coast Guard Unalaska, this is the Bennkah.*" There was a pause. "*We are Bennkah. We are Russian Tank Ship Bennkah . . . requesting immediate assistance. This is Mayday, Mayday, Mayday . . .*"

Mary furrowed her brow. Sonny turned and looked at her. He reached up and flicked the scan mode off, then upped the volume.

"That's why," he said.

*   *   *

Many leagues to the west, standing on the northernmost gravel beach on one of the out islands in the Aleutian chain, a native stood beside the boat he'd been working on and gazed across several miles of turbid ocean. Over the noises of surf and wind, he'd heard what sounded like explosions. Visibility was not good, yet he shaded his eyes and squinted into the spray. From a point on the horizon black smoke and flames poured up into the sky in great columns. The smoke came from the largest ship the man had ever seen. He was a fisherman. He knew these waters. He turned away and began hiking up the rocky path across the island to his settlement. The Chief must see this, he decided. The burning ship was aground.

And full of oil.

CHAPTER 13

Dutch Harbor and surrounding environs

THE GROCERY STORE that supplied food to a good part of the town and most of the fishing fleet in Dutch Harbor was only two blocks away from the wharf. It was a big prefab cavern of a building owned by one of the large crab syndicates and leased to Northwest Passage Foods, Inc., a chain-store conglomerate. The manager ran tabs for most of the fishing boats and the crew boats that worked the harbor and the surrounding waters of the Aleutian chain. Dutch Harbor, after all, was a community whose economy revolved around the sea. Yet at any time of the day the place was crowded with shoppers only marginally affiliated with commercial fishing. The stereo system inside the building played muted orchestral pap on the overhead speakers—tunes like *Hey Jude* or *Tie a Yellow Ribbon*—in a continuous, syrupy-yet-bouncy, almost frothy loop designed to lull the shoppers into a somnolent state of binge buying . . .

. . . except when the U.S. Coast Guard made an announcement over Channel 16. Then the automatic override on the VHF in the main office kicked in, and the volume went up.

So as Sonny Wade on *Skeleton* listened to the report, so did the supermarket patrons.

"This is the United States Coast Guard Unalaska, United States Coast Guard Unalaska, United States Coast Guard Unalaska . . . break!"

Everyone in the store stood silent.

On the muddy street next to the supermarket, a gas station languished, its proprietor old and unwilling to move his feet too far away from his tiny space heater. From the radio over his head he also heard the bulletin from the Coast Guard:

"...*reported a Mayday, a Mayday*..."

And across the street at the beauty parlor some of the ladies became transfixed as the military monotone of the radioman rang out through the clouds of chemicals. The radio was louder than the hair dryers and more vibratory than the old, rumbling water heater in the back room of the salon.

"...*Russian ship identified as* Bennkah ... *break* ... *and responding to* Bennkah ..."

In the dark recesses of Willy's Tavern, all ears were tuned into the repeated bulletin from the U.S. Coast Guard:

"...*All stations, all stations, all stations*..."

And in thirty other places around the port city of Dutch Harbor, people were tuned in ... so that almost everyone heard the news as it was happening.

This included the just-released crew of *Skeleton*.

Second Mate O'Connell was having a late breakfast with his 300-pound wife, Susie. Their radio was in the kitchen.

"...*Bravo, Echo, November, November, Kilo, Alfa, Hotel*..."

O'Connell grabbed his hat, kissed Susie on the forehead, and bolted for the door.

On the edge of town, over the bridge and up the two-lane access road that eventually merged with the highway, there was a modest little trailer home on a scrubby lot of gorse and stunted fir trees. The place, Dutch Harbor's only whorehouse, was owned and operated by a local crossdresser who called himself Jean. In the main salon, the radio had been bolted onto the lampstand beside the bar where Jean usually entertained. The radio's speaker wires spidered out into four tiny bedrooms that had been arranged by color. In the Pink Room, the speaker beside Cowboy's head sounded like someone hammering on a tin can. Cowboy was roused from his post-coital slumber.

"... *reported to be on fire and aground ...*"

He listened for a moment, then lurched out of the double bed he'd been sharing with a slightly pregnant Inuit lady named Sheryl. He began putting his pants on. Cigarette smoke pooled around Sheryl's flared nostrils when she made him pay up on his way out. Jean handed him his hat as he ran across the living room and through the double doors.

Back in town, at a pool-and-darts tavern called The Whale, Tick and Manny stood with the other patrons at the bar while the U.S. Coast Guardsman began to repeat his message for the third time. Everyone there was silent. They all knew what an oil tanker could do to the fishing banks.

"... *Location longitude One Seven Two West. Stop. Latitude Fifty Five North. Stop. Vessels in the area are asked to assist in possible life-saving operations. For further information switch to 22 Alpha. Out.*"

Manny set his beer down with some money, waved to the bar maid, and turned for the door. Tick finished his beer, drank the rest of Manny's beer, picked up and pocketed the two-dollar tip Manny had just deposited, and followed him outside.

The *Skeleton* was only five minutes away.

CHAPTER 14

WHEN SONNY WAS a kid, the most exciting day of the year was the opening day of the salmon season. He and his dad would spend weeks getting the gear organized and the boat ready, and on the night before opening day they would be down on the boat in their sleeping bags like two kids on Christmas Eve. After all, most of their money was made during the first week, and often a good or bad year was predicated on skill and luck and getting that first strike before the next guy. It was the same for the smelting season, too, and for any other critter's cyclic calendar—anything in the ocean that lived and died on a schedule made up by The Alaska Fisheries Commission.

When Sonny grew up and began commercial salvaging in a big way, that same excitement welled up in him with any report related to his new field of endeavor. Every broadcast was a potential horn of plenty, every announcement to mariners was an opportunity. Now Sonny paced the floor of his wheelhouse, listening to every repeated word. Finally he began speaking to himself.

"I can't believe this," he whispered. "There's no way." He'd read about the Russians' new super ship in one of the trade publications. It was the newest thing afloat. What sort of calamity could have forced the captain to issue a Mayday?

"That's a monster ship," he said aloud. "Ice-reinforced and just off the ways. Not in Russian waters, either. Probably full and down on her waterline." He turned to Mary, who stood silent, contemplating the miraculous timing involved in the bulletin. "Go to 22 Alpha, Mary. Let's see what's up."

She spun the dial on the radio.

All over Dutch Harbor, others were doing likewise.

CHAPTER 15

NOT FAR AWAY, 120 men and women of the United States Coast Guard, Unalaska Station, were scrambling. It was quite possible that in the long history of the Unalaska Coasties, such a catastrophic Mayday had never been contemplated.

Not that they didn't have their share of dramatic rescues. It had been a hard year, much like the years before. Unalaska Station was recognized throughout the services for its place on the map. The men and women of Unalaska Coast Guard were known for their heroic efforts in the face of lousy weather and unusually difficult terrain. Unalaska's rescue diving team was world famous. Its officer corps was made up entirely of people who'd actually *requested* to be there, and its boat crews were as disciplined and overtrained as any unit in any branch of the service. To do whatever it took in the face of long odds was ingrained in every man and woman from the commander on down.

But desire be damned. An on-site helicopter crew, part of a small squadron of HH60 Jayhawks stationed in Cold Bay, had just reported back to base as they flew above and upwind of the *Bennkah*. According to the pilot and crew, the damage they were looking down on was overwhelming and they claimed that the possible ecological disaster that might confront the United States was unheard of. There were no protocols for a fuckup of this magnitude. None.

The commander, a big, grim man named Franklin, was in his office across the tarmac from the cement dock. He stood at the window behind his desk. He'd already watched as his forty-four-foot crew boat sped off. Now he looked on as the two cutters, the *Dauntless* and the larger *Alex Haley*, made ready to cast lines. Men were running everywhere over the wharf. He could hear the pneumatic starters being keyed and the diesels powering up. Equipment was hoisted and lashed, lines dropped from bollards, radar scanners started their turns. Then thrusters roared to life and both ships began to swing their sterns out.

Franklin walked his eyes from right to left across the slush-streaked window panes. The weather was not going to cooperate. He could see waves in the distance, breaking across the bar. Warning flags were up. The bell buoy that marked the end of the jetty was clanging. Last November they had lost several divers and men in a dustup that had resonated all the way to Washington. Now he was forced to contemplate a repeat performance.

I'm fucked. Better get on the horn. We're gonna need some help.

CHAPTER 16

On the *Skeleton*, a small internal pandemonium had continued to take control of Sonny's mind. He was alone in the wheelhouse—Mary having disappeared down the companionway. He was wound up. He'd yanked a chart from one of the tug's pigeon holes and hammered the corners down onto the nav table. Distance and direction, sea condition and tide times were already logged into his mind when Mary appeared again.

She produced a pimento cheese and bologna sandwich on a plate and set it down in front of her father. "Eat," she said.

Sonny squinted into the top slice of bread and started doing the dive tables.

"Eat," she repeated. "If we're going to go insinuate ourselves into an international incident with the Russians, you'll need your strength."

Sonny pushed the plate away and turned his attention back to his chart. "Eighty-plus feet," he said to himself. "Call it fourteen fathoms."

Mary interrupted his musings again. "I mean it, Dad, The Hague doesn't feed up like a good ol' tugboat. The I.T.O. or maybe the UN won't—"

"Hush!"

Mary blanched.

Sonny reached out and took hold of his daughter. "That is," he started again, "I love you, kiddo. But you're a pain in the ass. Just like your mother."

Mary scratched her nose with her middle finger.

"Now," he said, turning back to his chart, "go below and check our fuel situation. Is the Whaler on the chocks? What do we have for groceries? How much—"

"Wait a minute!" shouted Mary. "First things first."

Sonny stood back, eyed his daughter.

"Uh, knock, knock. Hello? We need a crew?"

Sonny smiled. "They'll be here. They know."

"What makes you so sure?"

Sonny squinted and focused down his nose. "Look," he said, pointing out through the porthole in the side door.

Tick and Manny were jogging up the dock. O'Connell's pickup roared up behind Cowboy's sputtering old Jeep. In a minute the four of them gathered by the rail and jumped aboard. They all had their sea bags as they barged into the wardroom, shouting and pushing.

Sonny grinned. "I had a hunch, Mar. You know how that is. Sometimes you just get this feeling, you know, and well, like bingo, along comes this, like, hunch—"

"Shut up."

"Yes'm. But we gotta hurry. Dal Sharpe has ears, too. He's listening. I know it."

"Ya *think?*"

CHAPTER 17

Anchorage, Alaska

ACROSS THE WIDE thoroughfare that separated the water and the city of Anchorage's commercial docks from a half-mile of warehouses and storage yards, there stood a modern, concrete-and-steel, five-story office building that boasted the silver words *Sharpe Salvage* over the entrance to the marble-paneled lobby. Most of the commercial operations at this port had their offices in this building. Every suite on the first four floors was rented.

The entire fifth level, however, was off limits to everyone not working for the building's owner.

On that floor Dal Sharpe stood at a wide, rain-spattered picture window, facing the glass myopically. He ignored the view—the bustle of late-season commerce—and didn't bother to notice the settling-in of bad weather. Dal Sharpe—middle-aged, overweight rosacea-sufferer and ex-Navy Supply Ensign—was instead riveted to the sideband radio while talking on his Bluetooth, both jobs performed as a unit.

But multitasking was not a problem for Dal Sharpe. He was a self-made man, an impressive figure in the world of maritime commerce, and someone who more often than not took a hands-on approach to the business of staking claim to ships that had sunk, or had lost their funding, or had lost their resolve, or all three. He considered himself the bane of the maritime insurance business.

He never missed an opportunity to stick it to someone, and under-bidding was his bailiwick, which meant that government contracts were a primary source of funding as his company scoured the seas for riches, holding huge cargoes for ransom. As a businessman, he was rewarded handsomely, time and again, for his efforts.

He owned the entire company—never issuing stock—which meant that his private entity was a kingdom, a kingdom that held as its main asset the egotistically named *Sharpe-Shooter*, the most ver-satile salvager in the North Pacific, maybe the world. Three-hundred feet long, she was an amazing, multifunctional example of speed, power, and maneuverability. Working on the surface or in any part of the water column up to six-thousand feet, she was a beast. Her winches could lift more than any competitor's winches, her gyros could keep her on station in the most inclement conditions, her pure horsepower could stabilize more than any of the competi-tion's muscle, and her comfortable working range was larger than anyone's. *Sharpe-Shooter*'s hydrodynamics, hydraulics, pneumatics, and computer-generated schematics could plan out a more superior operation than anything afloat. And because she boasted 30,000 total horsepower that could be routed to her various operations ca-pabilities, nothing in the salvaging world could compete.

On this gloomy afternoon Dal Sharpe practically shouted to his captain over the Bluetooth. "Frank, for Christ sake, turn on the fucking radio! You gotta go! Now!"

* * *

In the officer's wardroom aboard *Sharpe-Shooter*, Captain Frank Brooks, young, ambitious, and handsome, paced up and back the length of the cabin. "Yes, sir. We're south now, sir, but we're oiling up and airing—"

Sharpe didn't let him finish. "Get your guys off their asses! Clear the helipad! I'm on my way! And do not let Sonny Wade beat you to that tanker!"

* * *

"I'm on it, sir," said Frank. He hung up the phone and toggled the ship's on-board intercom. "Attention! Attention now!" he shouted into the handset. "This is your captain, and this is no drill! Shifts two and three, on deck!"

He ran to the aft door and opened it. His voice rang out in the companionway and ricocheted off the steel walls of the officers' quarters. "Off your dead ass, Bacon! Let's move!"

A few seconds later his first officer, Jack Bacon, stuck his disheveled torso out into the companionway. He was still in his skivvies. His eyes connected with his captain's, twenty feet away. He turned back into his cabin and in the space of a few seconds he'd grabbed his pants, backed into the hall, and hopped, one leg at a time, to the wardroom, where he stood yanking on his zipper, nodding and blinking at his boss.

"We got us a ship, Bacon," said Brooks. "So we gotta move. Wake the chief. Kick Rudy off the helm. Turn this lady around two-hundred eighty magnetic."

Sharpe-Shooter's First Officer Bacon ran for the wheelhouse.

Frank shouted after him. "The biggest tanker in the world just ran aground! And not a soul to claim it!"

* * *

Seconds later the big salvager began her turn. In minutes she would be a dot on the western horizon.

CHAPTER 18

Dutch Harbor

ON THE DOCKS now, in front of *Skeleton*, a young man with a sea bag paced back and forth. He'd heard the radio report earlier as he sat at the bar across the street at Willy's. He'd ruminated in front of his beer, trying to get the nerve to cross back over and ask Sonny Wade for a job. Now he knocked on the side of the tug. Then he knocked again, harder.

* * *

Aboard the salvager most of the crew, Cowboy, O'Connell, Manny, and Tick, sat at the galley table drinking coffee with Sonny and Mary, talking about *Bennkah*. The air virtually crackled with excitement.

Sonny was mapping out their first moves when he was interrupted by the banging on the hull. He lifted his eyes to Mary. "There's that kid on the dock again. He's been crawling the pilings for a month. Hire him."

"No way, Pops," said Mary. "That guy doesn't know his ass from his elbow. He's a tree hugger. Collects samples, for Pete's sakes."

Cowboy chimed in. "She's right. I saw him yesterday down at the boatyard taking photos of Hog Grange's worm shoe on the stern section of his keel. Had a pair of tweezers, picking at stuff."

"I don't care," said Sonny. "Stu's gone. He won't be back. Hire the guy. We gotta go."

Mary stood and took her coffee cup to the sink and dropped it into the soapy water. She turned and glared at her father. Then she went to the door, stuck her head out, and yelled at the guy. "You wanna work?"

The man nodded. Inside his hoodie Mary saw a young, eager face and eyebrows that floated above the bluest eyes she had ever encountered.

"Why should I hire you?" she asked, stepping out on deck and closing the door behind her.

The guy offered a shy smile and pulled his hood back. "My name's Matt," he said. "I'm a King's Point graduate, air and mixed gas commercial diver rating, I can underwater weld, and I do not get seasick."

Mary shook her head, rolled her eyes upwards. She turned and glanced through the port in the steel door behind her. Her dad's back was turned. She heard his muffled voice, going over the known facts about *Bennkah* and the Mayday, line-by-line with the crew. He was anxious, ready to move but trying to seem thoughtful. Mary knew that pose by heart. She turned back and ran her eyes over the soaked guy on the wharf. He was more than qualified. But she'd always been a tire-kicker, like her father. And a little bit of a ballbuster.

"That the best you can do?"

He smiled again, weakly. "How about this: I'll work for free."

"Now, why would you do that?" she fairly snapped, her eyes narrowing.

"I have my reasons."

Mary studied him again. Six feet, brown wavy hair, ocean eyes, nice smile . . . and the price was definitely right. The door behind her opened and Sonny and Cowboy peeked out. She ignored them, locked eyes with the guy, and said, "You bunk in the wardroom, Matt, until O'Connell puts you somewhere."

Matt took a deep breath. "Thanks," he said. "You won't be sorry." He reached out and touched Mary's elbow. She whipped her arm away and her eyes became slits.

"Don't do that," she hissed.

Matt held up his hands. "My bad."

Sonny and Cowboy exchanged glances. Cowboy sang, "Watch out, boy, she'll chew you up—" His musical efforts were interrupted by a pair of headlights belonging to a big white Cadillac SUV idling toward them along the dock.

"Crap," said Cowboy. "Here comes Punkin."

O'Connell stuck his head out the galley door. "Party's over," he said.

CHAPTER 19

THE BIG LUXURY utility car rolled to a stop and the front doors swung open. Two men got out. One of them wore the uniform of the U.S. Marshal Service. The other man's name was Larry Johns—chubby, bellicose, red-lipped—he was the money guy who held the note on all of Sonny's equipment. *Skeleton*, *Bones*, the truck, the underwater equipment, everything that went with the operation had been financed by Larry Johns in a deal, he claimed, to help Sonny out of a jam. People called him Punkin behind his back.

Sometimes they said it to his face, too. Because, fair or not, Larry Punkin Johns was considered an outsider in and around Dutch Harbor and Unalaska. He owned more of the place than anyone cared to admit, and he wielded a power within the community that could only be bought. At any time of the season a half-dozen privately run fishing boats were in arrears to him and a half-dozen local small businesses were late on their payments to his loan company, Johns Financial, a privately held entity based at the offices of the local branch of the First Congress Bank of Alaska.

Although Johns was combative by nature and could be as ruthless as was necessary when he sat at his desk, he had still never been comfortable with the fact that he had no friends. He considered his business a service, after all. Yet every year he perpetuated his isolation more and more. Every year, to assuage his guilt, he gave five thousand dollars to the local Methodist Church, and made some of the city workers decorate the Christmas tree that he bought and mounted on the plaza in front of the combination Dutch Harbor City Hall-Courthouse-Police Station-Jail. So every Sunday the pastor was obliged to shake hands with Larry Johns, a task the pastor likened to shaking hands with the devil himself.

On this soggy afternoon, as he read from a prepared statement full of estoppels and wherefores, he wore his salmon suit and yellow silk tie, with a pair of blood oxfords not designed to do well in icy conditions. He looked like a fat, pink tent preacher wading in shit. A Punkin.

He finished reading his statement, then handed the mortified U.S. Marshal a plastic packet of signed red stickers to put on the conspicuous surfaces of all the equipment attached to the salvage operation. The stickers said, *"Impounded on this date* _____, *by order of District Judge Hon. Albert Slater Esq. and The United States Marshals Service."* The government man climbed onto *Skeleton*, pulled the backing off one of the decals, and stuck it to the wheelhouse door.

Sonny clomped out onto the dock, glancing left and right before locking eyes on Johns. Considering what had happened so far, and what might happen next, this day would be some kind of record. "You can't do this, Larry," he said. "Not now. Not today."

"It's done, Sonny. I've waited long enough."

The marshal prepared another notice and stuck it to the big McElroy winch on the bow.

"Larry, just listen—"

"Done."

The marshal jumped to the dock and plastered the driver side window of Sonny's pickup with a red tag. He began slogging down the dock to *Bones*.

"This is a mistake, Larry. I can—"

"You can't do anything!" Larry Johns shouted. "Now move back!"

Silence.

Cowboy traded glances with Manny, Tick, and O'Connell. No matter what Sonny owed or what he had screwed up in the past, the crew of the *Skeleton* never abided rudeness from outsiders. They crowded around, cutting off Larry Johns' escape route.

Larry cleared his throat. "You'll have a few days to get your personal possessions off," he said by way of apology.

They moved in closer.

Technically there was no reason for a red tag anyway. No federal laws had been broken. So Larry Punkin Johns was bluffing, at least a little. Maybe.

Or maybe if Johns could show that fines or federal taxes had been skirted, he might have the wherewithal to force the issue. Maybe he had such damning evidence, who could know? Investigations had been based on a lot less. And Federal District Judge Slater had bought property from Larry Johns in the past. They weren't friends—Larry had none—but in this climate a certain amount of back-scratching was unavoidable.

As far as Larry Johns was concerned, though, Sonny had nothing to offer. He couldn't even pay his debts around town. So Sonny Wade needed to know Johns was not going to wait until things got so bad that he had to pony up to pull *Skeleton* out of the muck. Sonny was out of gas. His time was up.

"A few days," Johns repeated.

"Hear me out," said Sonny. "I have something."

Johns' voice rose again as he said, "This boat, *my* boat, isn't going anywhere."

"Larry, just listen."

"You got nothing."

"I have something. Now please, just listen."

The *Skeleton*'s crew crowded around as Sonny Wade performed the best song and dance of his entire life.

CHAPTER 20

THE WEATHER BEGAN to gust up again. A few stalwart gulls rose up and circled, then perched themselves once more on the pilings and faced into the wind. At the west end of the wharf a group of natives had started a fire in an old oil drum. They stood around the blaze, passing a bottle, and complaining amongst themselves. More rain was on the way.

Sonny lifted his eyes to the dangerous-looking cloud bank approaching from the west and addressed Johns. "You might have heard there's been an accident," he said. "A big Russian tanker, supposed to be the biggest one ever built, sixteen-hundred feet long, seven-hundred-thousand tons summer weight. It's aground and burning, Larry."

Johns shifted his weight, raised his hands and interrupted. "Whoa, man. Just whoa." He offered an incredulous smile, wrinkling his pudgy little nose. "Sonny Wade?" he said. "Oil? Jesus, have you forgotten? Because I can damn well guarantee you Dutch Harbor—hell, the entire state of Alaska hasn't!"

Mary piped in. "That's not fair—"

"Fuck fair!" spat Johns. "You want to talk *fair*? Where's my last five payments? Who do you think has been paying your fuel bill? Your insurance? Your maintenance? Huh?" Johns tossed his head around. "Huh? I helped you guys! I gave you a new start when no one else would!" He stomped a foot down in the mud and looked with horror as the mire sloshed up on his suit pants. "Shit." The puddle rolled up over the tops of his shoes. "And do any of you have any idea how much crap I take from folks for even doing business with you? How *fair* is that?" He bent over and began scrubbing at the grit. He gave up and stood and shuffled to a dry spot. "The loan officers at the bank are on my ass, Sonny," he said. "It's over. It's been over. Besides, the Coast Guard won't let you get near any tankers—"

"Wrong," said Sonny. "Think for a minute."

Johns inspected himself. Sighed.

Sonny continued, "Remember what happened to the Coasties last May? Twelve guys died, Lar. They don't want to touch that crap. They won't last. The U.S. Navy will have to get involved and they're everywhere but here. They won't even begin to deploy until it's over. Two weeks at least."

"True." Johns thought for a moment. "But what about UNCLOS. The law of the sea. You know the Transit Passage laws—"

"Wrong again. That Russian ship is outside the TP boundaries. It's up for grabs. If I can get there and put that fire out, we'll claim seventy or eighty thousand tons of crude. That's tons, Larry. And I know how to do it. And you know I do. If we go now—right now— we can get to that ship first."

Johns took a few steps to his right and leaned against the driver side door of his SUV, his ruined shoes forgotten for the moment. "Except for one thing," he said. "Dal Sharpe."

Sonny paused for a moment, then pointed his chin southeast. His eyes rolled down and settled on the offending direction. "Sure, Sharpe is probably already sending his boy, Brooks. But you know and I know that the *Sharpe-Shooter* likes to hide. And they're always anchored within smelling distance of the friggin' whorehouses, and the whorehouses have to have a road to the mainland for obvious reasons. So, Larry, my guess is they're somewhere near Cold Bay, near where they think the action is, the pipeline and barge delivery crap. All those bids that I don't do anymore. I've got 'em by a hundred miles at least."

"A hundred miles!" said Mary. She shaded her eyes for emphasis.

"They're faster, but they have a longer way to run. I can beat 'em but we have to go now."

Johns retorted, "I doubt it. Besides, the Russians are going to want their ship—"

"And claim liability on a big-ass spill? On a possibly out-of-control fire so close to the U.S. Aleutians? Please, Larry, just think for a minute. They'll blame their own goddamn oil barons. Putin's rules. The cartel did it. Political lying is a feature of their Brave New World, their new capitalist state. That's what they do. Just ask someone from the Crimea."

The marshal sidled up on the other side of the SUV. He'd finished placing the red tags on all of the equipment. He looked a hundred years old.

Johns said, "You really think you can do this, don't you?"

"Hell, yes," said Sonny, sensing the tide turning. He blinked at his daughter while O'Connell turned away and bit his lip to keep from smiling. Tick scratched himself. Manny and Cowboy adjusted their hats.

The new guy, Matt, stood apart from the crew and took notes.

* * *

Johns took in the motley crew. *A bunch of sea trash. Most of them haven't carried their weight in two years.*

He rubbed the creases on his salmon pants and examined the purpling leather on the toes of his shoes—three hundred dollars in Seattle. Then he adjusted his collar, repositioned his tie. He turned to the marshal and asked him to get in the car. Johns locked eyes with the soon-to-be exiled captain of *Skeleton.* "You're a fool, Sonny," he said. "Always have been. But I'm going to let you die like a man. And take this bunch of fools with you."

They roared.

"On one condition!" Johns shouted. He smiled and stuck a finger in Sonny's face. "You come back here with my money, all of it, in two weeks. Or I'm taking everything you own, and that includes your deceased daddy's waterfront property, too." He opened the driver side door and climbed behind the wheel. "I'm dead serious, Sonny. I'll write up the contract and fax it to you." He pointed to his companion in the passenger seat. "My friend Harry, the marshal here, will verify this for me. You'll be living in a cardboard box with the rest of your hooligans when Sharpe whips your ass." He turned the key and the engine started. "And you'll leave the red tags on the equipment, Sonny, to remind yourself who's running things."

"I can do that," said Sonny. He stuck his hand up to the open window, but Johns refused to shake. Instead, he pushed a button on the arm of the door and the glass slid up and sealed the two men in.

*   *   *

The crew watched as Johns and the marshal drove off.

"Punkin sucks," said Tick.

Sonny breathed a sigh of relief. He turned to his crew. "This is it, folks. Do or die. Once we get under way, I want you"—he pointed at Matt—"to remove those fucking red tags." He then looked at his first mate. "Cowboy, you and Manny follow us in *Bones.* And grab those Inuits off the dock over there." He gestured to the half-dozen locals huddled around the trash can.

"Those guys are bums," said Cowboy.

"Yeah, but they're big bums. And big is what we're gonna need. So let's move. Like they say, 'to the victor goes the spoils.'"

Tick said, "What does that mean?"

Sonny jumped up onto *Skeleton*. "It means first guy there wins. Now let's haul ass. We got us a night ride through the Umnak Pass. O'Connell, oil up, air up. Tick, take the lines off. Get that kid to help you. Mary, tie the Whaler down, it's off the chocks. Cowboy, we'll do VHF channel one three. On a double click, go to six eight. Everybody chop chop, let's go!" Sonny touched his breast pocket, where he'd stashed a handwritten list of tides and times. He would need all the info he could muster if they were going to claim this ship.

"I hope like hell the Coasties are working on that fire," said Sonny to himself as he stepped into the wheelhouse.

CHAPTER 21

Великан

UNDER A BRUISED sky one of two U.S. Coast Guard C-130 pilots flew as low as he dared over *Bennkah* and let go his cargo of fire retardant. He rose and banked away as a globe of red dust fell like a heavy cloud and engulfed the aft end of the stricken ship, spreading out and blanketing fifty yards of the stern quarter. Flames shot up through the haze and black smoke roiled as if to tease the Coasties. Then the second airplane made its approach and dumped its load. Both would have to reload, a round trip that would take them an hour.

The entire spectacle, as high and far as the eye could see, was a glowing, billowing mass of uncontrolled energy, and even with the failing light, the Coast Guard air units were doing their best to at least contain the situation until more hardware and the cutters arrived. Small explosions erupted, great gouts of flame gushed from sources newly exposed as *Bennkah* sat immobile, fouling the bank unchallenged.

Eight hours later, in the middle of the night, both cutters were on station, plus a small rescue boat, two HH65 Dolphin choppers, and the forty-four crew boat. The fire was still a monumental mess, and every able body had been tasked to fight it. Huge pumps sprayed towering geysers of seawater into the firestorm. The *Alex Haley* had launched its boats, which soon began zigzagging, then backing hard into the smoke, trying to position six-hundred yards of nitrogen-filled boom barriers around the worst of the still-flaming diesel. So far, there were no reports of crude in the water, but that wouldn't continue if the fire wasn't eventually controlled. Heat begets more heat, and sooner or later, systems would fail and tanks would rupture.

The captain of the *Dauntless*, a man named Bolger, worked his helm, shouting orders and monitoring as much of the equipment as he could. As the on-site leader of the operation, it was his job to make sense of the chaos. He was breathing hard, sweat erupting from his forehead and running down his face, soaking his uniform.

"Captain, sir," shouted the communications officer. "C.O.'s on the line, sir. What do I say?"

Bolger took the proffered side band handset. He clicked the mike and began his report back to his commander.

"We got a mess here, sir."

"Has anyone spotted survivors?" said Franklin.

"We can't get close enough, sir. We've got spots everywhere, but it's dark as hell except near the fires. The seas are a mess, ten to twelve, four-second intervals. Fifty yards is the best we can do. Plus there's ignition and burning on top of the water."

"What about the crude?"

"None in the water that we can see, sir. Just fuel. And the ship is level aground, slightly bow up. Biggest goddamn ship I've ever seen. It covers the universe out here."

Franklin didn't answer right away. Finally he said, "You know the drill, Captain. If there are survivors, give it your best shot. I'm standing by. The Navy is on the other line. I've got a Sikorsky, one of those big forest service helicopters that scoops water, heading your way. Washington is already raising hell. Out."

Bolger shifted his attention to the *Bennkah*. Directly ahead maybe five-hundred yards he recognized the lights of one of the Coast Guard's twenty-eight-foot inflatable rescue vehicles from the *Alex Haley*. He turned to his second officer. "What's he doing in there?" he shouted.

"They said they spotted someone in the water, Skipper. I think they're fishing them out."

Just then an explosion rattled the windows and a funnel cloud of black smoke engulfed the smaller boat.

"Get on the horn," said Bolger. "Call them off. It's too dangerous."

As the radio ensign tried frantically to make contact, the sound of another explosion tore through the wheelhouse. Outside, amid the drifts, Bolger watched in horror as a rogue wave filled with fire and smoke rose up and launched the inflatable, flipping it on its end and dumping all five Coast Guardsmen into the sea.

"Goddamn! Goddamn! Gimme the goddamn mike!" He called his duty chopper: "WRFMobile, Whiskey Romeo Foxtrot Mike, we got men in the water. I repeat, men in the water, southwest quad, thirty meters from the big ship's hull! Everyone look out!"

"I'm here, Cap," said the copter pilot. "I see them. I'm gonna try to get in there and drop a cage—"

Bolger over-keyed his mike in his excitement. "Just hold on! I'm bringing the cutter around. Just stand by!"

"—hard to stay static. The wind, almost like mountain stuff—"

"Just fucking *stand by*!"

But it was too late. The copter pilot, trying to remain on-site to lower a rescue basket, was working his controls and trying to stay in place, but he couldn't compete with the downdrafts that came from every direction. At once a tunnel of high-velocity vertical wind shear took control of his stabilizers.

"We got trouble, Captain—" began the pilot.

The copter sideslipped and turned on its tail before it fell backwards into the sea on top of the other swimmers. The impact was horrific. There was a whoosh as the fuel lines caught fire, then a giant plume of white as the flames incinerated everything. The explosion temporarily extinguished the islands of floating fires in a fifty-meter radius. Nine men were killed.

At dawn the last of the bodies was pulled from the sea.

CHAPTER 22

Umnak Pass, Eastern Aleutians
NOVEMBER 26, 1600 TO NOVEMBER 27, DAWN

FOR A GOOD part of that evening, as *Skeleton* and *Bones* plodded west-southwest against seas that threatened to get bigger and more ferocious, Sonny lay in his bunk and wondered what was happening at the grounding. The reports on the radio didn't explain a thing except that the ship was still aground, still burning, and still threatening to waste the bank in tons and tons of oil. Sonny knew that *Skeleton* could never make it to the *Bennkah* and claim her on a direct heading. The northern passage was too wild and wooly in these kinds of conditions, with huge seas and poor visibility, not to mention the constant helm fight that goes with challenging high, powerful waves. They'd be hard-pressed to make twelve knots in such conditions. So Sonny decided to take the Umnak Pass west and gamble that *Sharpe-Shooter* was also south of the Fox Island group. With the tide on their ass and the seas knocked down to manageable heights, *Skeleton* and *Bones* would move right along. The stalwart old tugs were making lousy time now, but he knew that once they got into the pass they would pick up a ground-effect current and things would change. If they hugged the south side of Umnak, the large, volcanic island on the northwest side of the Foxes, they would make up time.

Sonny held his first powwow at 1900 hours during an abbreviated dinner of canned ham, white beans, and cornbread. He explained to the crew his thinking. And then he went over the next step. He knew that although they would make good time for a while, they would soon run out of island to hide behind. At some point they would have to cross over, to make the north side. They would have to sail up and around not only the western point of Umnak, but around the spoil island, a ragged line of cliffs and reefs that was damn dangerous. The whole area had become a graveyard for ships whose captains didn't heed the charts and refused to take the safe route around. The rule was, if you drew more than six feet, keep the western point abaft at least three miles. And even then the current could back and skew and run the unlucky sailor into the mud and onto the rocks, turning a good boat into scrap in a hurry. Between the island and the point there was a small channel the fishing boats used, but nothing with size could hope to navigate it. *Skeleton* would bear well off the point before heading north.

The thing was, Sonny explained, the guys in *Sharpe-Shooter*, wherever they were now, would face the same predicament. They were most likely steaming around the Fox Islands right now, balls-to-the-wall on a west-southwest heading, maybe making as much as twenty-four knots. But when they, too, made the point, they'd be looking at the same problem. And if there wasn't enough water under their keel, they'd have to go even further west before they could safely turn north and back to the *Bennkah*. They'd have to make a big, wide arc that might use up several thousand yards. That was where *Skeleton* was going to beat them. Because the tide was going to be falling. And *Skeleton* only drew seven feet.

At 2300 hours, as they neared Cape Idak, the easternmost point of land, Mary and Matt were on watch. They could feel the surge of power as *Skeleton* clawed her way through the current-lashed straits south of the headland. Then *Skeleton* gained three knots as they rounded under the diamond-shaped crown and slipped away.

"This is incredible," uttered Matt, hanging on to the bulkhead.

Mary had taken *Skeleton* so close, they could hear the roar and see the frothy spumes towering over everything, blowing through the rocks.

At 0300 hours, just off Otter Point, with O'Connell at the wheel, they began to pick up more speed. Still traveling west, they were now well inside the lee and over a shallow bank, a less-than-sixty-foot bottom curve that broke up the seas and turned the water into a twisted confusion of current-driven wash and white mares' tails. *Skeleton*, with all her horsepower to bear, could make nineteen or twenty knots in these conditions. And *Bones* was right beside her. It was like being flushed down a giant toilet.

But it didn't last.

At dawn Mary stood beside her dad in the wheelhouse, her face in the scope of *Skeleton's* old sixty-four-mile Furuno Radar. "I see them," she said. "Only target on the southern quadrant. They're a little south of due east, looks like . . . seventeen miles."

"Uh oh," said Sonny. "We might be in trouble. I needed twenty miles at least. That's a lot of time to make up."

"We need jet skis," said Mary.

"Jet skis, hell. We need jets," said Sonny.

CHAPTER 23

"Slow the fuck down, Brooks!" bellowed Sharpe over the radio. "Turn my fucking ship *into* the wind!"

Dal Sharpe's copter had been in the air for a little more than three hours. The pilot had found *Sharpe-Shooter* easy enough, but with the seas uncooperative and with the big ship racing west so close to land, the ground-effect wind fouled the approach, turning the water into a confusion of foam and roiling seas and the deck into a constantly changing platform. The pilot couldn't get an angle on the helipad. Even with four guys running around, offering up their handheld landing hooks, every time the pilot tried to put down, the big ship yawed, the crew couldn't secure the landing chocks, and the pilot had to veer off yet again.

Then the radio in the chopper sparked to life. Captain Frank Brooks announced, "We have them on radar, sir. *Skeleton*, just over sixteen miles, and we're closing, at, uh . . . two-seven-five degrees. Be advised, we're slowing and turning two points to port and standing by."

The big salvager began to turn south. One minute later the seas were on the stern. Two minutes later the copter landed. Dal Sharpe scrambled out of his seat and headed for the wheelhouse. He held his khaki ball cap in his hand. He never even ducked at the rotor wash. He had to hold on to the ladder stanchion as *Sharpe-Shooter* powered up and turned back on a westerly course.

When Sharpe entered the control center, there was a milling confusion around the duel navigation plotter screens. Several officers, including Frank, were calculating the vectors and counting up the times.

"They can't make it," said Brooks, when his boss stepped to the table. "We're at fifteen miles now, and if you compute the angles, we'll have 'em by a mile when we head around the island west of Cape Sugak."

"Fantastic," said Sharpe. He grinned and pointed at a spot on the screen. "That's where we turn north. And by the way, do you see that big black cloud on the northern horizon? Up in the chopper it's stupendous. That's money, Frank. A black cloud of money. Now let's run that bastard Wade down and cross over and get that ship."

"Boss," said Brooks, inspecting the proffered location on the chart, "I gotta say it for the record, you know. This spot you've decided on is a little iffy for this boat of yours." He tried to lock eyes with Sharpe. No use, he looked away. "We'll be at least a mile ahead of *Skeleton* when we hit that hole, Boss, so what I'm saying is that when the bottom starts to come up, maybe we could take off some headway, slow down some, just in case the tide is not as high—"

Dal Sharpe rolled his eyes. "I got the helm, Frank. Stand aside. I'll put you on when we're around the island."

CHAPTER 24

SONNY HAD WORKED up all the possibilities in his head. There was no way he could whip *Sharpe-Shooter* by taking the point and he knew it. This was an eyeball-to-eyeball race now. The *Sharpe-Shooter* was in sight, fifty degrees off the port bow, only three miles away, closing and pulling ahead on the exact vector that he had envisioned.

Brooks is a good sailor and follows the rules, thought Sonny. *But he's basically a coward. So he can't be the one pulling these strings. Sharpe himself must be aboard.*

"Dad!" Mary shouted, "They're gonna cut us off."

"Screw that," said Sonny. "Come take the wheel. Now!"

Mary was beside him in a flash, snatching the wheel's center spoke. Sonny turned to the old paper charts that he'd retrieved from his dad's fishing boat after his death. He remembered a bunch of shortcuts—his father's little tricks—that had caught them so many fish on so many opening days, shortcuts to the fishing grounds that used to confound the other fishermen. And he remembered one was at the end of Umnak, right in the middle of Sarnaga Island. If it was on the chart it would be in ink, not pencil. He studied the big map. He found a tiny squiggle and the coordinates. And he smiled.

Sonny turned around and grabbed the mike. He double-clicked

the VHF, then switched to six eight. "Cowboy," he said into the receiver.

"I'm here, Boss. Damn, this ain't no joy ride."

"Check your watch. In nineteen minutes I'll double-click the mike again. Switch back to one three, then shove that Caterpillar engine in the corner. I'll slow a bit, and you c'mon up and put your bow in my wheel water. Close as you can. Then we'll speed up together. Follow me close, son. Stay right in my track when I turn north. This little shortcut is called Bad Rock Bight. I'm gonna bump. My stern'll rise then sink and my wheels'll dig. Then you'll do the same thing. Then we're through. Piece a' cake."

"Roger on the cake, Skipper. My seat belt is fastened."

"Oh, and on the other side, if you see a pair of skinny little lead pipes sticking out of the water on your port side, those are my dad's uh-ohs. They're in two feet of water. He put them in with concrete. They mark a dogleg around the rocks. We miss them, we're shit city. This cut is only forty feet wide, Cowboy. About the width of those ladies you like to ride."

For the next nineteen minutes *Skeleton* and *Bones* fell further and further behind. Then Sonny, with Mary and Matt watching and O'Connell on the stern signaling to Cowboy, saw what he was looking for and keyed his mike twice. One minute later he spun the wheel north, seemingly right into the teeth of the bladed granite rocks of Sarnaga Island. *Bones* was right on his ass. A high wall of rock lay dead ahead. It looked like there was no place to go. Sonny's fathometer read forty-two feet under the keel.

Suddenly Sonny's VHF, now back on one three, sputtered on. The unmistakable alto shriek of Captain Frank Brooks rattled through the little speaker. "What the fuck you doing, Wade?"

Sonny grinned. He couldn't help it. He saw in his mind's eye the inside of *Sharpe-Shooter*'s wheelhouse. And he saw Brooks freaking, glancing over at Sharpe behind the wheel, a man—his boss—obsessed.

On *Bones*, Cowboy answered for Sonny. "What's it to you, Frank?"

Brooks howled. "Get out of here, Cowboy. Wade, is this some kinda joke? 'Cause we're not slowing down for love nor money. Sinking your bucket of bolts won't change that. It's over. You and Cowboy are just playing in the bathtub."

"Call 'em out, Mary," said Sonny, pointing to the depth sounder. "Matt, get out on the port rail. Get ready to look for those lead pipe markers as soon as we make the pass.

"Thirty feet," said Mary to her father.

Cowboy keyed his mike. "Fucker's worried, Sonny," he said.

Sonny keyed. "Not yet, but he will be."

Then Sonny blinked his eyes and grinned and envisioned Dal Sharpe and Frank Brooks listening to his exchange with Cowboy. He saw them wince. *What's going on?*

Brooks' voice crackled over the air. "Hey!" He began to speak. "Sonny, it's over. Don't be stupid. There's nothing but skinny water in there—"

There was a thump and a clatter and nothing. Sonny figured Sharpe must have slapped the handset out of his hired captain's hand. Two seconds later Sharpe keyed the microphone. Sonny wasn't prepared for what he overheard. His former boss, Dal Sharpe, in the throes of rage, had forgotten he'd pressed the key thumb. He was speaking not to Sonny but to Brooks in the wheelhouse of *Sharpe-Shooter*. The audio was broadcast in flat, angry tones that echoed in the electric air:

"I don't pay you to prevent suicides," hissed the salvage mogul to his hired captain. "I pay you to salvage ships. If that piece of shit wants to kill himself, let him."

Sonny blinked again, still listening.

"Now put Bacon and the crew outside on the rail," said the enraged owner of the huge salvager. "We need eyes when we go around."

The VHF went silent.

CHAPTER 25

AHEAD OF *SKELETON*'S bow a great immovable wall of rock and rubble filled the horizon. The little northeast-angled channel was still there, Sonny hoped, but even ten years ago the line of sight had been obscured by a shoal of debris. Sonny glanced west and saw *Sharpe-Shooter*'s stern. She was at least three miles ahead of *Skeleton*. But she was still going the *wrong* way.

"Twenty feet," said Mary.

"I see the cut," said Sonny. He clicked his mike. "Cowboy, don't go cold on me here. We got whitewater breaking all the way across the passage. Looks pretty. Like a chrome bumper on a Buick."

Sharpe broke in. He sounded happy. "Sonny, that's not a channel. It's a creek. You're a dead man."

"Fifteen feet," said Mary. She saw the new guy, Matt, standing at the rail holding his breath. Ropes of foam curled under the gunwale and buckets of spray fanned out from the bow. Fifty yards ahead, surging water poured over the rocks. Mary had no idea what the guy was thinking, but she knew he'd never imagined he might die on his first day.

"Lead pipes?" croaked Matt to himself, scanning the tiny channel as far ahead as he could see.

The wheelhouse door was hooked open. Sonny heard the comment. "My father put them in years ago," he hollered out the door.

"Yessir."

"I used to fish these shoals every summer when I was a kid. And don't call me sir."

"Ten feet under the keel!" cried Mary.

"Hang on, guys," said Sonny. "And if anything bad happens, someone snatch Tick out of the engine room. He's probably asleep."

* * *

On *Sharpe-Shooter*, the owner turned to his captain. He was angry again. "What is he doing, Frank? Why isn't he high and dry? Tell me, goddamnit!"

But Frank couldn't know. No one could know. Sonny had learned navigation from his dad, and he'd learned the Aleutians from his dad, and nobody knew these waters better than his dad. Period.

* * *

"Twelve feet," said Mary.

Cowboy's baritone filled the air. "Sonny, I got a lot of turbulence! Your wheel wash is sucking me down! My stern is starting to squat!"

"Balls, Cowboy," said Sonny. "You gotta have balls."

* * *

On *Sharpe-Shooter* Dal Sharpe cranked the wheel around north. The safer course had taken him more than a mile west of Sarnaga. If Sonny made this little pass, Sharpe-Shooter was suddenly behind. Way behind. "Frank," he said, "is the chief in his engine room?"

"Where else?"

"Call him up. Tell him to take the governors off the engines. Pull the slugs out, whatever they got on those MAN Direct Drives. I need more speed."

Brooks stared at his boss. He looked up into the sound-dampened ceiling. "You can't do that, sir. Something'll blow."

"Do it."

He sighed, then clicked the ship's intercom. "Smitty, you down there?"

"Yessir."

"Dal wants you to pull the governors."

"On the mains? No way."

Then Sharpe went postal. He pushed Brooks out of the way and stuck his face into the transceiver. He was so loud and so close, distortion fouled his transmission when he told the chief what he wanted.

"What?" said the chief. "You're breaking up."

Sharpe backed up a step, took a breath. "Smitty, I pay you. Now if you want a fucking ride home, pull the governors! Now!"

"I keep those turbos at 12,600 or less for a reason—"

"Now!"

* * *

"Four feet," cried Mary, and grabbed the handholds on the wheel bench.

Sonny braced himself.

"Two feet," she whispered. Her eyes went wide.

And *Skeleton* hit bottom.

Sonny held his breath.

Skeleton's bow rose up and skewed two points east, looking for water. Momentum pushed her onto the hump. One second turned to two then three. Wheel wash churned. Sonny had memorized the tide tables. He was counting on his tide tables. Seven feet, piece 'a cake.

Then *Bones* crawled right up on *Skeleton*'s stern, both engines roaring as both boats lifted . . .

. . . and like magic, *Skeleton*'s props got purchase and her keel dug a track in the mud that *Bones* couldn't miss, skimming along right behind . . .

. . . and suddenly they were in the shadows between two steep cliffs of rock, crewmen staring into the faces of shrieking birds . . .

. . . and then they were through and out the other side.

"Eight feet under the keel and dropping!" shouted Mary, hugging her dad's shoulder. "We did it! We killed 'em!"

"Hold on, Mar. We're not through yet," said Sonny.

"Pipes! Pipes! Pipes in the water!" screamed Matt. "Dead ahead!"

Mary looked back at the depth sounder. "Two feet!" she said.

Sonny wrenched the wheel hard to port around the two markers his dad had placed all those years ago. *Skeleton* started her turn.

"Haul ass!" shouted Cowboy over the radio.

* * *

On *Sharpe-Shooter*, every ear was listening to the drama. Sharpe was laughing out loud.

* * *

Then the unmistakable *skreee*—as underwater rock slid up the double-walled starboard chine of *Skeleton*. She yawed and her bow rolled fifteen degrees, then she bounced back into the channel and was away and free.

"Eight feet!" screamed Mary, ecstatic.

* * *

Then *Bones* hit and both Cowboy and Manny were thrown to their knees. The little tug raced forward. Her port bow slammed against *Skeleton*'s aft starboard rail. O'Connell, who'd been watching from the back deck, went down. For a long three seconds the two tugs were side by side in a forty-foot channel. Then *Bones* was pulled into the deep by the draw of *Skeleton*'s wheel water. She fell off and Cowboy stuck his nose up over the bench.

"Piece-a-cake, my ass," he groaned as he climbed to his feet. There was blood on his chin where he'd slammed into the deck. He took a minute to wipe his face, then turned to Manny. "Go below, make sure we didn't hole the boat. I think we slid by, though."

* * *

Down in *Skeleton*'s engine room, Tick rolled up onto his knees. He decided to go topside and see what had caused the commotion. He needed a cigarette, anyway. He pulled his earplugs. He climbed out into the weather, ran his eyes up to the bow, and there was *Bennkah* on the horizon, majestic and imposing. She was only a few miles away. He scanned the seas aft and found *Sharpe-Shooter* a thousand yards back. "Fuckin' A," he whispered, and dug into his pocket for a smoke.

* * *

In *Sharpe-Shooter*'s wheelhouse Sharpe was livid. He leaned over the ship's intercom. "Smitty, goddamnit, take those fucking governors off now!"

Chief Engineer Charles-Smitty-Smith tapped a switch on his

earpiece to turn the volume down. He wiped his hands on his rag and tossed it into the recycle bin. He'd already removed the plates over the air breathers and one at a time reached into the workings of the big engines with a screwdriver, unloosing the dogs of common sense. He pushed the button on the intercom. "Already done, Skipper," he reported. "Gimme a minute to get outta here before you blow 'em up."

Sharpe put his right hand on the duel throttles and pushed them to the stops. *Sharpe-Shooter* surged with newfound power. No way was Sonny-fucking-Wade going to win this race.

No fucking way.

CHAPTER 26

SKELETON HAD SURGED ahead for a while. The seas had begun to moderate some, ten-to-twelve-foot breakers turning to eight-foot seas on the port bow. But now the unleashed power of *Sharpe-Shooter*'s engines began to take control, and in a few minutes it was a dead heat. Calmer seas aided Sonny. Yet anyone could see what was happening. Inch by inch *Sharpe-Shooter* came abeam, then began to pull away, her awesome power too much for the old tugs.

Sonny took a deep breath. He could see in the distance the name on the giant tanker:

Великан

"Crap," said Sonny. "We're tapped out."

"We were close," said Mary. In spite of her tough persona, she felt tears bulge in her eyes.

Then *Sharpe-Shooter* passed *Skeleton* and *Bones*, and her entire crew, even the cook, came out on the rail and began to howl and jeer. One of the deckhands flung a bent arm with a fist at Sonny's group of guys. Two more gave them the finger. An Inuit standing now on *Bones'* foredeck looked like someone had stolen his lunch money.

Sonny cast his eyes over to the big salvager *Sharpe-Shooter,* now forward of *Skeleton*'s beam. The sight sickened him. Captain Frank Brooks was at the wheel again, and Dal Sharpe stood at the lookout, beaming with sublime satisfaction. "Look a' my tanker!" he shouted across, pointing ahead at *Bennkah* just over two miles away, still smoking, the biggest ship Sonny had ever seen, and a bigger prize than Dal Sharpe had ever won, that was for sure. Two cutters, the command ship *Dauntless* and the big powerful *Alex Haley*, and their escorts were hovering in the shadows of the gigantic Russian hull, picking up their equipment and taking stock.

On *Skeleton,* a suddenly weary and dejected Sonny Wade had almost decided to turn around, when without a warning of any kind *Sharpe-Shooter's* port engine blew. Black smoke billowed out the dry stack. The boat skewed around to port for a second or two before her starboard engine, unable to bear the extra load, also exploded, pouring a tumble of smoke out the other exhaust port. In one minute *Sharpe-Shooter* was dead in the water.

And *Skeleton* slipped past them to claim the prize.

Sonny refused to smile. He leaned out on the rail and found his daughter. "Mary," he said, "I need you to get down in the galley and power up the ship-to-shore. Look in the log, get the number of Lloyd's of London, San Francisco. Ask for Maggie Irons. We're claiming rights to this damn ship."

When they approached to within a few hundred feet of the smoldering Russian wreckage, O'Connell dropped a buoy off the stern. It said, "Skeleton Salvage Inc." One of the Coast Guard cutters powered up and turned toward them. As they went by, the commander removed his hat and nodded grimly to Sonny.

Sonny switched to channel one six and keyed his mike. "Salvager *Skeleton, Skeleton, Skeleton,* come in, U.S. Coast Guard *Dauntless.* Come in."

Captain Bolger introduced himself. He already knew Sonny by reputation. He said, "It's been a bad night, Captain Wade. We lost some men. I wish you luck. Most of the fires are out, except we haven't sent anyone aboard. Too dangerous. I'm sure there's pockets of ignition. Whatever toxic fumes that built up have been vented by Mother Nature's lousy weather. But watch your ass in there. We've got no crude in the water. Yet. Expect some company pretty soon. This is the United States Coast Guard *Dauntless*. Out."

Skeleton and *Bones* idled in the shadow of the great ship for a few minutes while Mary made the call. Finally: "Dad, I've got Maggie Irons on the line."

"Thanks, Mar. I'll be right there."

CHAPTER 27

Lloyd's of London, San Francisco
NOVEMBER 27, 1245 AST

THE WEATHER IN San Francisco was not much better than it was on the Aleutian Bank. Maggie Irons stood at the third-story windows in the offices of Lloyd's of London and gazed out over the wind-and-rain-shrouded bay. She'd been working for over twenty-four hours now and her vision was beginning to blur. She blinked heavy lids over green eyes, then she closed them for a minute and thought about how good a shower might feel. Maybe she'd get the chance before the morning was over. This was not going to be a good day, that much she knew. Throughout the previous night, reports of the *Bennkah* tragedy had been pouring in, and during that time, she'd been assessing the possible damage, not just in money but in lives lost and ocean water contaminated. Lloyd's, the largest maritime insurer in the world, prided themselves on always being on top of global events that might impact the world of commerce, and it was Maggie who was responsible for the information stream on this side of an increasingly complicated situation.

In times like these, she wished for a simpler life. Sometimes the workload and all the extra hours got to her. She thought maybe a second marriage, and kids this time, and a house by the bay. She thought about a little sailboat and a dog and maybe belonging to a theater group or an art class or maybe an elementary school PTA. She could catalog recipes and gain a few pounds. She could sleep!

Then she opened her eyes and took a deep breath. *No,* she thought. *I'm too ingrained for anything like that. I'm too pigheaded for my own good. And this job needs me.*

She glanced down at her once-crisp navy suit. There were creases now where there shouldn't be. She wiggled her toes inside her Manolo Blahniks and ran her fingers through her unruly auburn hair. Then she turned and glanced down into the hub of activity that was Lloyd's Eastern Pacific lab. Along the inner wall, huge flat-screen monitors displayed data—size, speed, position, and direction—of the global fleet of ULCCs—Ultra Large Crude Carriers—from Helsinki to Hong Kong, moving the lifeblood of the world. Down in the pit, men and women sat at their stations and monitored traffic through the ships' GPS/AIS beacons. Most of the data was as it should be except for the now empty icon that had been *Bennkah,* gone off the grid twenty-four hours ago. The reports of her foundering had been awful. Phone conferences and e-mails and computer readouts from colleagues all over the world had hijacked Maggie's multitasking attentions. The story from the Coast Guard had been nightmarish. The Navy had called eight hours ago. The Pentagon would soon have questions. The only obvious silence regarding *Bennkah* came from the Russians.

Maggie's owlish assistant poked his head in her office door. "You've got a call on line one, Maggie. It's a marine operator link from Skeleton Salvage, in the Aleutian Islands."

"Okay, David. I got it." She picked up the phone and pushed the button on her console. "Sonny, is this what I think it is?"

* * *

On *Skeleton* the crew had assembled in the galley, the conversation put on speakerphone for everyone's benefit. And the guys on *Bones* were also listening in.

Sonny put the phone to his ear. "Hello, Maggie. Nice to hear your voice again, too." Sonny had gotten to know Maggie over the years. He knew her enough to appreciate her smarts and her good looks and her professionalism. He went straight to the point. "I'm at the *Bennkah* grounding now, Maggie, and being the first—"

"Bullshit, Sonny. This isn't a joke. The governor of Alaska is on TV as we speak. You absolutely cannot be involved in something of this magnitude again."

There it was. That word. *Again.* Maggie had been there front and center during the turbulent days of his ignominious fall. She gave no quarter then and she wouldn't now. *But she knows me. And she knows what I can do.*

"That's too bad because I am involved!" fired back Sonny. He looked around and got thumbs up and nods from Mary and his crew. "And I am hereby invoking the rules of the sea set forth in Lloyd's Open Form, Maggie, and the rules of UNCLOS!" There was a moment of silence. Only static across the miles.

Sonny finally said, "I am recording this, of course." He panned his eyes around the galley from person to person. Shrugged. No recorders were on. There hadn't been time for such niceties. "And so is the Coast Guard, no doubt. The rights of salvage are—"

"Damn it, Sonny, no! No! You just . . . this is not . . . this is an international incident, Sonny. There are protocols. The U.S. Navy—"

"The U.S. Navy isn't here, Maggie. I am." He decided to bluff a little, see how it worked. "And you've just accepted my terms because you answered my call. And now, because I've just taken possession, I'm going to begin the salvage process on my end. I expect you to be my advocate on your end. That's your job, kiddo. And you know I'm right."

* * *

In San Francisco, Maggie massaged her eyes with a thumb and fore-finger. She reached down and picked up her coffee cup and took a sip. Cold. She put it down. This is exactly what she was worried about. Sonny Wade—too smart for his own good. But even though he didn't have the lawyers lined up, he wasn't bluffing. Maggie punched up the speaker on her side. She began to pace. "What's her condition?"

Over the speaker, Sonny said, "She's still smoking. Down on her stern, hard aground and listing a little. No engines or pumps. No discharges. No personnel on deck. Probably all dead. But time is important, Mag."

"Where's Sharpe?"

If Maggie had been using Skype, she would have seen Sonny screwing his face into a semblance of a smile.

"Sonny, where's Sharpe?" she repeated. Sonny had always been a one-off ocean expert. There was no one like him. *But sometimes if you've got the biggest balls, you don't need the biggest boat to haul them around in. Or sometimes the biggest balls get you in trouble. Beating Sharpe in a quick-draw contest could be a mistake.*

Sonny was trying not to sound amused when he said, "Sharpe is behind me, listening in."

"Sonny—"

"His mega ship was black-smoking like an old Mack climbing Denali when we passed her. Looks like she spun her blower shafts or worse, threw a piston rod or two. I don't have the specs on those big engines of his. But he was overreaching, Maggie. Engines have governors for a reason."

Maggie's assistant handed her a separate phone. "It's Sharpe," he mouthed before Maggie could switch hands. "He's on one of those Narco, air-to-ground rigs. He must be sitting in his helicopter, rout-ing the call through his company board."

Oh swell, thought Maggie. *Sharpe doesn't want to take his turn on the official phone.*

Over the quiet sounds of Lloyd's progressive lab all around her, Maggie could hear the sound of wind as Dal Sharpe yelled over his handset. "Maggie! Maggie, Dal Sharpe here! Sharpe Salvage. I want to reassure . . . that is, your job there is . . . Maggie, you there? Dal Sharpe here."

"Yes. Right. What can I do for you, Dal?" she asked into the vortex.

"Maggie, honey, your job, your legacy, your ass, even, as a Lloyd's of London actuary is on the line here. I'm sure Sonny is talking right now. But you're a lovely girl that's gonna get tied up in stuff that isn't so cut and dried, rule-wise."

"Oh c'mon, Dal, *honey,* I wasn't born yesterday."

He paused for a wind-whistling minute. When he came back on, his voice had changed. "I mean, Maggie, you let Wade take claim of this ship, and by God, I will see to it—"

"Is it true you're not there yet, Dal?"

"Who gives a fuck—?"

"Thanks, Dal. You've just made my decision for me." She hung up, picked up the other phone. "She's yours, Sonny. And I'll help you—"

Over the speaker phone a cheer rose up.

"—but there are strings."

"What kind of strings?"

"Hold a sec."

Maggie stepped out the half door and went to her weather desk, behind which was a NOAA weather screen of the entire North Pacific region. Over Japan there was a large disturbance boiling up and whirling away to the east. Maggie ran her eyes over the picture and scanned the readout at the bottom. She keyed her phone.

"There's a big low off Japan. Be on top of you in less than a week. You have five days to float. No more. Then it's a group grope."

"You can't—five days? Jesus, Maggie, you can't pump that much that fast. Something will—"

"Take it or leave it."

* * *

On *Skeleton*, phone to his ear, Sonny ran his eyes from face to face over the crew gathered in the galley. He looked out the window across twenty yards of sea at *Bones*: six shivering Inuits, Cowboy, and Manny, silent and intense in the little wheelhouse. Everyone listening in, ready to jump. First one ultimatum. Now another. What next?

But five days? If the load didn't come off right or if the stern was too wet or if the interior tankage came but the exterior didn't because of whatever . . . hell, the big ship had just, in effect, crash-landed on an alien planet. *Bennkah* was never supposed to actually touch hard bottom. *Bennkah* was an oversized, overweight development of marine engineers who studied for years and built complicated expressions of their field, based on models that never took into account things like hard bottom. And no one had seen the damage to the ship's hull yet, even if she was ice hardened.

Sonny said, "We'll take it. Anything else?"

"Only one thing," said Maggie. "No cure, no pay."

"Damn it, I knew it!" *Skeleton's* crew erupted, this time with groans. "No cure, no pay" was shorthand for fix it or walk away empty-handed.

* * *

Maggie heard the commotion. She raised her voice and said, "Talk it over and call me back in one minute or I'm going with Sharpe."

She hung up and stepped away from the weather desk, entered her space, and walked around to her seat. She sat. She picked up her coffee, sipped. Cold. She put the cup down. Stood.

I've gotten to know Sonny pretty well over the years. He can be as hard-nosed as anyone when it comes to the sea. And he's smarter than any salvager alive. In a pinch, I would go with him every time. Even with his limited resources. But he has that soft side, and that Honest-Abe approach to things, which is what gets him in trouble.

Can I deal with this? Can I depend on a man who isn't Dal Sharpe-ruthless?

* * *

On *Skeleton*, Sonny opened the galley door and hooked it back against the bulkhead. Reaching out over the rail, he motioned for *Bones* to come alongside. The seas in the lee of the great ship were calming. He gathered his crew as best he could and spoke. "You heard the woman, no cure, no pay. If we get her off the bottom in five days, we're gold. If we don't, we're done. Without pay. You guys know, if Sharpe ever gets a deal like this he bites and stalls and his fancy lawyers start chewing the scenery. We don't have that option. What's it gonna be?"

Sonny, Mary, Matt, Tick, O'Connell on *Skeleton*, Cowboy and Manny on *Bones*, with a handful of Inuits, all stood gazing in awe at the rising bulkhead of a smoking Golgotha the size of a city, if in dry ballast as high as a skyscraper and as capacious as two Rose Bowls placed end to end. The water surrounding the ship was a spider's web rainbow, a fuel-enriched plasma, alive with flotsam and smoldering debris.

And the hulk was full of crude. So far no spills.

Maggie must have been pacing the floor when Sonny rang her up. "In or out?" she asked over the speakerphone.

"Do you know how you can tell if there's crude oil in the water, Maggie?"

"In or out, Sonny?"

"You can smell crude. It smells like black earth."

"In or out, Sonny? I need to know this instant."

He paused. "I can't smell any black earth, Maggie. So I guess we're all in."

"You damn well better be, Sonny Wade."

Sonny smiled. "Now go, Maggie. Run off and do your business. I've got a fire to secure, five million barrels of crude to pump, and a big damn boat to float."

*   *   *

Sitting across the table from her father, a speechless Mary Wade couldn't believe what she'd just heard. Her father had been anything but businesslike over the air. He actually sounded like he was flirting.

PART II

PART II

CHAPTER 28

Aleutian Banks

BELOW THE EQUATOR and just off Australia, the sea is an aquamarine painting. They call it the Coral Sea, and it's formed in splashes of Technicolor that run riot and in brushstrokes that possess the full color gamut, exploding on the canvas in lively gradients so dazzling they startle the eye. Anyone who voyages out among these palisades is forever made humble by such excess.

But the power to inspire can also be seen in the more sedative, more subdued hues farther north. The light is different up north, less raucous, less defined by a yellow sun.

Looking south from the blackened hulk that is *Bennkah*, one would squint into white and gray melting into cornflower, then cadmium with touches of onyx and sulfur, and underneath, the power of jet and cobalt on a reflecting firmament of icy angles and foam: breadth and depth of sea and sky. Now though, overhead, there was a miles-long pall of black, greasy smoke, funneling off to the lee, destroying the vitality of the moment.

Midday on November 27, Sonny stood on *Skeleton's* old-fashioned widow's walk, panning the horizon from north to south. The weather had improved. The power of the sea subsided, but marred by the trespass of a ship so big it was an insult. *How could the richest oil people on earth explain such hubris? How could the Russian shipbuilders ever think it was possible to control such a beast?*

He adjusted his hat with one hand while reaching for the hand-held VHF on his belt. He clicked it on and signaled the men on *Bones*. They looked over and he responded with a wave of his hand and another click on his radio. "Cowboy, come get Tick and put *Bones* at the bows." He pointed forward to *Bennkah's* prow.

A pause, then a click. "You got it, Skip."

"And, Cowboy, stay cool."

"Okey dokey, smokey!"

Sonny heard the excitement in Cowboy's voice, an eagerness that might have to be corralled for the good of the operation. Cowboy was as good a boatman as there was, but he had a checkered past, mostly due to his personal open-mouth policy. He was too quick to anger, sometimes letting his emotions get away from him, not unlike O'Connell and even his own daughter, Mary. Cowboy had lasted on *Skeleton* only because he was so good at what he did, and because Sonny was a tactful boss when he had to be, someone who could appreciate the scope of Cowboy's skills. And truth be told, Sonny saw himself in some of Cowboy's past episodes.

Cowboy throttled up and *Bones* chugged forward, easing up alongside *Skeleton* just long enough to collect Tick. "Hoo boy, Sharpe's gonna be crying all the way to the docks," he said into his mike.

*   *   *

A few hundred yards away in the overheated wheelhouse of *Sharpe-Shooter*, Sharpe had found their working channel, VHF 68, and was puffing on his cigar, listening in. He inhaled the tarry narcotic tobacco like a newborn at his mother's nipple. He was sweating and his khakis had crawled up the crack of his ass. When he exhaled, a pall of smoke layered the air. He clicked his handset and broke in. "Sonny, this is Dal." He held the mike down for a beat and scratched it against his two-day beard. "And just so you know," he hissed, "we're not going anywhere. We're gonna sit right here until you guys do what you do best: fuck things up."

Sharpe heard his radio squelch as Sonny keyed his mike. The insolent captain of *Skeleton* was ignoring him, pretending to do his job, instructing his first mate, Cowboy. Over the air Sonny said, "We'll need a cable on that anchor, Cowboy, on your aft deck. Set the anchor abeam of the ship, way out, due north over the drop. It should be one hundred fifty feet deep at least, maybe a thousand feet out."

Sharpe was enraged. "You hear me, goddamnit, Sonny?"

"I hear you, Sharpe. All Dutch Harbor and the rest of the world hears you on that squawker of yours. Now get off this channel. My guys have work to do."

In *Sharpe-Shooter*'s wheelhouse, Dal Sharpe threw his handset down on the back of the bench and took a long pull on his cigar. He was livid. Again. He exhaled and turned to his captain. "When you guys get those engines on line, you stay right here. Right in their shadow."

"I know the drill, Boss," said Brooks. "The chief is already pulling the cover plates for a look-see. It'll take a day or so. Those cylinders are twenty-three inches. At least two heads have to be pulled. Probably four."

Sharpe hung his cigar on his lower lip. He ran his hands over his shirt, shot his cuffs, trying to regain some composure and respectability among the men. *What a way to lose. Hoisted up and spun away on my own petard.*

But letting *Skeleton* just cruise on by had been out of the question. He'd had to risk it. Who but Sonny knew there was a shortcut? How did he know?

Sharpe pulled Brooks aside. He spoke *sotto voce*. "I'm outta here for now, Frank. I'll be back tomorrow. Tonight I want you to put some guys overboard. A volunteer crew with some night-dive time and some muscle. We need a hawser in their props. Even a shot of chain—"

"No way," said Brooks, backing away. His face clouded. "I want no part of that." He took another step back and turned and looked out the forward windows. Two crewmen were on the bow putting canvas over some of the equipment. "You may hate the hell outta Sonny, Boss," he said, "but that's not my affair."

* * *

Captain Frank Brooks wanted so much to display a backbone. *No more stories; no more lies. When my men look at me, I want to be able to look back.* But it was true that he would do a lot of things to keep his job. After all, he was the captain of the most high-tech workboat in the Pacific. But soiling himself by allowing crewmen, able-bodied witnesses, to act as surrogates, was not an option. He'd had a history with Wade. He had been *involved* with him. There were complications dating back before the tragedy that ruined Sonny Wade. And besides, in spite of the unspeakable day that took Sonny down, everyone in the business knew what the man could accomplish. Most would never gravitate to dumb ropes-in-the-props pantomimes in order to one-up Sonny Wade. He was someone who could see through a clumsy, dirty trick or a subterfuge in a flash.

But there was more to it, Brooks knew. Sharpe had a long history of dirty tricks, starting years ago in the Navy when the guy was a supply officer and had control of more inventory than he should have had. He made his bones buying and selling things that weren't his and forcing issues that were better off left alone. All of that was part of Dal Sharpe's DNA.

* * *

Dal Sharpe, sole owner of the *Sharpe-Shooter*, the ultimate boss, stood for long seconds. It had been a shit-storm of a morning. And somehow he was losing control.

"Captain Brooks—!" he began, then paused to yank the cigar from his lip and bury it under his foot on the carpeted cabin sole. His voice, when it came again, was quiet and controlled. "Captain Brooks, I didn't make you the highest-paid salvage skipper in the world for nothing. And I can't fire you. Not now. And you can't quit. Not now." He looked out the windows, away from *Bennkah*, into the hazy distance. "But I better have this ship. I will have it. Or you will be sorry as hell you ever became captain of my boat. *Capisch?*"

Brooks remained silent.

Sharpe turned on his heels and left the cabin. He stormed down the centerline gangway, sweating, picking at the seat of his pants. He climbed up onto the helipad and in two minutes he was gone.

* * *

In the wheelhouse, Brooks bent down and dry-scrubbed the blue carpet where his boss' cigar had left a black carbon stain. He sighed and reached for the intercom. He ordered their anchor deployed, and before long the *Sharpe-Shooter* angled around to windward on her rode. She was a half-mile from the action as the engineers began their work below in earnest.

CHAPTER 29

At dusk, Cowboy and his crew finished placing *Bennkah*'s massive anchor into the deep mud off the drop. Manny and Tick had gone up the side of the ship's bow from their seats on a makeshift cherry picker and had been deposited at the anchor house with a cutting torch assembly and a pair of cable ends. They had had to release the huge chain from its dogs and set many tons of steel on *Bones'* sliding aft deck ramp. Then they used the power of her main Caterpillar to set it in deep water. Never underestimate the strength of chain falls and two-inch cable. Soon the paying out of Manny's rode-and-cable combination had begun, and the Inuits were officially at work.

Just before sunset the *Bennkah*'s anchor was firmly set, *Skeleton* had gone through one of many metamorphoses, and her crew of seamen had become salvagers. Gear had been hauled out, pumps commissioned, safety harnesses checked, Jacob's ladders made ready. Then Cowboy had rafted *Bones* against *Skeleton*'s chafing-gear-draped rail, and the crews had settled in on the two tugs. Most of the men stood on *Skeleton*'s aft deck and watched the sun cast its saffron glow on the smoldering hulk of the tanker—an eerily beautiful sight against the dark waters and the rocky islands to the south. Smells of Cowboy's cooking wafted between the boats.

* * *

Matt was standing alone at the port rail when he noticed Mary, who appeared and sat down on the first riser in front of the galley entrance. She seemed to be waiting for supper. He took a few tentative steps toward the riser. The last sliver of sun had cast its lumens through her thick hair, across her left cheek, placing its golden halo across her lean figure. As Matt approached, he admired her angles, the contours of her neck and shoulders as they rested taut and perfect. The view was worth the embarrassment of being caught with an over-long gaze. Matt had spent too many months burying himself in his studies. And his chosen vocation wasn't exactly popular with women, and even less acceptable with ones of the beautiful variety. They were nonexistent at the Merchant Marine Academy.

It really didn't matter, though. He had never had much in the way of social skills, stumbling through his young life with a purpose and fortitude that masked his shy nature. So he knew he risked acting the fool. *Leaning on the rail, ogling the captain's daughter.*

Mary peered into the gloom, tired-looking, apparently ignorant of her admirer's thoughts. She watched as some of the other crew walked around Matt and gathered to smoke and chat. The smell of frying steaks was overpowering.

Tick grinned at Mary. His reddish dreads hung down under his hat and over his shoulders. The front of his long-sleeved t-shirt wasn't hidden by his jacket. It said *IREE* in bold red and green letters. "Hi, Mar," he said.

"Hi, Tick."

Matt couldn't help but look on and listen in. Tick crinkled his nose up and said, "How you?"

But instead of waiting for an answer, the Rastafarian wannabe plowed ahead. You could tell the pair had known each other for a while. "I been thinkin' some weird things, Mar. Do you ever think about weird things?" His cigarette dangled from his right thumb and pointer finger.

She adjusted herself on the steel seat and sighed. "Always," she said.

"I mean, imagine if you were somewhere, you go out your back door and pick a mango. What would that be like, man? Or a papaya."

"Where you going with this, Tick? Are we back in the islands?"

Tick looked off across the water. "And what if, like, when you peeled your mango you ate it while you looked out at the sea and it was bright blue with a reef that had thousands of little colorful fish. Imagine that."

"Tick, we're in Alaska." Mary smiled. "And what about the papaya?"

"Papayas have pepsin, Mar. They're good for digestion. I read that. Probably nobody in Jamaica has indigestion. Impossible. And in Jamaica they have avocados, too. All over the island. Did you ever think about that? Avocados have a shitload of potassium, which is good for when you're out in the sun. Jamaica is full of sun. And millions of colorful fish on the reefs."

"You're weird, Tick."

"Or Trinidad. Trinidad has colorful fish, too."

Matt turned away from the conversation, a half smile on his face. He looked back just in time to see Cowboy—wearing an apron and holding a spatula—lean out the door. The big man placed a foot on the landing and looked over the group, noticing Matt, nodding. He settled his eyes on Mary and winked at her. "You and Tick'll make a swell Jamaican couple," he said.

"Or Trinidadian," said Mary, rolling her eyes. "When's dinner?" She pointed to the hungry men. "They be hungry." She gestured to Matt. "And our dishwasher's waiting."

CHAPTER 30

SUDDENLY SONNY APPEARED, nudging Cowboy aside, leaning his head out the door. "Smells like Sunday barbeque."

Most of the men turned.

Cowboy grinned at his boss. He tossed his spatula from his left to his right hand. "Gettin' there. And good job today, Skipper. I think," he said.

Sonny was proud of what had been accomplished so far, and the men could tell. Manny piped up. "Yeah, man. You did it."

"Dutch Harbor ain't gonna like it," said O'Connell, staring across at the gathering of Inuits on *Bones'* bow. The taciturn group of natives huddled, each drinking a beer, not smiling.

Sonny noticed O'Connell's disapproving tone and his meltdown stare at the natives. *Uh oh.* He stepped down onto the riser. He gestured toward the Inuits. "If we pull this thing off, they'll come around," he said, taking a seat next to his daughter. "And, oh yeah, O'Connell," he said, "chill out. Those big boys over there will be doing all the grunt work. The stuff you hate to do. You got a problem with that?"

O'Connell scowled and yanked at one of his ear lobes. "Yeah," he said. "I don't wanna split with no goddamn Eskimos. It ain't fair." He shot his eyes around the gathering.

Keep cool, thought Sonny. *I don't need any crew distractions.*

Ever since O'Connell had come up from the lower forty-eight and gone to work on Alaska's waterfront, the guy had felt short-changed. Nothing ever seemed quite right. And now, Sonny knew, O'Connell was miffed about an iffy promise that probably seemed way too insubstantial to count on. And he was being asked to work with drunks and people who hadn't paid their dues as he must have thought he had, and to hope for a pie-in-the-sky payday.

Cowboy didn't seem to see it that way, though. He jumped on O'Connell's attitude problem. "Settle down, money-grubber. I only promised them two hundred a day."

Manny broke in. "Besides, they're from here. So they have as much right to this haul as you do if you think about it."

"*You* think about it, Einstein," said O'Connell.

"I'm just saying—"

"Knock it off, you guys," said Cowboy.

Sonny listened to this last exchange without comment. Now he turned to his first mate, responding to a spatula tap on his shoulder. The look in Cowboy's eyes said a lot. He had questions on his mind. Probably the whole crew did. After all, Skeleton Salvage wasn't the U. S. Corp of Engineers or the Navy or some super-hotshot brain trust of geniuses. And nobody knew what was coming next. They understood the basics, but no one, including Sonny, had ever been in this position before.

Cowboy said, "Okay, so we got this big-ass ship. Now what?"

CHAPTER 31

SONNY RUBBED THE corners of his eyes. He'd been obsessing over the salvage process for some hours, but an actual list of steps couldn't be possible until they got aboard and completed a survey. And that wouldn't be possible until all the fires were out and the weird gasses had been neutralized. Invisible danger lurked in the details of such a large operation.

"You want the *Readers Digest* version or *War And Peace*?" he said, finally.

"Who's Warren Peas?" asked Tick.

When no one answered, Sonny bent his hands into a church steeple and leaned his elbows onto his knees. He said, "Short version, then." *How do I say this?*

"We've got the anchor set and the fires are manageable, I think." He pulled his eyes away from the group and scanned the big ship. The swell was moving *Skeleton* up and down in slow, three-foot undulations, but the side of *Bennkah* was rock steady. Sonny spoke slowly, thinking about each step. "We'll put teams aboard and go through every working deck, into every hole we can, to plug any fuel leaks or oil leaks. We'll get some barges—Mary's already been working on that—to start pumping the oil off and right her, weight-wise, to help with the buoyancy equation. Then we'll just keep nudging, cranking on the anchor chain, nudging, cranking, nudging—"

"Basically pump off the crude until she's light enough to pull her off the bottom," said Mary. Her face lifted and she leaned into her father.

"See how smart you are?" he said, adding a wink.

Tick chimed in, "But what do we do about the wind?"

"What we always do," said Sonny. "We make her our friend. She's a problem now, but in three or four days she'll clock around to the south. And if we're as far along as I think we will be by then, we'll let the wind do all the heavy lifting." He put his hands on his knees and stood and scanned the skies. To the east a few stars were starting to appear among the intermittent layers of clouds. The western horizon had lost its sun and was now a plum purple shot through with pink. He added, "And if this ship is ice reinforced, and I believe it is, there's a lot of steel at the bows and the chines and around the underwater running gear. *Bennkah* will hold up to what little strain we put on her as long as we don't get out of character or ahead of ourselves. The word 'float' is the operative word here."

Cowboy said, "I dunno, Boss. Sounds too simple."

"Maybe, maybe not. We'll know soon enough. Meanwhile, one of you will have to do exploration duty with the depth sounder in the Whaler. I'll need to know the exact course she came in on. I'll need to map the bottom. The furrow she made. How deep. I'll make a paper overlay, not just computer stuff."

Matt, who'd been quiet all day, suddenly stirred. He locked eyes with Sonny. "I'll do that," he suggested.

"Figures," said O'Connell.

Matt turned to him. "What's that supposed to mean?"

"Cool it, O'Connell," said Sonny. He looked at Matt. "If you mean the charting, thanks, but no. You can do the Whaler and mark the channel if you want. Use the handheld GPS and the sounder. I'll do the charting myself."

They all turned back to the ship. *The huge, fucking ship*.

Manny spoke for the first time. "I just don't see how . . ." His voice trailed off. His eyes went cloudy. He was speaking for the entire crew. Maybe after the excitement of the day and the race they'd won, a touch of reality had sunk in. No one had ever seen a beast like *Bennkah*. All day Manny had been looking at her, no doubt marveling at the sheer weight of such an animal. And Manny was an engineer. This ship's innards must be as complicated as anything he could imagine. And as huge. "I really just don't see how—"

Sonny knew what they were thinking. "Same way you eat an elephant," he said, shrugging, then spreading his arms to encompass the scene. "One bite at a time."

An explosion rocked the *Bennkah*, lighting up all their faces.

Sonny said, "Thar she blows."

"You sound like Ahab," said Manny.

"Yeah," admitted Sonny. "Sometimes I do."

"Just don't forget what happened to him," Manny added ominously.

Sonny smiled. His father had read *Moby Dick* three times, much of it out loud. He used to recite a passage from the novel whenever he had to endure something that defied logic. Sonny knew the passage by heart. *"For there is no folly of the beast of the earth which is not infinitely outdone by the madness of men."*

Sonny decided not to bore his crew with poetry. "You read too much," he said, then turned around and leaned his back on the handrail. "Any more questions before we eat and get started?"

Mary also stood. "Just one," she said. She fixed her eyes on the monumental ship. "What's *Bennkah* mean?"

Sonny took his hat off and scratched his head. "No idea," he said.

* * *

Matt, the rookie, tilted his face into a smile. He was the paper lion, the guy who didn't know "his ass from his elbow." No one had asked him anything serious all day. No one cared what he thought. He spoke up. "I know what it means." His voice was just loud enough to carry over the sounds of sloshing water and humming generators.

Everyone looked at him.

He ran his eyes over the group, then settled on Mary, who had unleashed her crystal blues in surprise.

"It means Goliath."

CHAPTER 32

A FEW MINUTES later Sonny joined his crew, assembled in the galley for supper. Everyone was seated, fired up, talking at once. Someone passed out cold beers. Sonny popped his top. "Enjoy these steaks," he said. "They just might be the last ones you'll get for the next five days. We're gonna be humping 'round-the-clock."

Mary stood at the rear counter, helping Cowboy, who was sweating over a hot stovetop piled with chow. She lifted a drawer out of its notch, pulled it open, grabbed a giant handful of silverware, and laid it out on one of the two tables. "Where's the other crew?" she asked.

Cowboy placed a platter of prime cuts on the port table. Mary followed with the potatoes, the peas, and two plastic bags full of sliced bread. A huge salad followed, along with butter and steak sauce. Cowboy said, "I left the Eskimos over on *Bones* with beanie weenies and a case of beer. They're happier than pigs in shit." He pointed at the steaks. "Everybody get a chunk of cow. Eat now, tomorrow you might die."

Manny did the honors. "Rib eyes. Wow. What is this, The Last Supper?"

"Might be. For me, anyway," said Sonny, filling his plate. "It'll be my ass if we don't make the deadline. I don't have a clue what everybody else will lose, though."

"Hey, we're all in this together," said Cowboy, still at the stove. Sweat ran down the side of his face. "But supposing we actually do make this deadline, Sonny. Do we get a medal or something? I mean, what's the bottom line?"

"You talking about money?"

"Is there anything else?"

"Pussy," said Tick.

"Son, you don't know squat about pussy."

Tick shrugged and started cutting meat. "Ain't what your mom said."

The crew groaned. "To answer your question, Cowboy," said Sonny, "we get everything."

The room went silent. The only sound was of water slapping on the hull and the distant hum of the diesel power plant down in the engine room. Outside, the night had descended completely.

Sonny continued. "Minus expenses, which are formidable. Wait until you see all the barge traffic Mary's calling up. And the boat cut, of course. I'll get two percent more than you, the captain's cut, and that's how it'll go, down the chain of command."

The crew exchanged looks, realizing how momentous this salvage gig was. Their lives were about to change, one way or another. Slowly they regained the use of their limbs. The scratch of utensils on ceramic filled the room. Finally Tick said, "Sounds good to me. I'm pretty damn sick of the dollar menu myself."

"So what are you gonna do with your share, my fine rasta-dreaded friend?" asked Sonny.

Tick spoke up in a lousy Rastafarian accent. He'd only been to Jamaica once with his mom and dad on a cruise ship a decade ago, so his island renditions left something to be desired. "Mon, I'm gwan go to Jamaica. Gwan roll me some spliffs. Gwan sit on a beach ..." He dropped the accent. "... then buy the damn beach!"

"I know what I'm gonna do," said Cowboy.

Everyone piped in. "Buy Grandpa's ranch in Oklahoma!"

"Aww, kiss my ass," he grumbled.

Mary said, "Well, I'm going to buy a dog. A big one. I'll call him *Bennkah.*" She looked down at her chest. "And then I'll buy myself some huge breasts."

Every man dropped his fork. Sonny's face turned red. Mary blinked into the silence and smiled.

O'Connell was the first to recover. He retrieved his fork and took up the thread. In the past he'd made it a point to ignore some of the things that came out of Mary's mouth. After all, she'd grown up with a bunch of men. He said, "I don't know what I'd do with any real money." He looked around the room. "I've been broke so long." He thought for a moment. "Get me some teeth maybe." He smiled, a sad clown smile through the brown work. "And maybe a king-size bed. Huge. As big as they make them. I've never had a nice bed before. Hell, my old man made me sleep on a pallet until I was eighteen. That is, after he was done beating me half to death." This last was spoken in almost a whisper. He took a sip of his beer and looked down into his plate.

When O'Connell didn't look up, a momentary pall was cast over the meal, the mood shift like a drawn curtain. Nobody wanted to patronize him, but nobody actually knew him that well. O'Connell kept to himself more than the rest. He didn't hang out in town with any of them, and he wasn't a man to spin his life into understandable blocks. O'Connell did his work and did it competently, and even if he groused sometimes, they all could be accused of that.

"How 'bout you, Manny?" he finished, still looking down. "What're you going to do with your jack?"

After a pause, Manny spoke up. His voice seemed more thoughtful than the others. He was an immigrant and had a history of nondisclosure. Still, he didn't back down. "I'll pay off my truck," he said. "Maybe fly down to the lower forty-eight, see my family. It's been a while."

Then Matt opened his mouth. An innocuous question. "How long has it been, Manny?" he asked. "Since you've seen your family?"

The table went quiet again. Finally Mary turned to Matt and said, "Manny was abandoned at a gas station off a California interstate when he was just a teenager. My mom and dad found him. Dad here became his legal guardian."

"Oh . . . I see. Well, it's none of my . . ."

"It's not what you think," said Manny. "I mean, my parents loved me and all. They just couldn't afford to feed me. Right, Sonny?"

"Of course," said Sonny, lying.

The air went flat.

No talking, just the sound of people eating.

Sonny rubbed his eyes and squinted into the new guy's face. *Why must there always be complications? And why now?*

CHAPTER 33

AT LEAST I broke the ice, thought Matt. *This new-guy stuff is getting old.* He decided not to back down. If he were more of a participant, maybe things would smooth out for him.

Looking around at such a diverse group—a group in work clothes, with smashed cigarette packs and Kodiak snuff can dimples on their asses, tan Carhartt overalls and boots stained with oil—he could see a difference between himself and everyone else, but the difference wasn't huge. His own life mirrored Sonny's in a way.

And his having to pay attention, but not too much attention because, as he thought, Second Mate O'Connell is a freak about his spot on the pecking order. And the best hands-on guy is a 6' 3" lump of gristle and Stetson named Cowboy who wants everyone to shut up and seems to have an occasional angry streak. The water bug, Tick, is a white guy with dreads and wears a hat that says *"Big Bamboo."* And now he finds out that the engineer-slash-mechanic is a sensitive immigrant from Mexico who doesn't want to insult anyone, but who was abandoned by his folks as a kid.

Bruised sensitivities be damned, though. These people would be hard for anyone to understand.

Like how about when Mary, the beautiful daughter, has just watched her father do something extraordinary, a feat of seamanship almost without equal, bringing two boats through such a tiny shortcut? But to hell with seamanship, at every turn she can't keep from jumping all over him for his bookkeeping failures? Who does that?

Matt kept going back to it, but it was true, he got the job here, in spite of the fact that no one gave a shit about his degree or his level of book learning. So now he knew, this wasn't a school. They didn't welcome you with open arms or bless you with a book of protocols and a uniform. He was alone, afloat by the grace of these guys, afloat beside an anomaly, a ship too big, full of too much ballast crude. *What the fuck?*

Tick broke the spell again. "So what's your deal, Matt?"

So now it was time for Matt to get personal. And he had brought it on himself with his question a minute ago. When he had signed on, he had done it for nothing. There was no split for Matt. How was he going to tell them? What kind of idiot would they think he is?

"He's working for free," said Sonny, looking down at his plate, grinning, chasing a pea with a fork.

Matt winced. *I'm a dope. And now I've got the whole boat even more suspicious than they were.*

Mary spoke up. "Like Daddy said, no cure doesn't mean a thing to our little sardine here. No pay is already the law of the land for him. This Last Supper thing we're doing doesn't even affect Mr. Matthew Fields, does it, Matt?"

Matt locked eyes with Mary. "It affects me. Just differently."

O'Connell, Manny, Cowboy, and Tick exchanged dubious looks. Then they all exploded. Because they all knew: nobody in their right mind would risk their ass for free. Something wasn't right. The crew all had questions and turned to Sonny for an answer.

* * *

Sonny speared the pea on his plate and popped it into his mouth. He felt all eyes on him and glanced up. "Okay, be cool," he said. His voice was just loud enough to cut through the scrutiny. He chewed his food and swallowed, taking a sip of his beer. He decided not to get into any personal stuff. *I'm not good at that kind of thing, and every time I try, it gets sticky.* He said, "We're all going to get this rainbow off the dock no matter who gets paid what, and we're gonna do it in five days or less. That's all any of you needs to worry about."

They eventually got back to their chow, even Matt. But the damage was done and questions remained.

Sonny repeated himself. "Five days or else. That's all any of you guys need to be worrying about."

"Do you really think Maggie will hold us to the five days?" asked Mary.

"I know she will. Huge ship, lousy weather pattern, limited iron and steel resources. She may be good-looking and all, but she's tough as nails when it comes to business."

"Yeah. I heard she left her husband's bedside—where he died, by the way—to oversee the Long Beach Bridge debacle," said Manny.

As the men kept eating, Sonny retreated into himself. He recalled the past, remembering that time period when the Long Beach span was sheared by a Lloyd's tanker and created a nightmare of epic proportions. He thought about the circumstances. He could narrow his focus and look outside himself. His eyes left the galley and scanned the huge ship beside them. His ship. And Maggie's ship.

Please, God, no mess for Maggie or me.

The moon would be up soon. He could probably find Maggie's shadow reflecting over *Bennkah's* form somehow. And he could almost see Maggie's face in the ether. He didn't know exactly if he had some sort of crush on her, but he sure as hell admired her. He'd seen her at work. And he knew that her intractable umbra covered a multitude of ships at sea. Her sihouette was everywhere, even on *Bennkah*'s wide high hull and her cathedral of a wheelhouse and her port and starboard landings, the moon in the details. Maggie was a looker, all right, but she had the ability to step outside herself. *Bennkah* was a living thing to her. *Tell me about your lives lost*, she would think. *Mothers, fathers, ol' uncle Pavel* . . . but no, the stories would be unhappy. All sailors' tales were unhappy. And Maggie was unhappy with them.

As if Matt were reading minds, he said, "She sounds pretty hard-core."

"And single," said Mary.

"Don't get any ideas," Sonny countered.

"Why not? She's not married," said Mary. "And you said she was good-looking. What are you waiting for?"

A long pause. The smell of burned diesel drifted into the galley from the outside air, circling their small flotilla.

Mary bore down. "Dad, you're such a dweeb sometimes, with all that hoping and praying Mom's coming back. That picture, Dad. On the dash? Mommy Dearest? She's not coming back. That ship has sailed. Besides, she doesn't deserve—"

"Mary, you don't understand—"

"Really? I had to live with all that crap, too, you know. The headlines, the stares, the whisperings. So trust me, I understand. We all do. You're the one who doesn't—"

Sonny slammed his hand down on the table. The lovefest was over. Mary had gone too far. Sonny had lost his cool, which meant that Mary would, too.

Sure enough, she stood, tossed her tray in the sink, and stormed out.

CHAPTER 34

SONNY LEANED AGAINST the railing on the catwalk over the wheelhouse. Behind and above him the eight-foot radar scanner went around and around, the screen marking time on standby below. Sonny shoved his hands deep in his pockets and hugged himself with his elbows in the chill night air. Overhead the clouds raced by, exposing an expanse of stars sometimes, or the moon already high in the northern sky. Dark, light, dark. He studied the effect. A strobe just for him and his confused aspirations, somehow related to a wife's desertion and abandonment.

Sonny knew he was a klutz with women. Even as a boy, he was too centered on a fisherman's life. He preferred a day of catching salmon to holding hands and munching popcorn at the local theater. Whatever he thought he'd understood about females, though, was destroyed when Judy left him. The roots had been exposed before, he supposed, when his mother was just a story told by a perpetually grieving father, stumbling through half-realized remembrances. Not surprisingly, his dad was equally inept with the fairer sex.

Sonny never knew his mother. She had died of ovarian cancer when he was a baby, and his father had blamed himself. After all, Dutch Harbor was a small, isolated settlement on the edge of the world, and there were no big-city facilities catering to such a stupefying disease. The family had lived on the water back then: a man, a wife, and an eighteen-month-old baby, in a house on a shore with a pebble beach facing the ever-changing northern exposure.

But after Sonny's mother died, his father had not been able to live in that same house. The memories were too painful. So they moved into a small trailer in town and his dad rented out the beach cottage month to month.

The years flew by, filled with work and weather and the trials of living as fishermen on the banks. But then, when Sonny was fifteen, a man and his daughter leased the beach cottage on a year-round basis. He was a landscape artist from Seattle, who chose Dutch Harbor and the cottage as a good place to learn to paint the sea. And his daughter was Judy.

Judy the beauty.

Love never found better pursuit than Judy, nor a more ennobling reason to learn the skill. Within four years, Sonny and Judy were married.

Then Sonny felt the tug of patriotism and joined the Navy, a five-year chapter in his life he never spoke of, due mainly to his abrupt departure from the elite SEAL program. Sonny returned to Dutch Harbor where he and Judy moved into the cottage on the sea. And suddenly life was grand. Sonny's dad working the docks, still living in the trailer, Judy's father now back in Seattle, painting his panoramic scenes of a violent sea. And Sonny and Judy so deeply consumed in their love they often wondered if they would simply disappear into it. Their love was like air, like water, like food. It completely sustained them.

Judy soon got pregnant, and nine months later Mary was born in the little Dutch Harbor hospital, while Sonny was halfway around the world towing scrap iron to Bombay.

The money was good, though. Great, in fact. And Judy endured the days alone with Mary, raising a young charmer, smart and quick and full of life. Their existence was rich and empowering, and Judy loved Dutch Harbor as much as she loved Sonny. Nothing could have changed that. When the family was together, the joy each of them took in their life far outweighed the time when Sonny was at sea.

Still, over the next decade, Sonny had dreams. One day they would be together as a family full-time, he thought. If things worked out, he could bring his skills home. He could be a Dutch Harbor fixture again, like when he and Judy were kids.

And it became a self-fulfilling prophecy, really, because Sonny was good at his work and an expert at offshore engineering problems that would baffle most other men. The marine-industry contractors that oversaw such operations around the world knew of him. Owners and managers did, too. So one day Dal Sharpe came calling with one of his tug operations, Skeleton Salvage, and Sonny became his go-to salvage captain in the North Pacific region. Sonny had been able to specify some things on his contract, one of them being more time at home.

"You're good with your hands, Sonny," said his new boss. "And I like the way you think. During the off-season you can stay in Dutch Harbor, run my maintenance, and save me a yard bill."

And so the winter ice-up meant down time: six months in Dutch Harbor to weld and paint and perform mechanical work on Sharpe's ever-expanding inventory of equipment. Then came the warm season, a time to work offshore, but only in his specified region. No more trips to the Mississippi or the coast of Africa.

For years the new arrangement was a success, and for the area, a blessing. After all, Sonny knew these waters. He could hire local people; he knew everyone in town. If you want to be a part of a community, you have to connect with it. You have to contribute in small and large ways, supporting the people that allow you space. So the life they had together grew with promise and opportunity, and Mary grew into a young woman of substance—a stubborn girl who had a mind of her own.

That's an understatement.

In fact, Mary was never the kind to hang out with debutants. She was a young lady who followed her father around, demanding access to his mind, which he gave freely. For Mary, high school studies and graduation became diving classes and welding classes and diesel engine seminars. She studied, applied, and passed the Coast Guard's Twenty-Ton Captain's License exam. One winter the three of them even moved onto the *Skeleton* to perform the maintenance together. They were a somewhat insular family, integrating their lives into Sonny's work. And Judy was proud as punch. She said so: "My daughter is not a cutout. My husband is not a layabout. I'm very lucky to have them both."

That winter, Mary found love and priorities changed, not just for her, but for Sonny and Judy, too. Compromises had to be reached, family responsibilities altered and agreed upon. The world was changing for Sonny, but all of it in a positive, life-affirming way.

Eight months later the disaster that now ruled Sonny's world happened.

I never saw it coming. There are no books to read to prepare for this sort of thing. I responded the best way I knew how. I just did what I thought was right. What Judy and I agreed was right.

Oil had fouled the bank. A massive spill. And Sonny was at the heart of the accusations and recriminations. Sonny was accused of some awful things. The entire town of Dutch Harbor was up in arms. The Wades received hate mail by the crateful, death threats, graffiti; oil-soaked carrion was thrown onto the front yard of the cottage.

One day Sonny found Judy alone on the catwalk where he now stood. She'd been crying, her head in her hands. She had just seen

Sonny's face on the national news. The taped footage was of him sitting in a witness chair, refusing to be candid about the facts. Pleading the fifth. Whether Judy had heard the story before or not, this was the official censure, open to the world. He was now involved in a government-fueled inquiry into his competence.

"I watched you," she said. "I watched you destroy yourself. Why didn't you tell them? Why didn't you speak up for yourself? For us?"

"You know why, Judy. We agreed."

"When will you learn? The SEALS, all those years ago. Washing out because of obstinacy and misplaced pride. And now this? This can't go on, Sonny."

But it did go on, because Sonny insisted, refusing to explain to the world the facts of the case. And his wife, his Judy, knew the facts. She shut herself away in the cottage and would not accept the reasons for not opening his heart to a world of jackals.

On Monday of that next week, Judy was gone. After all they'd been through together, she'd packed a bag and left on the ferry.

Sonny never heard from her again. His calls went unanswered, his clumsy letters to Seattle were marked "return to sender." His daughter's attempts were rebuffed by silence. A family of three became a man and his daughter trying to cope, even while Sonny's life became a public display of incompetence.

He blamed himself, though. He always blamed himself.

When the inquiry dust cleared, a no-fault judgment was issued, and Sonny avoided prison, but everyone in Alaska had an opinion: insurance firms and huge oil companies were covering up the truth. And Captain Sonny Wade was a fuckup.

A year went by. Skeleton Salvage was in receivership by then, not owned by Dal Sharpe anymore. He'd nearly gone bankrupt because of the disaster but somehow miraculously—even mysteriously—recovered and moved on to greater things. So a devastated-yet-resolute

Sonny, now alone but for his daughter, obtained a loan from Larry Johns' investment company and bought the operation. He would be his own boss. And some of the men that had labored by his side all over the globe wanted in, too. Success was just a matter of more work. He was convinced that his wife would keep tabs from wherever she was. She would see his progress. She would realize he was right about keeping their secret. And she would come back.

During the next few months, Sonny pushed himself harder than he ever had. By ice-up that year, he had rebounded some. He'd told himself that once Judy was alone, sadness and longing would rule her world. She had been embarrassed, mortified, and disappointed in Sonny, but she must have been fumbling with other emotions, too. Sonny felt betrayed. So did Mary. Yet Judy must have been so humiliated by the public tarring, loneliness must have become her only option.

"You have to tell them, Sonny," she'd said. "You have to."

But he never did. He couldn't.

"This can't go on," she'd said on the catwalk that day, only a few days before she ran away.

So Sonny's dreams turned into a self-destructive workload and a desire to separate his private life from his captaincy. On the outside he was the same man, but down deep he wished more than any-thing to be left in peace by a crew that couldn't understand what it was like to lose the love of your life because of a principal you could never explain or reveal.

Maybe there's still a chance.

Sonny thought about that and he thought about what he had to do now. He scrambled down from the catwalk and went below and climbed into his bunk. One hour, he thought. A little nap for one hour. To recharge his mental batteries. He lay down and closed his eyes. He listened to the hum of the generator. But sleep eluded him. He got up and stared out the window. He had a job to do.

And something to prove.

CHAPTER 35

DOWN BELOW IN the crew's head, Mary stood alone in front of the sinks. She had bolted the door behind her and now she gazed at herself in the mirror. She wanted to cry, not for herself exactly, but for the girl in the mirror who always had such high hopes. She wondered when the hammer would fall this time. Crying was out, though. The most therapeutic solution was work, even though it might be fruitless. She had to stand up for her dad. Giving in was what Dal Sharpe would want.

She filled her cupped hands with cold water, splashed her face, dried off with a paper towel, and left the room. Five minutes later she leaned against the outside railing, gazing up at a full, red moon exploding over the sea to the east. The visage exaggerated the sheer size of *Bennkah*.

In a moment, Matt ghosted up beside her. He must have been finished with the dishes. No telling what he wanted. To try an inane approach or a joke, maybe, who could tell? He seemed to want respect. Fat chance. It was way too early for that.

"What a sight, huh?" Matt said, casting his gaze upwards. He'd been standing there a few moments as she completely ignored him.

"What do you know?"

Matt scratched his head, inept and powerless. "Sometimes none of us knows," he tried. "I'd like to find out, though. About you, that is."

In the distance a puff of smoke went golden, an incandescent flare-up on *Bennkah*'s deck.

Mary dropped her gaze. The beginnings of the former anger spiked. "Matt, get out of here, okay? Get out of my face. Go polish the compass balls or something. Fuel up the Whaler, whatever, just go. I'm in no mood."

"Look, I'm sorry—"

Suddenly a growl erupted and an orange glow floated over *Bennkah*'s deck. A billow of black smoke shot up over the super-structure. Within a few seconds an intercom clicked on. Sonny's voice broke through. "We've got fire in the stern. And it looks like more than a marshmallow roaster. Let's roll those ladders. It's game time."

*   *   *

Mary and Matt scrambled. Within two minutes Sonny had winched Tick up onto the high deck with tethers, and the crew began stringing Jacob's ladders up the sides of the great black hull. A half hour later high-power arc lamps burned amidships and even in the companionways of *Bennkah*. Water gushed over the stern, spraying from the Inuit-manned outflow of *Skeleton*'s four-inch pump. Smoke was everywhere. The crew was on their own amid the destruction, yet everyone had an idea what was needed. They had all donned their fire suits and grabbed the Halon handhelds to chase down remnants of flame, breaking through warped hatches, smashing CO_2 pipes, unleashing the water cannon on *Bones* and starting to flood the forward decks. Engines roared, pumps rumbled, steel on steel made a carillon cacophony that rang out over the entire area.

Some of the men decided to explore. They were without specific directions yet, so crawling the ship, however dangerous, was hard to resist. And extinguishing smoldering fires below decks was a job that had to begin sooner or later.

* * *

Tick raced down a companionway, following the halogen glow of his flashlight. He was the most agile of the bunch. And heedless of the danger. He'd immediately found a midships stairwell and descended two decks with nothing but his light and a pry bar. Smoke drifted in the gloom. *This is gonna be fun.* He ran aft down the centerline until all the bulkheads were paint-peeling black. He stumbled over a stack of bodies in front of one of the doors, but they were so charred, they were barely recognizable as human. Eventually he found the crew's quarters and began rifling pockets, going through drawers and lockers—the ultimate scavenger hunt for the ultimate scavenger.

* * *

Elsewhere on the ship, another crewmember was engaged in a similar enterprise: in the wheelhouse, a man in a soot-covered fire suit examined a cache of papers, trying to read Russian script through his fogged face plate. Exasperated, he ripped his head cowl off and exposed himself as Matt, squinting into the documents, everything around him a charred ruin. *Man, we'll have to tag, document, and detail all these corpses. They're everywhere.* He put his handheld radio to his mouth and reported in.

* * *

In *Skeleton's* galley, Mary worked the SAT phone, a job she had started earlier. She had a list of oil barge companies before her, calling in her markers for the oil brigade that was soon to arrive. At her father's request she asked one of them to gather some body bags from the Coasties. "Get your butts in gear," she told everyone, "while this weather holds steady."

Sonny handled the small winch that delivered supplies back and forth. And he monitored the radio, listening to reports from Cowboy, Matt, Manny, and O'Connell from various points on deck and inside the ship. The oil containment reservoirs seemed to be in good shape, especially toward the bow. But there were so many, more than they had anticipated, both interior tanks and exteriors, reservoirs that used the skin of the ship as their outer bulkheads. It would take a few hours to map and catalog every one. And there was an inordinate amount of heat, seemingly surrounding the midships sections of the hull. There had been no ship-operated release of any fire retardant, no Halon powder or CO_2 signatures seen anywhere. So they had used their own Halon hoses, at least on and near the upper decks.

At dawn a group of weary men evacuated the ship. They marched down *Skeleton's* rail and climbed into the galley and sat. They were dirty and exhausted. And hungry. Mary had a stove full of eggs and sausages and potatoes, and a platter full of biscuits. "Help yourself," she told them. "Coffee's in the pot." They filled their plates and began to chow down.

Sonny descended the stairs from the wardroom and stuck his head into the galley. "Alright," he said shouldering his way through the group, pouring himself a mug of coffee. "How are we doing?"

Matt spoke up first. "We have to put a detail on the bodies. They'll be a problem if we don't." He handed Sonny some burnt documents, a box of folders, a couple discs. "I found the schematics, though," he said. "What's left of them. A CO_2 tank is just forward of the number four oil reserve, fifth level down. It's as big as a house."

O'Connell interrupted. "So what?" he said. "It's worthless, kid. The pipe's mostly melted aft of centerline. There's no sign it was ever deployed."

Matt said, "Maybe we can pump it ourselves." He turned to Sonny again. "I also found a computer terminal in good shape in one of the forward fire stations. There's a lot of info on one of these machines. I hooked it up to one of ours. I need some time to figure it out, though."

Mary said, "Yeah, well that's a bummer. Because, guess what? We don't have time! Or haven't you heard?" She sipped her coffee. Over the lip of the cup she shot Matt a withering look.

Matt grabbed a biscuit and slathered it with butter.

He doesn't look very happy, thought Sonny. *I wish my crew could get over this personal snipe-a-thon. Mary's supposed to be mad at me, not Matt.*

Through a mouthful of food Cowboy said, "Hey, why we still burning, anyway?"

Manny said, "Halon can't do it all. Ship's too big. And the powder's screwing up the machinery. But the CO_2—if we could just get a hose—"

"Enough Halon can do it," interrupted O'Connell. His face was black with soot. "This isn't a big inferno anymore. It's little flare-ups."

"The reason we're still on fire is because there's still fuel to burn," Matt said, glancing around the room. "And all that water we're pouring on everything isn't working."

The crew went silent. Sonny could almost see the incredulity. *Who the hell was this guy?*

"We need more water then," said O'Connell, finally.

"I got six-foot seas curving around the bow," interjected Tick. "You can have some of that. It's a royal pain in the ass when you're working a water gun."

Sonny said, "The seas will clock around with the wind, Tick. Trust me on this. They will help us. But we need to get some of the *Bennkah*'s systems up. We need a charger on her auxiliary batteries. Manny, find her auxiliary storage depot. A few lights down below would be tits up."

"It's on my list."

Matt said, "Look, I'm no mechanic, but at the academy I learned that Halon powder, like Manny says, will get in the breathers of any generator—"

"I know, I know, so for now we'll flood and pump. Relax, fish. We'll flood and pump. You're gonna go for a ride in the Whaler, anyway, this morning, okay? I need those depths." Sonny stuck his face out the door and panned his eyes across *Bones* to the Native Alaskans who were scarfing sandwiches and coffee. "Cowboy, how are things holding up with our guys?"

"They whine a lot, but other than that, so far so good," he said.

"Let's let them collect the dead Russian crew. Gotta be done. Mary's got some bags coming."

Just then a muffled explosion rocked the boat. Everyone ran for the door, still eating.

"Here we go again," said Cowboy.

CHAPTER 36

CAPTAIN FRANK BROOKS, a half-mile away, binoculars to his eyes, watched from *Sharpe-Shooter*'s rail as *Skeleton*'s crew spilled from their galley. He exchanged a brief, faraway wave from someone running to his station along *Skeleton*'s rail. These circumstances were not what he had hoped for, but neither were they a complete disaster. If he could teach his boss to stop pissing upwind, all they had to do was wait until Sonny ran into trouble with that old equipment of his. He would *ask* for *Sharpe-Shooter*'s help. It was November twenty-eighth. Still plenty early.

Just wait. Chill out. Let Sonny work out the kinks. Then swoop.

* * *

On *Skeleton*, Sonny began poring over the charred schematics that Matt had found. Even in Russian, they could tell him things. Numbers don't lie. Unless these had been cooked somehow, which didn't sound likely considering the scope of such a ship and the fact that this signature Russian endeavor floated a lot of politics and even more oil.

Before long Mary poked her head in the door, smiling. She mimicked a cavalry charge with an air bugle. Sonny stuck his head up and followed Mary's eyes out the window to a column of three empty oil barges and a tug heading toward them, just now passing *Sharpe-Shooter*. Another convoy was three or four miles away.

Sonny clasped his hands together and looked heavenward in a display Mary had never seen before. He nodded to his daughter. "You stay here and see to things. I'll go over and start the crude pumping."

A few minutes later Sonny had made the climb up one of the Jacob's ladders to the decks of *Bennkah*. He stood high atop the carnage with his radio and coordinated the oil barge lineup. He knew how important it was that the right order of cargo removal be maintained. No strange hull mischief could happen, not yet, not until he had a map of where the crude was and how *Bennkah* lay on the bottom.

Amidships, O'Connell barked orders to some of the Eskimo crew, who began pulling plates and getting the hoses ready. An oil barge could accept a ten-inch ID hose, and *Bennkah* had lots of them strung on loading davits and lying in alleyways fore and aft on the pumping deck.

Down on *Bones*, surrounded by the sloshing lee waters of the Bering Sea, Manny worked the little tug's throttle and the wheel, even as she lay at her anchor. He was trying to maintain some stability as Tick continued to pump water, but the power of a continuous jet provided off-putting thrust that tended to turn the boat this way and that. Nothing trumped pumping water, though. And on a tanker the size of *Bennkah* they could hope that gravity would allow for a continual soak, pouring down through the decks, even in places inaccessible to the men.

* * *

Elsewhere on the ship, Matt, with Cowboy and one of the Inuits, all of them in full suits, prowled along the dark corridors. Matt wielded

a ball peen hammer, occasionally banging on a bulkhead, listening
for echoes. Fire pooled in spots amid the burned-out machinery,
yet there didn't seem to be any reason for such heat. "Thump," went
the hammer 99 percent of the time. No hollow ringing; the tanks
were all full. *So far, so good.* Cowboy cataloged the Russian cunei-
form numbers stenciled on each tank into a notepad.

Later, Matt, who was playing hooky from his Whaler job, separated himself and splashed down into a deeper area, following
a column of black coded pipes, looking for any usable CO_2 discharge valves. He started when a small fire suddenly erupted and
inundated him with smoke. *I gotta find some usable CO_2.* He turned
back and climbed the steep gangway, then through another series
of hatches, running along another water-soaked explosion of fire
until he reached the deck and the mid-ship fire station, where he
staggered and sat down hard, his suit black from smoke and fire.
He ripped off his mask. Face sooty and hair singed, he sat there
catching his breath. Suddenly, from far away, he heard the Eskimo
crew cheering.

When he investigated, he found that oil had begun to flow from
the ship into one of the barges. He carted his weary body over the
rail and went down one of the ladders to find the Whaler. Six-foot
seas were going to make this next job a bear. He removed his fire
suit, donned his slickers, jumped in the boat, and sped away. The
trough on the bottom of the sea would not map itself. He had to do
this job right. He didn't need more grief.

* * *

On *Sharpe-Shooter*, Captain Brooks took it all in. He lowered his
binoculars. *It's early. It's still early. One screw-up and the ship will be
ours.*

CHAPTER 37

AT NOON, SONNY leaned on a convenient section of fat pipe, sharing it with his just-arrived daughter and O'Connell, drinking coffee, watching Matt out in the Whaler and enjoying the sight of the crude being pumped from one of the interior tanks. With a ten-inch hose, the oil was not sluggish. A hundred yards aft, a pair of roustabouts from one of the tugs were lowering heavy, black body bags over the side into one of their lifeboats. Mary noticed, sighed, and turned away. She sat between the men and tried to pour shots of booze into three cups. Death was never pretty. But pumping oil was a great sign that things were going right.

"It's too early to celebrate yet," Sonny said.

"Not for me," said O'Connell, gritting his stained teeth. The creases in his face were black with soot.

Mary gave O'Connell an extra shot. "Breenco Petroleum has just signed on," she said. "They have four or five barges, ten thousand barrels apiece. So we have these three pumping now, and Breenco tonight. And Lucky Diamond is on the way with their stuff. Plus two more companies are trying to free up some of their equipment. We might be floating this girl by tomorrow."

Sonny said, "Let's not get ahead of ourselves. We don't know how much water we have to displace. Ten or fifteen feet at least, so we'll be pumping for a long time. But that's good. Real good, in fact. And

the stern is up again. Manny and the Inuits packed the rudder housings with monkey shit last night. They wrapped things really tight,
and now the bearings on the shaft have sealed themselves. This
morning, when she was pumped almost dry, they put a come-along
on both rudders and set them amidships. She's towable, we get her
off."

The trio sat and watched as the Eskimo crew worked with abandon. Big black hoses vibrated with surging oil as the barge below
settled into the sea inch by inch. The smell of crude hung in the air,
an unmistakable reek of black mulch—the smell of money. Back
toward the stern a quartet of pelicans stood on the superstructure,
their wings spread, drying in the last of the direct sunlight. The sky
had started to cloud over again. Cold rain was a few hours away.

Mary looked at her father's face. "You need a nap. Your face looks
like a dried fig."

"Not yet," he said. "We're too close, baby girl. I gotta get back to
Bones, spell Manny. We still have fire, Mar. And when's your fish,
Matthew, gonna get me those depth specs?"

"My fish? Hah! Hiring him was your idea, not mine."

"Yeah, well, he was prowling this ship all day, you know. That's
not what he was hired for." He pointed astern. "So he's still out
there, late with the numbers."

"I know. But he's been freaked out over the flare-ups. Decided
there's a cricket in the woodpile. Maybe a Russkie did a dirty. He
was looking for more paperwork last night up in the burned-out
wheelhouse. He looked like one of those body bag guys. Crispy.
Face sort of green, like the Statue of Liberty. Got caught in one of
the smoke flumes, I guess."

O'Connell spoke up. "Something wrong with that kid. Nobody
works for free. I don't trust him."

Mary said, "Yeah, I wonder about him myself."

Sonny stood and lifted his shoulders and exercised his neck muscles. He buttoned his jacket and prepared to leave. "He's got energy," he said. "Just keep an eye out. And I could use a read on the hull, too, so we know where to pump. I was gonna send Cowboy, but Matt'll do fine. But don't let him go alone, Mary. In fact, why don't you go and put your rubber jacket on. Get someone else to monitor things topside. O'Connell here can do that."

"Sure, why not?" she said, "I could use a dip."

CHAPTER 38

A COLD, SPIKING rain had settled the seas when Mary and Matt entered the water and adjusted their buoyancy compensators for the descent along the hull of the great ship. Very little current disturbed their trajectory and they were able to see more than they expected, even though they had been put in the water on the windward side. On a pathway all the way to the bottom, there was no indication of hull damage or oil discharges midships. The hull seemed stuck fast, also, so there was little silt to lessen the visibility on the bottom, which was twenty feet at least. When they reached the chine at roughly eighty feet deep, they swam aft and slowly up, along the fat welds, looking for anything obvious. Within ten minutes they were at the stern of *Bennkah*.

Mary stood in her re-breather on a piece of ripped steel at one of the huge prop blades, adding a sense of size to the tableau. They were now at forty-five feet and the seas were slightly less subdued under the counter, so what backwash there was made for an exhilarating yet subtle ride. Mary leaped away and pirouetted through one of the big bent Kort Nozzles, then danced around the monster rudder assembly like an otter. As she swam, what air was generated around her body drew big, flat air pockets that expanded beside her and made silver plates, scattering and rising up with the curls of smaller bubbles.

She perceived Matt watching her as he floated apart from her. She pretended not to notice he was practically gawking. She'd been told she'd cut an impressive figure underwater. The look on Matt's face confirmed it.

Then she saw Matt wave for her attention. He pointed at his gauges. He wanted to get started inspecting some of the damage on the lee side, following the scar along the starboard hull where rock had insinuated itself in wide streaks and where debris had torn a huge gash along the aft quarter, ripping through the outside plates in some spots. Mary saw him and swam to his side. With a thumbs-up she signaled "okay," and together they began their inspection.

Matt and Mary crept along, feeling with their hands and examining with their eyes. They signaled to one another. Since *Skeleton* wasn't equipped with modern underwater microphones, Mary had to read Matt's reaction to the damage in his face, and she telegraphed her unease likewise. Together, as they moved over the distressed sections of steel, they became convinced the area looked unstable, even though the actual chine was solid and there were no large dimples or declinations that might signal rib failure or separation from the skin. What she did see, however, was the peeling away of an aft section of the stern quarter right where *Bennkah* met the mud, and a long scar of slightly indented hull that looked to be the result of rocks. At the midships row of painted numbers, they again exchanged grim looks. In some places the four-foot-wide trough that had developed was eight inches deep.

They were halfway up to the bow, in seventy-five feet of depth, when the thick double-walled steel they were touching actually cavitated visibly, pushing water. There was an ear-splitting groan and a huge vibration that caught them by surprise. It sent Mary head over heels, knocking her mask and regulator off. Clouds of silt welled up, blinding her. And because Mary couldn't see, the laws of neutral buoyancy confused her for a moment. She reached out for her breathing apparatus, but it wasn't where it was supposed to be. Up was not up, and fore and aft were meaningless directions. She turned to where she thought the hull should be, but it wasn't there. She rotated her body and swam the other way, but to no avail, and the clouds of silt allowed for almost no visibility.

Somehow, not realizing it, she had drifted several yards away from the hull. She began to release air, watching the bubbles rise. *Up is this way*, she thought, yet she was running out of oxygen and close to panic. She'd been diving since she was fourteen, but always in a more controlled setting. She didn't like to admit it, especially to her father, but lousy visibility coupled with wide-open waters scared the hell out of her. Drifting off into the cold was her nightmare. She was starting to have involuntary movements of her chest muscles trying to suck air. She could hear herself making high-pitched noises of panic.

Then Matt appeared out of the gloom with her mask and air gear in hand. He fixed his own regulator into her mouth while he untangled hers, then handed her her mask/snorkel unit and exchanged breathers. She sucked air for a long moment, closing her eyes, refusing to look at Matt until she regained her composure. She felt exposed. She couldn't let that happen. Soon she began to settle down. She cleared her mask, opened her eyes, and found herself face-to-face with Matt, sixty feet underwater. Embarrassed, she pushed him away and made for the surface.

They ascended in a line, making their regulation stop at thirty-three feet for the tables, then broke water, swam the hundred yards to *Skeleton*'s stern, and climbed onto her dive grating together. Their suits steamed white in the pelting rain. Then she stood by as Matt gave Sonny the bad news.

CHAPTER 39

"The running gear is useless, sir," said Matt. "Some of the outer layer of steel is even peeling away. The shaft bearings are torqued, the props are bent to hell, there's a pair of what looks like Kort Nozzles that are mostly torn away, and the rudders are there, but I wouldn't trust them. Lots of steel, though, except further forward where the tankage starts."

Mary nodded. "Yeah. What he said." She could tell her father was impressed with Matt's assessment. She was, too.

"We found what seems to be lighter-gauge steel and less reinforcement. I don't know much about tankers, though. It's double-walled, but all the real steel is aft and, I assume, on the forward quarter where it would meet the ice. I don't know how much is left at the scar." Matt ran a towel over his face. "It's almost like they were sailing two ships, one for the ice, one just to pass an inspection. Again, I don't know how much hull is left at the scar."

Mary interrupted. "We can shoot it, Pop. An X-ray will tell us how bad it is."

Matt and Mary had removed their gear and stepped into the heated wheelhouse to get out of the weather, but they were still dripping wet.

Sonny grunted with disapproval. His right hand had closed over his mechanical pencil tight enough so that his knuckles grew white. Turning on his right foot, he bent over his chart table and made several notations in his just-completed map of the bottom and of the hull lying in the trough. "On smaller ships they sometimes use full tanks with baffles to stiffen things up," he said. "Or they run stringers from tank to tank, fore and aft, that a diver wouldn't be able to feel out, and shooting the hull wouldn't find. We won't have time to X-ray the hull, anyway," he decided. "If she splits, we are dicked." He turned back to Matt. "How deep are we in the mud? Is the hull down there warm or even hot compared to the undamaged areas? And knock off the 'sir' crap."

"It's not so bad in the mud there. The ship carved a channel for more than a mile—you can read it in the specs I wrote out in the Whaler—then her rudders caught something, maybe the nozzles, on an outcropping of rock, and she skewed sideways. There's some silt rising up on the lee side, so a temperature differential is possible. But no hot spots like you're thinking. Like leeching from an engine room still burning. The hull is actually moving some. We didn't see it at first, but it is. If we can turn her back into her own track, who knows? And the windward side was undamaged."

Cowboy had been grabbing a bite to eat in the galley. He climbed the stairs and approached the group now, sandwich in hand. "Hey," he said. "I was just on the windward side. I saw seventy-eight feet on the markers. They're starting to rise a little on the bow. That's what the big shift was a while back. I put a double click on the anchor capstan." He turned to Mary and Matt. "You must've gotten an earful down on the bottom. Scare ya?"

"Nah," said Mary, lying.

"Shift? What shift?" said Matt.

Mary turned completely around, trying to hide her red face from Matt's eyes. *He might have saved my life down there. I can't let him make it a big deal.* But it's good, the tumult that had turned her world upside down was only because *Bennkah* was getting lighter.

Matt stood stone-faced, trying not to smile while Sonny spoke.

"It's the afternoon of the twenty-eighth. Somebody tell me, where's that Japanese storm front now?"

"I got it." Mary gathered her phone and did some calculations. A tiny NOAA app popped up on her screen. She studied it. "About two-and-a-half days out, give or take."

After a pause, Sonny decided aloud, "Let's keep pumping oil until we can raise her off the mud."

CHAPTER 40

THE DAYLIGHT HAD abandoned them on *Bennkah*'s deck, but the rain had stopped for the time being. Early evening sounds now consisted of transfer pumps and thumping hoses under buzzing spotlights so harsh you couldn't stare into the cones without eye protection. The rubber snakes full of oil were dancing on deck, working their couplings, no doubt beyond specifications.

Sonny stood at the rail outside his wheelhouse. Across the way he heard one of *Sharpe-Shooter*'s engines power up, then shut down. She would be back on line soon, too. Another dose of salt in the wounds of life.

Everyone was reporting to Sonny, each intent on their own sphere of responsibility.

The Eskimo crew had made peace with the barge men and together they continued to pump oil. Everyone was getting very tired, dangerously tired, yet even in the pressurized environment, and until they experienced at least one more groan of disapproval from the ship, no one wanted to freak out, every one of them hoping that Sonny would keep them safe. They pumped on a grid designed by Sonny to keep the strains away from amidships. A checkerboard pattern seemed best. And the barges were starting to stack up in the lightly fractured waters of the lee side. A traffic jam of sorts was under way.

On *Bones*, Tick had taken the helm, battling wind and chop, trying his best to keep things moving, helping the barge tugs get their property under control and ready to tow. Tick's mind may have been in the islands, but when he had a task to perform, his hands were on the job. A good thing, too, because a particularly nasty wave blasted the forward section of *Bennkah*, crashing up, sliding down the side of the hull then rolling down the lee and leaping over the moored oil barges. Tied together as tightly as cable winches could make them, the barges acted as a unit, floating over the waves. Still, it was critical that as many as possible get under way to make room for more. It was a matter of control. As Tick used *Bones* to push the flotilla one way, he watched two men, barge riders, separate their string of three and begin to pay out the big towing hawser while their tug pulled steadily away to the south and east, beginning the almost two-day trip to the depot. A few minutes later another tug sidled up to claim her cargo.

Matt was again deep inside a slightly lighter *Bennkah*. He stood on top of the big CO2 tank when *Bennkah* decided to shift again. It had been a tiny movement, but weariness made Matt's knees bend and he fell on his ass. With another groan, the big ship moved a second time and steadied.

Cowboy, who was up in the anchor room, took a turn on her anchor windless. Using a walk-around lever on the capstan, he tightened the screw one, two, three more clicks. He gave Sonny a radio thumbs-up, even as the huge ship voiced its complaint.

Under the water, a scarred section of hull expanded and contracted loudly with the different pressures between the hull and the interior. At once the first drops of oil could be seen leaking from a fissure the width of a human hair, sixty feet down in the water column. A few minutes later, a tiny trail of crude made itself known on the lee surface, looking like a small, thin black coil on the surging water. *Skeleton*'s deck lights were on. Sonny and some of the crew spotted the telltale as they leaned against the rail eating. They saw a spider of black, refracting through the tops of the small green waves that bounced off the side of the ship.

"Looks like Manny's pomade," said Cowboy, trying to release the tension.

* * *

Two hours later and a mile away on *Sharpe-Shooter*, a helicopter approached and landed on the helipad. Sharpe himself climbed out and made for the wheelhouse.

CHAPTER 41

CAPTAIN FRANK BROOKS was worried. All day he'd been waiting for a setback to Sonny's salvage operation, and all day he'd been disappointed. He'd counted the full barges of crude being dispatched and calculated as best he could the weight of the oil that had been pumped. "They're gonna float her, Boss," he told Sharpe. "I watched her roll up twice now. And they've got power on the bow. The anchor's dug in. *Skeleton* might do it."

"Bullshit!" said Sharpe. He picked up the VHF handset and called *Skeleton*. This time of the evening Sonny's crew would be around, some of them asleep in their bunks. They'd been at it almost nonstop. It was getting around that time. Fatigue was surely setting in.

When Sonny answered, Sharpe didn't beat around the bush. "Gotta hand it to you, Wade, you really know how to pick 'em. Looks like you've been pushing your crew pretty hard, too. But there's some ugly things being said, Sonny, about your judgment calls. A little bird told me there's a bad spot in that hull."

* * *

Back on *Skeleton*, Sonny drew a sharp breath. He'd seen the oil slick roll up, a tiny thing that could be a harbinger for more tiny things in any kind of inclement weather. Did Sharpe know about the leak? Or was he just guessing? In a grounding of any kind there's going to be damage to a hull. And if he was talking specifics, how did Sharpe get any details so fast? He wasn't alone in the wheelhouse. He turned to the guys to read their faces. They all shrugged.

"No bad spots, no breach, Sharpe. We're doing just fine. We haven't moved her yet, but she's lighter. Why the call? Are we just chatting or what?"

"A chat, Sonny. A sociable chat. *USA Today* wanted my expert opinion. I gave it to them. I told them my crew was standing by with support and a chopper and as much hardware as we needed in case the *Skeleton* fell on its face. How close is that hull to cracking open, Sonny? You want to be the guy on the cover of *Time* when that happens? Again?"

He's heard something, thought Sonny. "What's this about, Sharpe?"

"I'll call you on the cell."

A few seconds later Sonny's cell phone rang. He answered.

"What do you want, Sharpe?" Most of *Skeleton*'s weary crew had now gathered, listening in to their captain's side of the conversation.

Sharpe said, "I know you've worked hard here, Sonny, and I'm sympathetic. You've got bills. You've got people to pay. You've pumped some oil and done some real good things. So let's get real for a minute. Now's the big push. This is make or break time and you're out of steam, or damn near. I know there's a weak spot in that hull. So I'm going to give you a hundred thousand dollars. I'm going to accept the liability, which is considerable—"

Sonny covered the phone with his hand. "He wants to pay us to leave. A hundred thou."

O'Connell opened his eyes wide. "I say we take it."

"Really?" Sonny made a face, disappointed.

"Why not?" he said. "Gift horse, worth two in the bush."

Matt chimed in, perturbed. "You're mixing your metaphors."

O'Connell snapped, "What are you, gay?"

Sonny said, "Sharpe would get the best of everything, guys. If something bad happened, he could blame us." He put the phone to his ear. "You're goddamn right about the liability, Sharpe. And there would be plenty of risk to you." He covered the phone, looked at his crew. "He's getting excited."

There was a rare silence on the other end, so Sonny took the opportunity to sign off. "Let me discuss this with my associates. Get back with you in five."

* * *

On *Sharpe-Shooter*, Sharpe closed his cell. He turned to Brooks. "He'll take it."

"I don't think so. I worked side by side with the man for ten years. I know the guy. He won't take it."

"Yeah, well I hired the guy. Built my entire business around him until he damn near bankrupted me with his colossal fuckup. Nobody knows what he is or isn't capable of more than me. Trust me, Sonny Wade will take the money, turn tail, and run."

Brooks picked up the binoculars and scanned *Skeleton*'s rail. "You got the 'turn tail' part right." He gave the lenses to Sharpe, who put them to his eyes and witnessed seven *Skeleton* crew members with their pants down, asses out, mooning Sharpe.

He was not amused.

PART III

CHAPTER 42

In the wee hours, Sharpe had taken a shower and changed his clothes. He'd had a bite to eat with the crew, making small talk, discussing options. Now he made ready to climb into his helicopter, a process that wasn't suited to his body type. The weather was damp and he had the kind of form not designed for too-tight pants. As he strode the platform, his khakis found momentum and rode north. His matching shirt also strained to contain the load, and jammed both his armpits with pleats of material. He'd gained a size or two since he was in the Navy.

Frank Brooks watched. He stood on the helipad trying not to laugh at his boss.

Sharpe, though, missed any humor that might have evolved at his own expense. He was still thinking about that phone call to Sonny. He had decided that what happened a few hours ago was an insult, never mind the idea that turnabout is fair play and it was his own crew who had begun the taunting business. Once aloft in the passenger salon behind his pilot, he powered up his iPad. A file appeared—SONNY'S SALVAGE AND RESCUE. He opened the file and scrolled down with his finger. He stared at the screen, thinking. Then he pulled out his cell and dialed.

* * *

In the depths of *Bennkah*, a fire-suited man crouched atop the CO_2 tank. His phone rang and he dug through his suit and retrieved it from one of the lined pockets. He flipped it open. "Go ahead," he said.

* * *

Later, as the chopper flew through the night, Sharpe leaned back in his chair sipping scotch, smoking a cigar. He looked like the cat that swallowed the canary. He called his captain, mostly to hear the sound of his voice and to make sure he was awake.

"Any changes?" he said.

"Nope." Captain Frank Brooks sounded like his mouth was full, a late snack. On *Sharpe-Shooter*, which swings the shifts every four hours, the cook puts together a midnight deli that's as good as it gets—fresh-baked bread, sliced meats and cheeses of all kinds, with deli-style condiments and salads. It's a known fact, working tugs everywhere are really controlled by the man or woman who runs the galley. "Looks like they might get her done with a couple days to spare."

"I wouldn't bet on it," said Sharpe. He blew a perfect smoke ring.

Both engines were a go now, both oiled up, both purring as only huge diesels can do. And Frank had been working with the third-shift crew, checking the systems, deploying spuds and anchors, using air combos, controlling drift with gyros and thrusters, trying to do anything to keep everyone on their toes. He was an able captain, Sharpe knew. A waiting game was no fun.

Sharpe said, "Call me immediately if something noteworthy happens. Then call the press."

* * *

It was now early morning. At the bow, in the anchor house on *Bennkah*, the anchor hawser was moving and groaning with the slight motion of the ship. Each link of chain was fully a foot around and hardened, so it took a lot of power to see any movement at all. The fire-suited man from before, obscured by the darkness, sparked a torch. He leaned over and began to score one of the steel anchor links.

The ship moved ever so slightly, the strain tremendous.

CHAPTER 43

AN HOUR LATER on *Skeleton*, Mary climbed down a companion-way and made her way to a door. She knocked, and in a moment Matt stuck out his head, still wet from the shower.

"You decent?" she asked.

Matt nodded, tried to smile. Their eyes met for a moment before he dropped his.

"Because I can come back. It's awful early. Still way dark. I can see you later, I guess. I just wanted—"

Matt stumbled. "Come in. Uh, well, if you give me a second, ma'am—"

Mary flared. "Cool it, Matt. Just . . . cool it, okay? No ma'ams or sirs or any of that crap." She took a breath. "I came here to say I'm sorry. You know. For working you over that night after dinner. I get mad easy. I go off. I don't know where it comes from."

"You were okay. I mean, you were upset, I guess. And I was butting in . . . like a fish."

"Yeah, well I don't control myself very well sometimes."

"Hey, you've been great in the water."

"Thanks, but we both know that's not so true."

They exchanged sheepish smiles. She noticed those eyes of his again. *Damn.* A silence equally as uncomfortable as any other ensued. Finally Mary shook herself and said, "Okay, well, so anyway, get your clothes on, grab a towel, and meet me in the salon in ten minutes."

"Salon?"

"Yeah. The wardroom. I'll see if I can do something about that burned-up mess on your head. Your hair looks like my Great-uncle Sal's back."

Later, in the salon, Mary covered Matt's bare shoulders with a towel. She began cutting the singed hair off slowly. Touching his neck. Turning his head. Leaning down over his left ear.

Matt seemed paralyzed. Mary knew that the act of touching someone was not a simple thing. And being the one doing the touching was even more complicated. She had little experience with guys, especially handsome guys, but she knew that between a man and a woman all sorts of things could happen. So she noticed as he did his best to stay still and let her make the moves. When she leaned over him, she saw his face blanch as he smelled her skin and pretended not to be swayed by her nearness. She saw a bead of sweat on his forehead. She could hear his mind working: *There's no connection other than utility. She's just being kind.*

Never mind need or want or loneliness.

Mary reached her hand over Matt's forehead and pulled the comb into the curls and snipped with the scissors. She told herself that it didn't mean anything, really, touching this man's head so gently. She was just doing a favor for a guy she didn't know who got her out of a tight spot.

"So why are you here, diver boy?" she said. "You never answered that question."

"It's just not something I need to say in front of everyone." Two of the windows were ajar and wisps of sea air slipped into the room, around the corners of the bulkheads, cooling the place and filling the shadows with slight movements.

"I mean the truth is, I just want to learn the business. I want to learn the operation. That's all," he said.

"You could have gone over there on the *Sharpe-Shooter*. It's a damn sight nicer rig than *Skeleton*. They're always looking for guys that can dive and weld and splice a cable. And they pay good. Hell, they even have Wi-Fi."

Matt turned his head, trying to look at Mary and not screw up the haircut posture. He said, "Yeah, but who got here first? Without blowing up his engines?"

"Good point." She trimmed a lock of hair and it drifted to the deck. She finally smiled at him. Then she accidentally took another snip, just as he was readjusting again. He felt the tug and heard a sharper, *deeper* clipping sound in his right ear. A giant clump of hair landed on Matt's lap.

Mary put her finger on a large patch of exposed scalp. "Whoops."

"Aw, geez," he said.

CHAPTER 44

AN HOUR BEFORE sunup Sonny sat alone on watch. His crew was dog-tired, most of them taking naps, Mary and Matt occupying themselves in the wardroom. The barge crews were doing their swing shifts, pumping oil according to the plans, and things had been going surprisingly well during a brief calm that had taken hold. There wasn't a breath of wind over a dark sea undulant and slick with premonition. Sonny knew it wouldn't last. They'd probably get a bout of weather soon. Intense calm usually was a warning. Yet for the time being the eastern horizon was just beginning to paint itself. On such a tranquil morning the sky would soon be clear and yellow, shot through with brighter hues. It would arrive but it wouldn't hang around long, soon displaced by a nor'wester, heralded by black and foreboding shelf clouds packed with wind and rain.

In the west now, Sonny saw dark blue going to purple where reflections of a late moon dipped into the sea. The only sound other than machinery was made by vessels creaking at anchor, loose rodes swaying with the ambient swell.

Sonny got up and stepped down into the galley. He had made a decision to call Maggie. Now he contemplated his feelings of guilt. After all, he was alone. What were his responsibilities? Calling Maggie at this time could be seen as disingenuous—what if Judy tried to contact him, even as he was standing there, talking with another woman?

Cheating.

But no, Judy wasn't trying to find him. She wasn't trying to re-connect with her old life. Inconvenient truths could be brutal.

He punched numbers on his SAT phone. Over the miles, he heard Maggie pick up. The quiet on either end of the line was mes-merizing. Finally, "This is Maggie."

"You keep strange hours, too, huh?" said Sonny. "I thought I'd be going straight to voice mail."

"Yeah, well, I'm not sleeping much these days, Sonny."

"That's why I'm calling. Got a nice nudge earlier. She pointed up three or more degrees on the compass. Sometime tomorrow maybe we'll move her."

"God, that's a relief. You, or I guess *we*, are in court, now. Sharpe has been leaning hard on us here. Causing bad feelings. He's gone to the TV stations, all righteous and concerned, worried about Alaska's future and the future of mankind."

"And the seals and the fishes and the birds and the bears. I know, I know."

"My face is on the cover of the *New York Times*, too. Seriously. I'm accused of trying to help you destroy the ocean for profit. And of course they dredged up all that other stuff from the past."

"Of course."

"One good thing, though. The Navy has refused to respond so far. They say it's a job for the Coasties, but the Coasties say there's no cause for alarm as long as there's no oil spill." She paused. "Sonny, is there any oil in the water?"

"Not a drop," he said. Technically there had been a bubble of black goo but it was negligible enough that he decided not to worry Maggie about it.

"Fantastic. That's what we've been saying in court. And satellite surveillance can't pick up anything so far. How about the press, out there? Are they circling?"

"Once a day. It's calm now, but it's been blowing about thirty knots out of the north, so they don't stay long."

"Good. They're all a bunch of chickenshits, anyway." Maggie shifted gears. "What about Sharpe's crew? Where are they?"

"A couple hundred yards away, on the hook, watching. Like vultures. Earlier they pulled their gear and did a couple ride-arounds, supposed to make me see that they're fixed and ready to roll." Sonny shot his eyes out the darkened windows. He could see someone in the *Sharpe-Shooter* wheelhouse. Somehow Brooks must have known he was being looked at. He gave a wave. Sonny waved back.

"Keep the faith, Mags."

"Goodnight, Sonny. And please do not screw this thing up."

"No way, Maggie. Not for the world."

"Oh, Jesus, Sonny, that might be what's at stake here."

Maggie hung up.

Sonny looked at his handset and placed it in its clip. He leaned back in the old barber chair and thought about the call, the voice.

He thought about Maggie.

CHAPTER 45

FIFTEEN MINUTES LATER Matt appeared in the wheelhouse. "Hit the rack, Captain Wade," he said. "It's my watch."

Sonny had been dozing in his chair, watching the morning arrive. It was usually a gentle process in northern latitudes, but as Sonny had forecast, on this day the wind had begun and the signs of rain were in the air. The sun had wanted to come up and show itself, but was now hiding behind dark layers of clouds. The night was not releasing its hold. He clicked on the overhead light and turned his head and was surprised at what he saw. Matt had a buzz cut.

"What happened to you?" he said, raising his voice over the groan of the wind.

Matt tried to grin. "Long story."

"Looks like a short one to me," quipped Sonny, smiling.

Matt nodded. "It's only hair," he said. He leaned against the aft bench and jammed his feet against a bulkhead. The *Skeleton* was starting to rock.

Glancing outside, Sonny couldn't help but notice Frank Brooks across the way watching them through the windows in *Sharpe-Shooter*'s wheelhouse. Curiosity was one thing, but this constant in-your-face scrutiny was disrespectful.

Matt cocked his chin. "What's his story?"

Sonny answered as politely as he knew how. A couple days ago he wouldn't have opened up to Matt at all, but he was beginning to like the guy. He was a hard worker and he was smart. He'd proven that when he'd found *Bennkah's* paperwork and the computer stuff and his underwater work was top notch. Sonny and the crew might have been too rash in judging him before the facts were in. "Frank Brooks? Good sailor. Hard worker. Former future son-in-law."

Matt widened his eyes. "Ah." Then, "What happened?"

Sonny hesitated, smiled to himself. He removed his feet from the wheel bench and stood and stretched his legs and his torso, reaching out with his hands to steady himself in the now noticeable pitch and yaw. "We all used to work for Sharpe, Matt. Not Mary, but the rest of us. Like one big happy family. We were Sharpe's boys. But to make a short story shorter, after Sharpe fired me, I bounced around a little bit, and eventually I started my own outfit here on *Skeleton*. Some of the guys jumped ship and joined me. Not Frank."

Outside, sounds of engagement meant the barge crews were working through the weather, uncoupling one barge and plugging in another. Engines roared, a small tug broke away to realign the fleet.

"Why not Frank?"

Sonny offered a sad smile. "Sharpe made him an offer he couldn't refuse."

"But Mary could."

Sonny nodded. "Blood being thicker than water and all."

"Now I understand why he's always looking over here."

"Yeah, I don't think he really enjoys Mary cavorting with you."

"Cavorting? Hah. That's a good one."

Sonny paced the width of the wheelhouse, looked around for his coffee cup. This kind of discussion wasn't something Sonny was good at—making guesses about his daughter's possibilities regarding a relationship. After all, he had failed at women. He picked up his cup and stepped down into the galley to the coffee urn and filled it. Matt followed. "You'd be surprised," Sonny said. "For Mary it's cavorting." He sighed. "Look, I know she comes off as a hard-ass. And that's my fault. She didn't used to be that way. But deep down she's a real softie. And I miss that part of her."

* * *

Outside, the wind began to gust harder, a temporary blow presaging the rain. These kinds of weather events could be seen on the weather map as long spirals of activity, literally spin-offs from the main storm now just a few days away. The men who had been working on the barges retreated into their protective cabins. They knew this little storm would be over soon.

On the weather side of *Bennkah* the northerly winds struck her flat planes of steel at a perpendicular angle, putting a huge strain on the anchor, which was holding the bow of the ship just so. In a normal situation everything would have been fine. But hours ago, someone had decided to up the ante. In the anchor room, one doctored link on the hawser chain creaked open then peeled apart on one side. It began to gape at thirty degrees before the hook shape at the outside end of the link grabbed and held. The sound of stressed metal competed with the wind whistling through the noninsulated room. Tons and tons of pull were now being exerted on what was left of the link. It couldn't hold. It began to bend again, and as the gap got wider, the strain got larger. Suddenly the air was rent with the most horrendous screech—like some lurid banshee lament.

On *Skeleton* Sonny heard the uproar. He dropped his coffee cup in the sink, turned in his tracks, and ran to the wheelhouse. He listened to the sound getting louder and louder, like a freight train descending.

In the *Sharpe-Shooter*, Brooks also heard it. And most of the crews on all of the boats stirred. Sonny's VHF buzzed. "Sonny, that better not be what I think it is," said Brooks.

Crewmen were still in their bunks below. Sonny looked at Matt. "The anchor chain." He yelled out, "Hang on! Everybody hang on!" Then Sonny hit the air horn and tabbed it down. So did Brooks over on *Sharpe-Shooter* and the captain of one of the little barge tugs. The cacophony was overpowering, but not so loud as to mask the *crack* of *Bennkah*'s chain parting completely and sliding into the sea.

And *Bennkah*, her hull pointing at almost ninety degrees off the wind, fell off at least fifteen degrees more, which was all the progress that had been made during the past three days. In the process she keeled over and righted herself in one movement, a 1600-foot monster generating a twenty-five-foot wall of white water directly toward *Skeleton*, *Bones*, the barge flotilla, and a little farther out, *Sharpe-Shooter*. Sonny stood on the balls of his feet. "Prepare for the big one!" he shouted. He grabbed the wheel with one hand and double clicked his radio handset with the other. "Cowboy, you and Tick look out! Get inside, now!"

Then *Skeleton* was caught in the suction. She slid down and forward, forcing a big swag in her anchor chain, then she rose up and up—

—and then the wave broke over her bow, kicking her to port fifty or more degrees, sluicing water down her decks. They rolled down precipitously, dipping a rail as her bow shot high in the air, then dropped like a rock, *whump*, with the flat of *Skeleton*'s front third taking the dead-on hit. Sonny held on through the deceleration and ended up on his knees, but still gripping his seat stanchion.

Matt, though, landed on the deck so hard he bounced and slammed his head. He was knocked cold and carried away for a few seconds—the gauzy eternity that makes ears ring and minds lose grip. When he came to after what seemed like forever and tried to open his eyes, all he saw was the sparkling, liquid silver of concussion in the margins of his vision.

In the next few minutes, all over *Skeleton*, *Bennkah*, *Bones*, and the barges, crew members picked themselves up and checked for damages. Most were not hurt. Some were.

Sonny sat down hard in his captain's chair. The alarm was sounding. He looked around at the mess in the wheelhouse. Something disastrous had just happened, and there was absolutely no explanation for it.

CHAPTER 46

A GOOD SAILOR spends his whole life rehearsing in his head what he should do when the unexpected occurs. But in commercial endeavors, as in all walks of life, the unexpected hits most often when the timing is most inconvenient. Like when much of the crew is in bed, or working a monotonous shift in the middle of the night.

On a summer evening many years ago when Sonny was eight, fishing somewhere off the banks with his father, a cluster of burrs on the half-inch cable that they used to crank their nets aboard grabbed Captain Wade's shirtsleeve and began to wrap the cloth on the spool of their Stroudsberg winch. In the blink of an eye, Sonny's father had a broken arm. He could have lost it altogether, except a small boy had the wherewithal to kick the PTO handle in and stop the cable as it began to pull his father's arm around the spool.

* * *

Now, on *Skeleton*, while Sonny sat in the wheelhouse in his dad's barber chair adding up the pieces, others in the flotilla began to stir. If someone were to look down from above, the collective scene might have been hard to piece together. Each boat had its own serving of drama, each unfolding at the same time.

In the crews' quarters of *Skeleton*, Manny and O'Connell,

disconnected with the action in their sleepy off-duty world, had been tossed like rag dolls across the width of the bunk area. Yet except for a few bruises they were okay. Down the hall in the head, Mary had been lucky, too. She had been showering, so when she sat down hard, the enclosure had prevented any real damage except to her pride. *Skeleton*'s on-board crew had weathered the catastrophe.

Over on *Bones*, though, one of the Inuit crewmen hadn't been so lucky. He had snapped his femur, wedging it between the steps of a companionway landing. The bone protruded through his pant leg—a compound fracture. Cowboy would have to tell Sonny and get some first-aid pronto.

And on *Sharpe-Shooter*, Brooks had also gripped the wheel and held on, but some of his hovering crewmen hadn't been as fortunate. First Mate Bacon was thrown to the deck with others, then dashed against the rear bulkhead as the big boat dipped her rail before riding up and over the foamy breaker. In the engine room, Chief Smitty popped a tooth on one of the brass rails around his power plant. The galley was strewn with debris, and cuts and bleeding were a problem among the deckhands. Amazingly, nobody had gone overboard.

Among the fleet of boats, when the wave passed, the most noticeable aspect was the cacophony of shouting and sirens and warnings in the form of intermittent engine room alarms and list alarms. *Skeleton* alone had topped out at more than thirty degrees of heel, so when her wailing siren went off, it could be heard across many hundreds of yards of water.

Most of the barge crews were okay. The fuel barges had been aft of the major movement. Only two were taking on oil at the rear quarter of *Bennkah*. And so it went.

* * *

On *Skeleton*, Sonny knelt down and looked Matt over. "You all right?" he said.

Matt's eyes fluttered. "I think so, yeah. Dizzy."

Sonny yelled out to his crew below. "Everybody okay down there?"

Soon they began to stagger into the wheelhouse. Manny and O'Connell in undershirts and Mary in a jumpsuit, her shoulder-length hair wrapped in a towel. Outside, the wind had already moderated and the new freshets of rain had knocked down the seas. Ahead and to starboard, the crew on *Bones* were stirring. It looked like her anchor had come ungrounded, then hooked again. So Cowboy and Tick were on the bow, making sure they weren't adrift anymore, although they would be powering up and rafting up to *Skeleton* in a few minutes. The Inuits were gathered in a group. That's when Sonny noticed they seemed to be tending to a wounded man.

Skeleton's radio came to life. "Sonny, damn it," said Brooks. "You screwed the pooch again!"

Sonny keyed his mike. "*Again*, is it?"

* * *

In *Sharpe-Shooter*'s wheelhouse, Brooks went suddenly quiet. He'd fucked up. He'd opened his mouth once too often.

Sonny finished, his anger easy to read as it came through the speakers. "Careful what you say, Frank. Or you'll regret it for the rest of your life. Trust me, I know."

First Mate Bacon stood slowly. "What's he mean by that?"

"Nothing," said Brooks quickly. "Don't worry about it." He keyed his mike. "All I'm saying, Sonny, is we got a mess over here."

Over the radio: "That's not all you're saying, Frank. But it better be all you *say*. Or else. Copy that?"

Brooks' heart began to pound. He licked his lips nervously. He hung up his handset and thought about what his boss had said the night before from the chopper. Almost like he knew something was going to happen. "Fuck," he whispered to himself. "Could it be?"

*   *   *

On *Skeleton* Mary touched her dad's back. She was silent for a moment, maybe trying to decode the subtext between her father and her former fiancé. "Dad, what's going on—"

"Not now, Mary." On the mike. "Do you understand me, Captain Brooks?"

"Yes, sir. Yes, sir, I do."

Sonny did a slow turn to see who was there. With *Bones* coming alongside, his whole crew would soon be present. There would be some investigating, and he was a disaster referee from way back. He needed to gauge his crew, also. Find out who knew what. Except for the oil pumped, three days of work had just been wiped out and many thousands of dollars' worth of ground tackle had been lost.

*   *   *

There was also a new problem. One that could derail all of their efforts and make a mess of the whole operation. On the starboard underbelly of *Bennkah*, at the fissure that Mary and Matt had explored, a tendril of oil began to bleed into the sea. If someone were to inspect the area, they would see a slight indent, where ocean pressure was pushing against the rift.

Things were about to go sideways fast.

CHAPTER 47

OVER THE RADIO, Cowboy transmitted, "Hey, Sonny, we'll be there in a minute, but one of my boys has a busted leg. Compound fracture. We gotta get him to a hospital."

Sonny rubbed his face. *Nothing's ever going to be easy.*

He snatched up the mike. "Okay, Cowboy, I hear you." He motioned for Mary to retrieve the kit bag. "I'm getting you some morphine." He thought for a moment. "See if there's a boat driver over there among the Inuits, Cowboy. Let's try to get one of those guys to take the *Bones* back to Dutch Harbor, drop the wounded one, and head straight back. Do you hear that? Does *Bones* have plenty of fuel? If not, we'll have to pump you some. And set up the GPS with the proper waypoints. I know the navigation part won't be hard; they're all Dutch Harbor guys. And coming back'll be no sweat. It'll be easy to see *Bennkah* on the horizon from twenty miles. But we need to make life easy for everyone."

The big engine on *Bones* roared to life, it's dry exhaust pinging and rattling, spitting carbon into the night. One of the Inuits responded on the radio. Presumably the guy with the most experience. He seemed all too familiar with the radio workings. Two of the crew were already at their posts. Ready to pull the anchor that had reset itself. "Copy that, Captain Wade," said the man. "My name is Joe. I'll do my best."

Sonny hung up. He turned to Mary. "Take the first-aid kit to *Bones*, give the guy with the broken leg some morphine, and leave enough for at least another dose. Make sure they wrap that leg up right. See that they tie the guy into one of the lower bunks. Steaming back to Dutch Harbor is gonna hurt like hell, morphine or no, if they don't get him cushioned properly. Be careful stepping over the rails. Then come back here. Everybody else sit tight until I get back."

"Where are you going?" she asked.

With the coincidence of an anchor letting go—a huge, brand-new anchor and chain designed for many thousands of tons of weight—the calamity that just happened didn't make sense. The wind had started to blow, but the seas had not had time to get rowdy. "I'm going to find out how the hell the anchor chain parted on a new ship," he said, donning his slickers. He grabbed a flashlight and went out the door. A minute later the crew heard the Whaler power up. They exchanged glances. It was going to be a long day.

* * *

After he was gone, Tick spoke up, addressing Mary and for the benefit of all in the wardroom. "We're back to square one, ain't we?" he said.

Mary ignored him. She stood at the open door, looking out over the water to the lights of *Sharpe-Shooter*. Brooks stood there watching. Was he gloating? Hard to tell from where she was. But he was not a man to take lightly, and he had a boss that beat all.

* * *

Sonny was fueled by adrenalin now. His heart hammered in his chest as he climbed the rope ladder. Up and up he went, one step then another, up the side of *Bennkah*. He stepped over the rail and stood for a moment with both feet on the deck. Then he began his trek to the bow. The rain hadn't been heavy enough to wash the decks properly. The work crews had fouled all the surfaces, leaving greasy black carbon everywhere. And there was so much debris from the fires, he had to make his way to the centerline gangway, a street-sized fairway right up the middle of the ship. Visibility was poor. It was still early morning, so any sun that was going to show up would be on the northern horizon, and the cloud cover washed out any colors and put everything in deep shadows. He could have turned on the lights, except wasting generator power in unpopulated sections of the ship was not smart. He decided to wait and see if that would be necessary.

At the threshold of the anchor room a length of chain blocked his way. A brass rail kept seamen away from the big capstan/chain hauler. Even so, Sonny could see his crew's walking rig attached to the gear. He also could pick out the big black hydraulic lines running away in the dark. He clicked his flashlight and a bright halogen beam illuminated the immediate area. The massive hauler took up a big portion of the room. A twisted block of dog-end chain lay across the assembly like the limbs of a steel octopus. Then there was the broken link. He bent down and trained his light on it. At the break, it was blackened with acetylene and oxygen.

Whoever did this used so much heat the temper was destroyed.

He took another step inside. The noise was outlandish, like a macabre, iron cathedral, the running gear descending through access points, down into the depths, pinging and clanging with metallic resonance.

The anchor itself had been lost, attached still to the other part of the chain that went down the starboard hawse pipe, one of two channels as big around as three men. He noticed that in the port channel the secondary anchor was still dogged in place, unattached to any chain. He would have to get Manny up here to rig it and get it ready as a replacement.

Sonny squatted and went over the broken link, stretched into an odd configuration by the force. He saw sabotage, pure and simple. Blackened carbon detritus marked the scar where someone had destroyed the steel. He flashed his light around the room. The cutting torch was there, marked with "Skeleton Salvage" and the name of the oxygen company that supplied the gasses. It would have been easy. The tools were right here.

He stood. He felt like he was in a bell tower, the double-eye chain hanging down into the depths. The sound a death knell. The idea that he couldn't trust his own crew was devastating. But there was no denying it . . .

. . . someone on his crew was working for Sharpe.

CHAPTER 48

ONE HOUR LATER the crew that had assembled in *Skeleton*'s main salon moved forward and took their places in the wheelhouse. The rain had abated and the seas had calmed even further. Cowboy had spotted an oil slick, so for a time they were anxiously comparing notes, trying to figure out what to do. Now the quiet was a telltale of despair. No one had any ideas. When Sonny entered, his face was set in stone.

O'Connell was the first to breach the silence. "Well," he said, "what'd you find?"

Sonny was too angry to speak at first. He spotted the framed picture of his wife on the floor, facedown, glass cracked into a spider's web. He bent down and retrieved it and placed it back on the wheel bench. He lingered for a moment.

"How'd our Eskimo look?" he asked.

"He'll live," said Cowboy. "We doped him up pretty good. They've been gone for an hour. The downwind draw means that *Bones* can go as the crow flies, flat seas, good speed. They'll be back tomorrow."

Sonny nodded. He scanned the faces of his crew. "We got a problem."

Manny said, "I'll say. We'll never get paid now."

Tick said, "And all because the damn anchor chain broke."

"That chain didn't just break." He pulled his hat off and ran his hands through his hair. "Someone broke it."

The crew exchanged astonished looks.

Sonny reviewed the details. The anchor chain on a large seagoing vessel is made up of figure-eight links that fit into a precise pattern and are hardened to the nth degree, but not so hard as to be brittle. The only way to get into the links is to apply heat, and a lot of it, to break the temper. Even forty-year-old chain will retain most of its inherent strength as long as it's not compromised with a torch or something similar.

Matt said, "Sabotage?"

Sonny looked squarely at Matt. There were too many questions roaring in his head now for him to be circumspect and wise. Fuck wise. What the hell had this newbie been doing these past three days, wandering all over the ship? And why was he always the first to stick his nose into things? Sonny stepped up in his face. "That's right, kid. You know anything about it?"

Matt blanched. "Are you kidding me?"

O'Connell stood up fast, a scowl painted on his face, rage emanating from his eyes. He had never liked Matt, anyway, and to see Sonny up in the kid's face gave him a reason to speak up. He turned to the rest of the crew. "It had to be him. Snoopiest bastard I ever saw, and I knew it all along." His eyes bore into Matt. "I knew he couldn't be trusted!"

Cowboy stood. "Why else would he be working for free?"

"And he's a welder," said Manny.

The mood grew from bad to worse. Cowboy, O'Connell, and Manny started yelling obscenities at Matt. He'd destroyed their chance at the prize of all prizes. They moved in. Matt started backing away, looking to Sonny for help. But there was nowhere to retreat and Sonny wasn't helping. Not now. Matt's face turned red and felt raw as his eyes darted around the hostile room. Cowboy and O'Connell finally stood him up against the bulkhead, fists balled, like a scene from an old Western.

Cowboy spat out the accusation. "Tell us the truth, fish. You fuck with the anchor chain?"

"Hell, no!"

"Then tell us why you're working for free."

O'Connell said, "Yeah. Are you a ringer? Do we have to go union, dude? You a scab? Are you working for someone else?"

Matt's eyes went wide. "Mary?" he pleaded.

They all looked her way, but she said nothing. She looked confused.

"For Christ sakes, Mary—" Matt tried to get off the wall, take a step toward Mary, but before he could take a step, Cowboy let loose with a big right hand, knocking him down. Then O'Connell kicked him in the gut. Manny stepped up, opened his palm, and slapped Matt hard across the face. Then he hit him again for good measure.

Aw hell, thought Sonny. *This is all I need. Open warfare on the boat.* But he had somehow lost control and there was no turning back. Cowboy and O'Connell and now Manny couldn't be stopped, and Matt had to withstand a salvo too sudden and too violent for any one man. He fell to his knees as he tried to cover up, but his efforts were pitiful. Matt might have been a lot of things, but a fighter wasn't one of them. Finally Cowboy snatched Matt up and pinned him against the wall again, his fist ready to take him into orbit.

Then from the back of the room, "It ain't him."

Quiet.

Everyone turned.

"What'd you say?" asked Cowboy.

All eyes were on Tick. "I said it ain't the fish. Set him down."

Cowboy eased back, let Matt fall against the bulkhead.

Sonny said, "Okay, this is getting crazy. What do you know, Tick?"

Cowboy said, "I swear to God, if you've got something..."

Tick stood in the middle of the room and turned all the way around. His face was more distressed than Sonny had ever seen it, and his hands kept gripping themselves like someone who was guilty but not guilty. "I just—"

"Goddamnit, Tick!"

"Okay, okay!" He wiped the sweat from his forehead and blinked his eyes. His hands began to shake. He turned to O'Connell. "Tell 'em, Connie," he whispered.

Another silence.

Tick pointed at O'Connell. "Tell them, goddamnit!" he said again, this time a little louder.

CHAPTER 49

O'CONNELL STUMBLED. HE turned white. "Tell them what? What you talking about?"

"About the calls. Tell them."

Cowboy's arms fell to his sides. Manny put a hand to his face.

"What calls?" tried O'Connell. He faced the crew and gestured at Tick. "You can't listen to this jelly brain—"

"What calls, Tick?" said Sonny, easing to the fore.

Tick took a step and sat down hard on the rear bench. The skin of his face wrinkled up and his eyes squinted shut and his forehead went shiny and slick as his mouth moved. When he spoke it was barely above a whisper. "I was wanting to call my ma. Wanted to give her some good news about what we were doing." He roamed his eyes over the group, then dropped his gaze to the floor. "She's always thought of me as a fuckup. I wanted to prove her wrong, you know?"

Sonny exchanged looks with his daughter. This wasn't going to go well.

"I tried calling but I was out of minutes." He looked up. "So . . . I borrowed O'Connell's phone—"

"You sneaky little fucker!" O'Connell lunged out at Tick, but was subdued by Cowboy.

Mary said, "Finish!"

Tick said, "I accidentally hit the wrong button. Then I see 'incoming' and I see this number come up on the screen. And not just once. A bunch. And it looked familiar. But I couldn't quite place it. So I went ahead and made my call and didn't think nothing of it again. Till now."

"Whose number was it?" said Sonny.

Tick looked at O'Connell, whose face was turned to the floor. "Dal Sharpe's. I remember it from all those years we worked for him."

O'Connell tried to mount a defense, but it was too little too late, and everyone remembered how he'd tried to implicate Matt. A sneak who would ruin someone else's life to protect his own. After a minute he gave up. He put his hands to his face. "I had to do it," he said. "I had no choice. It was that or prison."

"What the hell are you talking about?"

"I can't tell you, Sonny, but if I could, I would. Trust me—"

"What? Trust you? You're my goddamn second mate! What kind of operation runs on some fucking sort of espionage and backstabbing...Trust you?" Sonny collapsed in his chair. *Goddamnit, goddamnit. I'm an idiot. I can't see the forest for the trees.* He gripped the bridge of his nose with his right hand and squeezed. *You think you have a handle on things. You think everything can be solved, like a math problem. Or like a puzzle. First you do this, then this and this and this. And pretty soon there's an answer and everybody's happy. The poodle jumps through the hoop. The seal spins the ball on his nose. The rabbit appears from out of the hat.*

He ought to be smarter than this. Sonny turned to Cowboy. "Tie him up. Tight. Put him in the anchor locker. And get his phone. At some point we'll contact the U.S. marshal. This is a high seas crime. Fuck this guy. Someone could have been killed."

Sonny left the wheelhouse. Matt followed, but as he left, Mary tried to say something.

"Matt, I—"

"Don't bother." He pushed past her. His face was bloody. He was limping slightly, and his voice came in raspy, careful words. He must have been choked to the point of bruising. He'd taken several shots to the kidneys, too, Sonny knew, and someone would have to tend to the guy's ribs. There was no boat to send him back to Dutch Harbor.

* * *

Meanwhile, in the water, a growing spider's web of crude undulated in and out along *Bennkah*'s waterline.

CHAPTER 50

AN HOUR LATER Sonny sat at the galley table, his eyes shot with blood. Tick, Manny, and Cowboy stood idle, arms uselessly dangling, grim. Mary poured herself a mug of coffee, the aroma of which wafted around the room. Everyone was tired. Everyone felt like the rug had been pulled from under them.

"So what are we gonna do?" she asked.

Sonny didn't answer. He stared out the door. The weather was going to be pleasant—a calm before the front that was coming. The sky was showing itself in laces of blue and white, drifting above an expanse of blue sea. A flock of seagulls had moved into the superstructure of *Bennkah*, doing what seagulls always do, arguing over whatever sea gulls argue over. Away in the distance a line of islands formed their own little cloud formations. The only thing marring the scene was man-made. And the more Sonny tried to wrap his head around the whole man-made mess, the more he realized it didn't look good.

"I say we call the authorities and tell them what happened," said Mary. "I mean, that's a major breach of a serious law—"

"We do that and the feds will be crawling all over this operation and we'll get screwed right out of the only chance we have to finish the job," said Sonny.

"We've only got two days, Dad. Do you think it's even doable now?"

The silence in the room said it all, what they were all thinking, including Sonny. But before he could answer, a response came from the open door.

"Of course it's doable," said Matt. He stepped in and headed for the coffee. His face was a road map of what just went down, but his voice had cleared and belied any hurt. "Right, Captain Wade?"

Sonny looked at him and almost smiled. He felt anything but confident.

Matt started reading off some of Sonny's wins like he'd been studying the man, which, as it turned out, he had. "I mean, c'mon, what about *Seawise Giant*? The *Santa Anna*, that big schooner? *John Jacob*? You kicked ass on all those jobs."

"How do you know—?"

"James Russell."

A name from Sonny's past.

Matt said, "Admiral Russell talked about you all the time. He showed us the insurance reports on the *Shintu Maru* grounding a few years back. Two other outfits gave up on that wreck. And the other one, the old one, The Monrovia-flagged ship *Lea Carol*. That cargo was in two hundred fathoms. All that pressure. That was amazing."

"Manny was on that," said Cowboy. "I was, too." There was a hint of pride in his voice.

"You used a bell on cables, right? Had to figure out how to position the boat so you could pull from the stern without tipping her." Matt's fat lip made it hard for him to talk. He had repaired his face some—now sporting a bandage under his left eye—yet he wasn't finished saying what he had come to say. "That stuff is in the textbooks now. I had to take friggin' tests on your recoveries and how you accomplished some of that stuff."

"Dad made a computer model with one of those old Commodores we had on board. I was just six or seven back then."

The room grew quiet. A minute went by.

Matt sipped his coffee and locked eyes with Sonny. "But the world's not the same, now, Cap. This business is going to be important. I'm thinking really important. Like Fukushima Power Plant important. Like global warming, global climate change important. The coastlines are more fragile than they've ever been, and you guys can call this job a blue-collar, backbreaking stinker of a job all you want, but everything's about to change, and it's going to change in my lifetime. I know it. I can feel it. And I can learn here. From you. Admiral Russell told me so."

Sonny was stunned. "So that's why you're willing to work for free?"

"Damn right. Because I want to know what you guys know. Because you guys aren't just good, you're damn good."

Sonny looked at Matt. He almost smiled again. Outside the seagulls were squabbling. A trio of pelicans flew in formation a foot above the calm water.

Cowboy clapped his hands. His grin was from ear to ear. "Alright, then," he said. "Where do we start?"

Sonny ran his eyes around the room. He was quiet for a long moment. The beginnings of a new confidence tried to take control. "We set the other anchor and start pumping oil again. Only this time we have to use *Skeleton* to set the anchor. Let me go talk to the barge people. No cure, no pay. We've got two days."

Mary squinted into the glare of the morning sun. "That's not all we've got." She nodded across at *Sharpe-Shooter*. "We've got an asshole that won't go away." She pointed with her pinkie and they all turned and watched as Frank Brooks jumped into his inflatable workboat. In a minute, a double white line of foam fell away behind the ultra-modern Zodiac all the way to *Skeleton*'s port rail. Then Brooks was there standing in his boat, bending his knees in the swell, looking around, listening, smiling, motor idling.

Sonny greeted him with a curt nod. The crew was by now gathered behind Sonny in the salon. "What's kicking, Frank?"

"I just wanted to say . . . uh . . . you know, sorry for popping off this morning about that anchor. I was out of line."

"Yeah. Funny thing about a lie. Tell one long enough and you'll begin to believe it yourself."

Brooks looked down at his feet, embarrassed. Behind Sonny's back, Mary exchanged what-the-hell glances with the rest of the crew. They all shrugged, none of them understanding where this was coming from.

"I know one of your guys got busted up pretty good. Everybody on *Skeleton* okay?"

"You asking because you give a damn or just taking notes for Sharpe?"

Brooks seemed contrite. "You know better than that."

"Do I?"

Mary stepped forward. "We're all fine, Frank." She turned to the crew. "Right, guys?"

"Aye," said the crew, in a ragtag unison, four guys nodding, closing ranks behind their captain, trying to cover for O'Connell's absence. But there was Matt's black eye and ravaged face. And Brooks was focused on it.

Sonny put his arm around Mary to seal the deal. "Like the little lady said, we're all set here."

Which Brooks decided wasn't true. "Maybe. Maybe not," he said. He gestured toward *Bennkah*, pointing to the thin coil of black goo rising up from the side and drifting towards the *Skeleton*. "Good luck with that," he said, a touch of irony in his voice. He sat back down and drove away. "Good luck," he said again, but only to himself. His outboard engine was loud. No one heard him.

Sonny gathered his crew one more time. "One of you guys cook us something to eat, will you? I've got some things to work out." He looked out at the black line of crude. Then he turned and retreated to his quarters. He had some thinking to do.

CHAPTER 51

TEN MINUTES LATER the satellite phone rang. Cowboy was closest, but he acted like he didn't hear it. Mary didn't pick it up. Tick went to the rail and lit a cigarette. Manny said something about oiling up the main and ran off to the engine room. Finally Sonny stepped from his room and picked up the offending machine. Without preamble, he said, "Look, Maggie, I know Sharpe or Frank has called you about the oil—"

"Sonny, don't talk, just listen." He envisioned Maggie standing at her picture window overlooking San Francisco Bay. Her voice sounded calm. Too calm. Her nerves must have been frayed. For the first time since he'd known her, she sounded vulnerable.

Sonny moved away from Cowboy and Mary, stood in a little pocket of quiet near the engine room dog house. "Go ahead, Maggie," he said.

"Sonny, I've been in this business a long time. A helluva long time. I followed my father into it. He followed his. Did you know that?"

"I did not know that, no."

"It's a hard job, Sonny. It really is. Stress levels off the charts. Thankless. But the thing is, I love it. I eat, sleep, and drink it. I do."

Her voice had started to crack. Sonny realized she was putting herself out there for him and he had nothing to say. It had been years since he'd been trusted with a confession. He stumbled. "I know you do."

"Sonny, promise me it will be okay."

Sonny ran his eyes out the doghouse vents, out past the door to the big shadow of *Bennkah*. She was listing again, hard on the bottom. The oil was starting to spread from the little breach in the side. "I promise," he said, not knowing if it was a lie, but hoping against hope that it wasn't.

"That's all I wanted to hear." There was a click on the line and Sonny was alone. He had no way of knowing, but Maggie had just been in a meeting with Sir Herbert Albertson, the executive who headed up all of Lloyd's of London operations in the western hemisphere. His chopper had just departed the San Francisco headquarters helipad.

* * *

"Maggie," he'd said, "are you sure about this Skeleton Salvage thing with Sonny Wade?"

She'd assured him she was. "And don't worry," she said, "I have Dal Sharpe waiting in the wings. He's insanely jealous and chomping at the bit to take control. So there's that. A backup plan."

Sir Herbert Albertson nodded. They were sitting in her office. He'd just flown nonstop from London Heathrow and was still in his first-class attire: a dark, silken warm-up tracksuit paired with brightly colored Adidas that all Europeans seemed to wear.

He was cracking fresh Dungeness crabs that he'd requested from Fisherman's Wharf. Bits and pieces of shell and juice were spilling onto her desk, but he didn't seem to notice. Maggie watched but wasn't eating. How could she?

"God, I love these things," he said. He tore off a piece of bread from a loaf and dipped it into the crab juice. "And this bread with the disgusting name."

"Sourdough," she said.

"Yes. That's it. How can something that sounds so revolting taste so good?"

It was a rhetorical question. So Maggie waited patiently. She knew there was something grimmer her boss wanted to say. One doesn't fly ten thousand miles on a $15,000 plane ticket to deliberate the qualities of sourdough and Dungeness crab.

He polished off the one cold Anchor Steam he'd found in her office refrigerator, dabbed at the corners of his mouth with his bib, stood, and looked at Maggie.

"I probably don't need to say this, Maggie, but the stockholders insisted." He paused. "If this salvage operation doesn't work out, your employment at Lloyd's will be terminated."

"Always so wonderfully goddamn refreshing to hear," she said through the most insincere smile she could muster.

"Don't shoot the messenger, Maggie." He wadded up his bib, tossed it in a wastebasket, turned, and left her office and headed for the helipad.

* * *

Sonny walked up the starboard rail and entered the work area. He saw Matt first. "Matt, how close to the bottom is that scar?"

"Close," said Matt. "Maybe six feet from the mud, maybe less. Then it extends vertically along an inner beam. I don't know how far. Probably a welded seam. But, sir, uh . . . Captain, water is heavier than oil. If we move the ship, she'll implode. Could be a hundred thousand gallons of crude in the water, depending on how far that rip extends before it's over."

The crew went to the rail. They all watched as another bulb of oil exploded onto the surface. They knew the hull was about to give up the ghost.

Sonny snatched up a pair of binoculars and focused on the *Bennkah*'s hull as the crew grumbled amongst themselves. In a minute he put the glasses down.

Sonny said, "Hey you guys, listen up! This is important."

The crew went quiet. They were all now contemplating the disaster that might surely destroy their livelihoods and maybe their lives.

Sonny's voice was steady. "Matt, I need you to isolate that one holding tank. It's starboard, exterior number eight, I think, but we have to be sure. Just get the number. Now listen, we have to get the reciprocal tank's inspection plate, so find out from the barge people if they've been pumping from there—"

"Dad," interrupted Mary. "This is going to be a mess. You know that. And we'll all have to eat that crap over again—"

"No!" Sonny cast his eyes over his crew. "We're going to fix it. You got that? Anybody who doesn't believe it, get the hell out of here now."

The silence was encouraging.

"Okay then. Cowboy, when you get the inspection cover off the other tank, I'll need a hole cut into the plate and a flange welded to it, six-inch, the pipe itself extending down through the plate a few feet, with a wheel valve bolted in place on top. If we don't have the hardware here on *Skeleton* you'll have to scavenge it from some of *Bennkah*'s deck apparatus."

"Got it."

"The reason that tank is burping, people, is because the ship moved and the hull cavitated. Like Matt said, oil is lighter than water, so the pressure gradient is going up inside the tank. The oil we are seeing is not a slick, it's a warning. Not a death knell."

Manny nodded like he was starting to get it. "So we have to find a way to equalize. We have to let the oil out."

"Yes and no. The pressure on the tank starts from the bottom, right? Seawater entering the tank. There's a lot of atmospheric pressure, two-and-a-half atmospheres down at sixty or seventy or more feet. I'm sure that tanker engineers have dealt with equalizing pressure situations for years, with vents and the like. But in this case we have to do everything ourselves.

"What I mean is, on top of that holding tank there are two big valves, plus a couple of two- or three-inch breather vents for gasses, not liquids, that are used during a normal offload. The breathers should be closed now. First thing we do is make sure they're closed. Okay, one big valve allows oil to be pumped in when they're loading. One allows oil to be pumped out. Except the pump-in valve has a one-way-only fitting on it somewhere inside the tank. Like a check valve. Oil goes in, it can't come out the same pipe. We won't be able to get into the tank now to remove that check valve, so that outlet is useless to us. We'll have to make our own. When we open their pump-*out* valve a little at a time, nothing but seawater will come out because the suction inlet is all the way at the bottom of the tank. So seawater will pour until there's no pressure. And when the pressure is equalized, we'll pop the pump-in plate and replace it with the one Cowboy is going to make. And we'll have a valve that will release from the top of the tank. We'll have to do things fast, because when we equalize the pressure, even for a few minutes, the hole in the tank down there will get bigger. All that pressure at seventy feet. But as that tank fills with more sea from the bottom, the oil will flow out the top, all the way up to almost sea level—"

"And we'll put a hose on that valve and let it flow into one of the newly emptied tanks," said Matt.

Suddenly they all got it. You could see confidence radiating outwards from the core.

"Bingo," said Sonny.

CHAPTER 52

BACK IN SAN Francisco, Maggie sat at her desk and stared at her computer screen. She'd had far better days, that was for sure. Some members of the international press had followed her home late last night and camped out on her doorstep. They wanted a statement. Some kind of admission. And a pair of representatives from the Maritime Commission had been calling her, trying to scare her, claiming they were going to subpoena her for some unspecified, upcoming hearings. The governor of Alaska, a man out of his depth, was leading a political charge, too. He had no facts, so on television he had pursed his lips into an ignoble moue, and in unctuous asides for the world to hear, disclaimed responsibility for any Russian oil, ranting about the Alaskan EPA Standards Commission not being given routes and times of Russian oil carriers—never mind the Automatic Identification System units now installed on all commercial ships—and demand the United States Armed Forces get involved at once.

A scenario that Maggie knew would not work.

Then her boss shows up.

I'm stuck. I have to depend on Sonny. And I know he's not telling me the whole story. He's never been very talkative at the best of times. If guilt were an apple, Sonny would be the worm, living in his own cave, eating the walls a bite at a time.

Or I could go with Sharpe.

Maggie had been there when Sonny Wade's life fell apart. That disaster was mind boggling, worse than the Long Beach Bridge fiasco. Except there was doubt. What did happen that night? What were the circumstances? This was before GPS/AIS recorded every move a ship made in the sea. And Sonny, stoic and single-minded, nodded his head in that witness chair, and with a dignity remarkable in the face of such scorn, refused to allow anyone to pursue any mitigating or redeeming facts about that night. It was as if he *wanted* to be destroyed. It was as if, in turning in on himself and his disillusions about his private life, he invited the hatred that rained down.

Maggie knew about Judy Wade. Sonny refused to talk about his personal life, but the details bled through. The quiet that attended him every day during those hearings was a marker—like a bell buoy—that rang and rang, the harder the wind blew.

I learned about Sonny during those days. I learned to respect him. But why?

Maggie had had her own ignominies to deal with back then, too. Her ex-husband, Ron Jackson, was a self-styled aeronautics engineer who one morning fell to earth from two hundred feet when the garage welds on his home-built, ultralight plane failed. *What a trip, as they say.* The jokers at the little airport called him a meat bomb. At the hospital they told her that Ron's broken spine had not killed him. They said his liver was so enlarged, it had burst like a rotten peach.

Ron, she knew, was what the doctors called a functioning alcoholic.

So Maggie watched as the hospital attendants wrapped the body and took it away. She went home to their town house and accepted a call from *Chevron*, and within an hour she was on a jet to the site of Sonny's Alaskan oil spill, which somehow translated to a venal disregard for her husband's condition and a reputation that dogged her still, even when she changed her name back to Irons.

So I know about Sonny Wade. I know more than he thinks I do. I know there's more to the story. And in spite of his reticence, I like the guy. And I trust him.

But when she'd called him a few minutes ago, she needed assurances. This thing was bigger than she was. She needed words from Sonny. She needed him to stand fast.

I hope to God he will.

CHAPTER 53

IN THE WATERS of the U.S. Aleutians, later that day, Sonny and his entire crew stood on *Bennkah*'s deck. Manny held the tools that he and his boss would need: a pair of huge wrenches, a pry bar, and a pair of cheater pipes. Gulls circled in the air and the sea smelled of brine and weeds and a faint aroma of heavy earth, the unmistakable odor of light, sweet crude.

Sonny and Manny examined the inspection plate at their feet. Twelve one-inch bolts around a steel flange the size of a large manhole cover. The one that Cowboy had welded up was identical, except it had a six-inch ID pipe coming out the top and bottom, with a valve assembly incorporated into the fitting, the kind you could feather open and shut by turning a wheel. Cowboy and Matt were several yards away manning the discharge pipe. Mary and Tick stood back, ready to jump in at a moment's notice.

Sonny tried to lighten everyone's load a bit by teasing Tick. The resident rasta hadn't taken a bath in a few days now.

"Tick, you smell flammable. Is this a new thing? Even the crude oil on deck is running away from you."

Tick scratched himself and rubbed his stubbly cheeks with his right hand. "Oil ain't nice, Sonny. Except on salad and Manny's hair. I'm saving fresh water and soap for the big push." He shrugged and turned to Mary. "Ya know, Mar, I been thinkin' about—"

"Not now, Tick." She exchanged looks with her father. "Keep your head in the game. Both of you. This is serious."

Sonny may have been reticent about personal issues, but at the job he was in his element. He turned to his first mate. "Crack your valve, Cowboy. Tell me what you got."

Cowboy began to turn the wheel on the pump-out. The suction from this valve went all the way to the bottom of the ruptured tank. He turned the valve and turned the valve . . .

. . . and he got oil. But in a few seconds seawater began to spew out at high pressure.

"Water!" shouted Cowboy. "I got water!"

"Open her up, Cowboy, all the way!"

Sonny turned to Manny. "We have to get this plate off before Cowboy's seawater turns to crude. But if we undo these bolts too fast, the pressure will blow and take both of our heads clean off. You sure you want to do this?"

"Hey, two heads are better than one," said his chief mechanic.

Sonny grinned as he and Manny took their wrenches and began to crank.

At the discharge end, Cowboy and Matt held fast to their valve as gouts of foamy sea washed over the deck. They were both on their knees, trying to maintain some leverage despite the lubrication factor. There had been a certain amount of oil still in the pipe, and when it had evacuated it had made a mess. Gripping the equipment was like holding on to eels. Now the valve was wide open, but with four hands on it, Cowboy and Matt were prepared to feather it at the first sign of pure black crude, except by now they were covered in the seawater slurry of the first few seconds. As they struggled with their end, two of the big nuts on the other plate were removed, one by Sonny, one by Manny. They both moved their wrenches to the adjoining nuts.

Soon four had been removed and the big rubber gasket under the flange began to fail, spitting black. Sonny couldn't get out of the way in time. Within seconds he was covered in oil and so was Manny, who wiped his face with a rag and smiled through the noxious crude.

Tick and Mary stood wide-eyed.

While Sonny worked, he talked. "Keep it coming ... keep it coming ... keep it coming ..."

"Yessir ... Yessir ... Yowza ..." said Cowboy.

Slowly the pressure began to dissipate. Two more nuts came off, then two more still. The pressure was almost down to nothing as Sonny and Manny freed the last bolts. Then it stopped altogether.

Cowboy said, "I'm getting oil. Oil! We're—"

"Shut it! Shut it!" said Sonny.

Cowboy and Matt cranked their valve shut. Then, with Manny's help, Sonny pried their plate up and removed it, replacing the original with the one Cowboy had made. Over two hundred pounds of newly engineered inspection plate slipped over the hole and down onto the one-inch bolts. Together Sonny and Manny began to twist the nuts back on.

Four of the nuts were tight just as oil began to bubble out.

"That's us," said Mary as she snatched Tick by the shoulder and pushed. Together they grabbed the business end of a six-inch ID hose that now led into an empty tank. As black crude began to gush, they stuck it into the valve pipe and toggled it shut and grinned at each other, covered in oil.

Deep underneath *Bennkah*, the torn steel bent inward as the hole widened to accept the sea. A loss of pressure from inside allowed the crack to conform to stress patterns dictated by the depth. But there was no harm, no foul. And more importantly, no oil. All the crude was now floating up inside the damaged reservoir, pumping itself into an adjoining holding tank as the water filled the void from the bottom up.

On deck, an oil-covered sextet, Sonny, Manny, Cowboy, Matt, Tick, and Mary, were beaming from blackened ear to blackened ear.

"How'd you know all that stuff, Dad?" asked Mary. She crinkled her nose and looked across at Matt and the others covered in goo. The seagulls were circling overhead still, gazing down on the display. Across the water, *Sharpe-Shooter* sat. A pair of binoculars could be seen sticking out of the pilot house.

"I didn't. I'm just like you. Making things up as I go along. Now let's get this other plate bolted onto that hole over there."

"You did it," said Manny, patting Sonny on his back.

"*We* did it," said Sonny.

CHAPTER 54

SETTING *BENNKAH*'S SPARE anchor had taken the rest of the afternoon. The rain had appeared again, a passing band that let loose an icy drizzle and made them wish for that next cup of coffee. By the time it was over, they were finished. And exhausted. The sky was violet turning to yellow in the west, with intermittent regiments of stars ranging across the heavens. On the northern edge of the sea a faint green glow could be seen, the beginnings of the Aurora Borealis that would light up the sky in the wee hours. Sometimes atmospheric disturbances affected the earth's magnetic field. The approaching storm was allowing the electrons in the upper atmosphere to be seen farther south than usual. For the next two nights, at least, the sky would be a light show.

On *Skeleton*, Tick and Matt were in good spirits as they held a high-pressure hose and blew grime twenty feet into the air while Sonny watched. He had told them that the decks were starting to get scary dirty what with all the oil and soot, and a little house cleaning wouldn't hurt.

"We're getting closer, aren't we?" said Matt.

"Yup," said Sonny. "All's left is to keep cranking on the new anchor when *Bennkah* wants to move, and when the wind comes around, pull her free."

The galley door opened and a rain-suited Mary emerged with

a tray of sandwiches. She passed them out. "Chew slow," she said. "That's the last of the lunchmeat. But on the bright side, we've got peanut butter to spare in the galley. And lots of crackers." She checked the sky, then turned to her dad. "NOAA weather said the storm is building and moving fast. So no more barges are going to be out our way until it's over."

"That's okay," said Sonny. "We don't need them. By my calculations the barges that are here and still empty can fill up and go, and she'll be light enough. She might be light enough now. All we need is some wind and *Bones* and we're good to go."

Cowboy had been on the radio with *Bones* most of the past hour. Now he approached the group. He had a sour look on his face when he turned to Sonny. "That's gonna be a problem," he said. "*Bones* ain't comin' back."

Sonny felt like he'd been punched in the gut. "What do you mean—"

"Those fucking blubber-eaters left *Bones* at the dock. They said she's gonna stay there, too, 'til they get their money. I knew letting them anywhere near liquor would fuck things up. They've been drinking. Now they're winos again. They want their pay."

Most salvage operations have a home office. Maybe a trailer or something with a phone and a copy machine and a desk where someone does the books. Sonny, the lousy businessman, had none of that. Sonny did all of his work out of the wheelhouse on *Skeleton*. Sonny couldn't believe his ears. He started pacing back and forth. He stopped, locked eyes with Cowboy. "You never paid them?"

"With what?"

"Are you kidding me?"

"Whoa, whoa, whoa, Boss. Get your head out of the sand for once. You can't lay this on me. This is all you, Sonny. You're the captain. If you'd paid those guys, I wouldn't have been on the radio for an hour. I'd have had something to offer. As it is, we got no one in Dutch Harbor now, anyway, so if you'd have been doing something other than oil distribution equations, we wouldn't be in this mess. *Again.*"

Sonny stood, speechless. "Again, is it?" he finally said.

Sonny turned his back. *Shit.* When the Inuit crewman had been injured, he hadn't been thinking. For some reason he never put his mind to work beyond the immediate problem, and in this case he figured that the emergency took precedence. At least now he *hoped* he'd thought that. How could he have forgotten the contractual stuff? Why hadn't Mary said something?

Still, though, arguing with Cowboy was no way to solve a problem. He had to have *Bones.* And Cowboy was in his face as usual, which was getting old. Everyone was tired, he knew that. But it goes with the territory. And saying anything you want to say to the captain gets tiresome.

A crack in Sonny's rock-hard veneer showed itself. He turned back around. "Fuck you, Cowboy."

A trio of words he immediately regretted. He watched as a band of color started at Cowboy's ears and spread down his cheeks and neck. The big man opened his mouth and closed it. Sonny knew that Cowboy had never been one to vocalize about high concepts like trust, and as his history showed, he'd never been one to take what he considered undeserved lip from a boss. Even Sonny Wade. Plus, Sonny knew he was on tenterhooks because the crew was pissed at every little thing, mostly at him for buying into the whole *Bennkah* thing in the first place. Nothing worthwhile is ever easy, especially when the competition is up your ass and you're too single-minded or too weak to do something about it. And too addle-brained to keep up with the contract labor.

Sonny watched as Cowboy maneuvered himself into what he

must have considered an offensive position. There might as well have been a pool table and a jukebox there on the deck. The angry man looked down into Sonny's face. "Fuck yourself, Sonny!"

Sonny saw Matt take one look at the situation and decide his bosses were serious. He tried to step in. He'd already proven he wasn't a fighter, but he must have thought the voice of reason might help. He held his hands up and stepped between the two men. "Alright, that's enough."

Cowboy stuck his hand in his face and shoved him, ass-over-elbows, into the gunwale. "Back off, punk," he said.

Then Mary offered her opinion. It was a question, really, directed at Cowboy. "What's wrong with you?" she shouted.

"Shut up, bitch," said Cowboy, which was all Sonny needed to hear. In a flash, he drew his fist back and punched Cowboy in the side of the jaw, staggering him.

Cowboy wasn't staggered for long, though. He came at Sonny and threw a haymaker. Sonny ducked it easily, then took a shot from up inside and connected with Cowboy's ribs. He followed it up with an overhand to the other side of Cowboy's jaw, dropping him to a knee.

Matt raised himself on one elbow. He shook his head and looked up in time to see Cowboy on one knee, steeling himself, balling his fist and sending a powerful uppercut into Sonny's groin, doubling Sonny over. Then Cowboy stood and held his knees for a moment, breathing hard. He rolled his shoulders back and approached Sonny, who was rising from the dead.

Cowboy, for some unknown reason, never quite trusted anyone, which was what made him a bar fighter. He tended to be accusatory. No one in his mind was ever innocent. There were no Boy Scouts. And when he was angry, he displayed his feelings however he could. Sonny had given it his best, but now Cowboy began to rain monster shots onto his head, standing him up, nailing him again and again.

Sonny blinked through the blood and concentrated on keeping his feet. But Cowboy's size, his power, and his disposition were too much for him. Over and over, as if in slow motion, he watched Cowboy's fists pounding him, punching him again and again until—CLICK—Mary had appeared out of nowhere to stick a .38 in Cowboy's face.

Sonny blinked.

"Stop it, Cowboy. Now. *Bitch*," she spat through clenched teeth.

Sonny, through the fog, saw Matt looking at him. When Sonny went to his knees, he approached.

Cowboy fell back and leaned against the bulkhead, chest heaving. He looked down at his fists. He raised his head and squinted through the sweat. "You brought this on yourself, Sonny," he said. "All of it. Just like before." He turned and went up the rail and climbed the stairwell to the crews' quarters.

"I'm outta here. Takin' the Whaler to *Sharpe-Shooter*. This time I ain't goin' down with the ship."

CHAPTER 55

THE LAST OF the barges were gone. Quiet had invaded the evening.

Mary took the ice bag and placed it on Sonny's forehead. Together they stood in the salon and watched through the starboard ports as Tick and Cowboy piled their things into the Whaler. Sonny placed his elbows on one of the tables and positioned the ice over his eye and held the bag there, just as Manny came through the salon with his sea bag.

Sonny said, "Et tu, Brute?" He didn't bother to raise his head.

Manny reached the door, opened it. "Yeah."

"Why?"

Manny turned and faced his former boss and the man who'd given him a home when he'd had none. "You *are* Ahab," he said. Then he turned back and pushed his bag out the opening and down to the deck. He met Tick at the aft rail and together they tossed his stuff into the Whaler where Cowboy sat. In a moment they were gone. Mary and Sonny followed their progress as they tied off to *Sharpe-Shooter*'s stern platform. They watched as Brooks invited them aboard. The skies were dark, the northern lights just beginning to fire up for real as Brooks looked across and nodded to Sonny. In a few minutes the Whaler was returned by a pair of crewmen. What had started out so promising was now officially over, all because Dal Sharpe blackmailed O'Connell into doing something outlandish and dangerous. And it had obviously worked.

Back in the wheelhouse, Mary turned and faced her dad. "I checked on O'Connell," she said. "He's okay—frightened a little bit. I gave him something to eat." She paused. "Let's call Maggie. Cut our losses. Then go home."

Sonny couldn't look at her. "Home?" he said, as if speaking a foreign language. Mary dropped her eyes. She must have realized they had no home. *Skeleton* would be repossessed. And their property on the north side of Dutch Harbor, the beach cottage that had been a Wade legacy, would be confiscated by Larry Johns.

Sonny placed his hands on the wheel and gazed through the windows at *Bennkah*. "I'm not leaving, Mary. I'm staying until this ship is off the bottom."

Mary stood back and sagged her shoulders in defeat, leaning to one side like a washerwoman carrying her pail. She turned away from Sonny, shielding him from the tears coursing down her cheeks. Exhaustion had taken control. Sonny could see it. She was giving up. She wanted this chapter in her life to end. "Dad, there's no way—"

"Goddamnit," he whispered. "There's gotta be a way." He stepped to the side of the wheel and leaned against the bench. He ran his eyes across the eastern horizon, then south where a few tiny pinpricks of light glowed from late-season fishing encampments on the islands. When he looked north his face took on an unnatural sheen, reflecting the eerie green and purple and red emanations that filled the sky over *Bennkah*. "There's gotta be a way."

Suddenly the VHF burst on. The transmission was poor, but Sonny could tell it was Matt. "Guys," said the voice, "you need to get over here right now. I found it!"

Sonny picked up his handset. "Found what, Matt?"

"Ground zero."

CHAPTER 56

On *Bennkah*, Matt squatted on his haunches, sweating profusely. What he'd found had stunned him. For a minute he didn't know how to respond. He'd been disgusted at the histrionics on *Skeleton*, but instead of sticking his nose into the melee and getting nothing for his efforts, he left. He decided to go exploring on the lower levels of *Bennkah*. In no time he'd found himself all the way down as far as he could go and aft of midships, prowling the center gangway between the tanks. He'd never been this far down into the bowels except at the stern rudder room, but the air, although very warm, had cleared itself of fumes, and he could breathe okay. So far he didn't have to wear a mask and deal with the fogging, which never worked very well when you were using a flashlight.

When he felt a good bit more heat radiating from an unexplored section of tankage, his curiosity was piqued. He'd continued down the hall to the epicenter of the high-temperature gradient. On one of the tanks, the hottest of the lot, he saw what he thought was a small inspection door, unlabeled, with a simple latch on the left-hand side. He flipped it open, burning his fingers as he did so. Behind the door he'd found a window, or more correctly, a screen of some sort. He stuck his face up to the glass and was staggered by what he saw.

Sonny's voice over the radio startled him. "Earth to Matt."

Matt decided that there was no way he could explain or give

directions over the radio. He had to go get his boss. He keyed his VHF. "I found ground zero, Sonny," he said. "Get ready. I'll be up there in ten minutes to get you. Bring the spotlight. And bring gloves." He began to run.

Soon Matt was leading Sonny and Mary to an oversized fire station hatchway on *Bennkah*'s deck. They began to descend, Mary and Sonny carrying flashlights, Matt now equipped with a battery-powered spot. "You're not going to believe what you see," he said. His voice echoed through the steel caverns.

"This better be good."

"That's not exactly the word I'd use."

They descended one level, then another and another, the light glow from the electric sky slowly fading, the air growing warmer. At level five they went through the first of a series of wide, watertight doors that had been left open. They could now follow Matt's sooty footprints down and down. Everywhere they looked they saw evidence of fire and water, swiftly turning what once were clean new bulkheads to char and rust.

Matt began to talk. His voice echoed off the walls. "There was always this heat problem that I couldn't figure out," he said. "Not so much the fires, but the weird stuff. Paint peeling off the bulkheads up above, steam explosions where water would find unreal temperatures, smoke funnels, things like that." He paused. "Right now we're just forward of the center of the ship. This stairwell goes down all the way to the keel. It's dark as hell down there, so we'll have to use our lights."

"What are we going to see?"

Matt thought for a minute. "I can't really put it into words. But I think it's evidence of something you can't imagine. You know I've been going over the ship's computer records, trying to find out what happened. I listened to some Russian audio phone records and heard one of the engineers dealing with a raw water problem and a fuel problem at the same time."

Mary said, "You speak Russian, too?"

Matt smiled in the dark. "Nyet."

Mary rolled her eyes.

"I used an Internet translation website. We're getting pretty good access off the satellite feed. Anyway, one of the engineers said something about polar bears in the baffles. And he used the word 'again' as if it had happened before."

They descended another flight, dropped through another door, down through a netherworld of blackened bulkheads and misshapen steel.

It was getting very warm.

Sonny said, "There are no baffles in a sea suction."

"Exactly. But according to the plans, this ship only has one sea suction. A huge thing, looks like a carburetor with eight ports. The guy wasn't talking about baffles. He was talking about diverters. And the computer was doing the diverting. The computer routed the seawater somewhere else."

Mary spoke up. "So the main generator got hot?"

"Yes. The computer sent the water to a more critical location. Are you guys familiar with how a nuclear plant works?"

Sonny froze, his feet stumbling on one of the risers. As he grabbed for a handhold, Mary ran into him. They exchanged looks and turned to Matt, who had stopped just ahead. His face was grim. The temperature was climbing.

"Just the basics," Sonny offered. "Fuel rods submerged in water are pulled from their shielding and the atoms start to bounce around and create heat." He slowed his words as he thought it through. "The super-hot water is pumped through a heat exchanger—"

"—and clean water absorbs the heat and expands and turns a

turbine." Matt was sweating so profusely now he had to stop and mop his face. "But you have to dump the old, spent rods. And they're still hot. The Russians have been suspected of using the Arctic—their Arctic—for years."

They went through another open, watertight hatchway and Matt turned them aft, down the lowest alleyway on the ship. They followed it for fifty yards. The entire length of the corridor was roasting. The walls were dull-black and the steel had given way in places, angle iron pulled free from welds, diamond plate warped up and curled. They came to a landing and stepped up. On the port side of the hallway there was the small inspection screen covered by a door.

Matt stood back so Sonny and Mary could see the door. "My guess is this ship is not just an oil tanker. It has an entire compartment full of spent fuel rods. Very hot spent fuel rods. From what I could make out, the crew didn't know it, only the captain. And the computer, too, which automatically diverted more water to a heat exchanger designed to cool—"

Suddenly a whooshing noise exploded out of the darkness. Something sounded alive. Matt stepped to the door and opened it, being careful not to burn himself. With a palm he invited Sonny and Mary to look.

"What you see is a lead-lined compartment, maybe the size of six ships' cargo containers. The kind you find on freighters, stacked together. The dimensions are on the computer. The rods are intact, but the heat from spent fuel is still formidable, as much as two thousand degrees Fahrenheit. The entire well is flooded and radioactive. This is a core. And the Russians were going to dump it in the American Arctic. In the wheelhouse there was probably a panel of some kind that activated the release. Like a big elevator that descends through the bottom of the ship, then ejects the whole unit."

"My God," said Mary.

"It's an engineering marvel. But a moral and ethical nightmare. It's an environmental abortion to end all abortions. Much worse than Russia's so-called 'Lakes of Crude' they have deep in Siberia. This thing is not local. It's global."

Sonny put his face right up to the screen. "And all that plumbing in there, the core is surrounded by a water jacket of seawater to keep it cool."

"Right. But like I said, the chief engineer didn't know about it. Only the captain, who was monitoring the computer. So they had a perfect storm on the ship. The heat set off an internal alarm, water was diverted, fuel lines blew—"

Mary finished the sentence. "And the computer shut down the fire control system throughout the ship because it was programmed to expect heat."

"Exactly," said Matt. "Then a real fire starts in the engine room, but there's no way to localize it because all over the ship, a monkey has taken over the sensory equipment."

Sonny was thinking now. "So the captain sees his ship going up in flames. He does what he can, but there's no hope for the ship. And he knows he's carrying a catastrophic nuclear box. What does he do?"

"By now the ship's systems are all down," said Matt. "He can't pump water through the jacket anymore. Imagine what he must have thought."

"An explosion?" asked Mary.

Sonny met her gaze. "A steam explosion. The most powerful kind. It would literally cut the *Bennkah* in half."

Matt finished the thought. "So not only would we have one of the worst oil spills in the history of the world—"

"We'd also have nuclear waste strewn across twenty square miles of ocean floor."

The sounds inside the core began to get louder. The heat was overpowering.

"There's a principle here," said Matt. Together the three of them looked again into the little window. "If water heats up, it rises, becomes a gas and goes through the cooling coils. Cool water comes up from the bottom to replace it. The captain must have seen that. But on a ship going twenty knots, a sea suction is useless without pumps. Inertia takes control. Water flows along the hull, not into an open port, especially if it's facing aft and has some kind of armored diverter fins on it to protect it from the ice. The cavity could even have filled with gas, making it air-bound."

Sonny said, "So without pumps the captain has to stop the ship. With no engines. God almighty, something this big would take miles and miles to stop."

"Unless you run it aground," said Matt.

Sonny put his face right up to the window. It was Jules Verne–esque, at once lethal and surreal. "We've got to get water to this thing," he said. "Soon. At first light."

"Yeah," said Matt. "It's only a matter of time."

"Yeah, well, there's a problem, Matt. Except for O'Connell in the anchor room, I don't have a crew. It's just us, now. And the fish in the sea."

When the trio climbed out onto the deck it was midnight and the sky was on fire with ionized particles. They hoped it wasn't a harbinger of things to come.

PART IV

CHAPTER 57

Aleutian Banks

NOVEMBER 30, EARLY MORNING

THE AURORA BOREALIS doesn't typically display itself as far south as the Aleutian Banks. When the solar winds flare up, the visible skylights at the magnetic poles usually reach as far down as the Arctic Circle, no farther. On this night, though, an exception was made. In the northern sky, huge veneers of nitrogen blue and oxygen green melted upwards into a dazzling kaleidoscope of ochre, coral, and red, moving and curling into one another in vertical sheets.

There has always been speculation about the cause of the phenomenon, but one point has been repeated time and time again by the men who ply the waters in these latitudes. When the lights show up, it's time to head for the dock. Solar winds be damned, somewhere there's a storm brewing. Whether it's local superstition or not, mariners of every stripe have heeded that advice for centuries. Now, on *Bennkah*, there was a different kind of storm brewing. And heading for a lee shore would not protect anyone from the catastrophe that could ensue.

"This is huge, Dad. Bigger than us," said Mary. The three of them had returned to *Skeleton*, retracing their steps through the darkened corridor and up all those flights of stairs. By the time they emerged onto *Bennkah*'s deck and climbed down one of the rope ladders, then into the Whaler and across the narrow gap to their own boat, the electric sky was almost as bright as day.

Moments later they stood together around the galley table, Matt and Sonny drinking coffee. Mary had gotten a can of mineral spirits from the paint locker and was wiping the black, greasy stains off of her wrists and forearms where her gloves had failed to protect her. Sweat had dried on her skin and she felt like she hadn't showered in days. "Like you said, Matt. This is global." She passed her rag to Sonny. "We need to call the Navy. Now."

"I agree," said Matt, standing in his jeans and t-shirt on a pile of flame-retardant clothes that used to be his fire suit. He was also sticky with old sweat.

Sonny said, "We don't have time. And we don't have anything to offer them. It'll take them a day to get here, much longer to assess the situation and send for experts and underwater equipment. Field radiation teams or Navy SEALs aren't rigged for this kind of thing. And the storm will be here by tomorrow sometime. If you don't believe me, check the sky. Looks like a Peter Max canvas. The wind is already clocking around. It's only two points off the bow now, and soon it'll start to crank up."

Mary screwed the lid back on the can of solvent and slammed it down on the wheel bench. "Then what do we do?"

Sonny looked at his daughter and held his hands up. He knew she was upset, but this was no time to get physical, at least with him. It had been getting worse and worse lately. Maybe Cowboy had rubbed off on her. Maybe *he* had rubbed off on her. Or maybe the idea of three in a boat, forced to save the world, was just too much to deal with. "There's only one thing we can do," he said.

"What's that?"

"Beg."

CHAPTER 58

AN HOUR LATER, after a small verbal tug-o-war with *Sharpe-Shooter*'s Officer On Deck, Sonny, Mary, and Matt found themselves in a conference room aboard *Sharpe-Shooter*. Captain Frank Brooks sat at the head of the long table, accompanied by First Mate Bacon and by Manny, Cowboy, and Tick, all of them looking on with skeptical interest. In front of the group, mounted on the aft bulkhead, a huge screen displayed Dal Sharpe's Skype face: sleep-wrinkled, unimpressed, an image that resented being woken up and told that, unlike when he went to bed, things may not be going his way anymore.

Sonny sat at a control console in front of the computer camera and began to explain. "Sorry about the timing of this, Dal, but it had to be done." He cleared his throat. "As you know, when I was awarded this job it was pretty straightforward. Stop the bleeding and pump some oil, turn the ship out of its track and float it, more or less. It wasn't going to be a treasure hunt or any sort of deep-sea excursion. We weren't looking at mechanical or electrical salvage, at least not right away. We put a lot of water on a lot of heat. We dove and checked for soundness. We had to deal with only one leaking tank after an anchor mishap; hopefully that's fixed. And as you know, I had to contend, not very successfully, with some crew issues. But last night my new second mate, Matt, went down to the bottom level on *Bennkah*, one of the sections that we hadn't been able to access before because of heat and air issues, and found something that I never thought was possible. I also never thought I'd be here asking this, Dal, but I need your help."

Sharpe looked incredulous.

Sonny took his hat off. He was sweating, but his voice was clear. "Are you familiar with how a nuclear reactor works?" he asked.

A few minutes later he finished his pitch. He'd been frank and uncompromising in the way he'd laid it out. This was a possible catastrophe to end all catastrophes. The Aleutian Islands and the Bering Sea would be affected for the next millennium, as untold amounts of radioactivity slowly destroyed the world they all lived in. He needed help, and he needed it now. This was beyond any petty rivalries. This was beyond money or jealousies or anything that had happened between them in the past. This next twenty-four hours could change the course of history.

"So there you have it," said Sonny. "As I speak, that core is getting hotter."

Dal Sharpe took the time to clip the end of one of his Cuban cigars and light it. He was wearing a maroon bathrobe, and now he excused himself and went into his sleeping quarters. He emerged a minute later, buttoning his khaki shirt and kicking into his too-tight khaki pants. He repositioned himself in front of his Skype equipment. Cigar smoke billowed. "Who else knows about this?" he said through the cloud.

"Nobody. I haven't had any time. I *don't* have any time." Sonny tried to guess what Sharpe was thinking, but came up empty. There was a tight-lipped smile on the man's face, and for a moment, he seemed to be examining the diamond signet ring on his left hand.

Finally Sharpe looked up and brought his face closer to the computer camera. The image filled the screen. "What's in it for me?" he said, his smile growing wide.

Sonny sighed. He knew it might come to this. And he was prepared. He'd known Sharpe for years, ever since the man had gotten
out of the Navy. A couple years later he had a pile of unexplained
capital to invest. The whole world, to Sharpe, revolved around
money and the acquiring of money. Sonny didn't care. He needed
some help and he needed it now. "Everything," he said.

"Meaning?"

"Everything, Dal. All the credit. All the glory. All the oil." Sonny
swallowed hard. "All yours," he finished.

Sharpe blinked his eyes. They looked reptilian on the big screen.
A beat turned to two and his smile turned in on itself. "That's a lot
of money, Wade."

"It is. Millions."

"And I could . . . I mean, I would own you." He inhaled cigar
smoke deep into his lungs. "Maybe I'd even buy *Skeleton*. I could use
it as a garbage scow. I could *sink* it, goddamnit." An instant of rage
displayed itself. "Because you'd be the fuck out of my life, Wade.
You'd be dancing in someone else's movie. Bagging groceries and
drinking Sterno, if there is a God!"

Sonny tried to calm him down. "Sharpe, we don't have time for
this. This is an operation that'll take both of us. We have to get
water to that sea suction. We have to get *Bennkah* off the bottom
to do it. Then we've got an engineering problem that might take
more advanced gear than we have on *Skeleton*, and the Navy or the
Coasties, especially the Coasties, won't be able to help for days,
which can't happen. I haven't figured it out, yet. This is just spit-
balling. But you've got that diving bell on here. Maybe we could use
that—someone inside it to direct operations. Maybe I can hook up
a suction, like a treasure hose rig. But I can't get it down there that
deep. You can. You have your spud anchors. They can go down over
a hundred feet. We could reverse the blower on one of those spuds.

And also, I don't have the type of modern dive gear with underwater voice capabilities on *Skeleton*. You do. We'll need a team of guys, three at least, to go up under *Bennkah*. The sea suction is a single unit, huge, on the port side, the north side. But it's too close to the mud and silted up pretty bad, I'm guessing, which is why I need help pulling *Bennkah* around when the wind comes around. There's a ton of heat, Dal. On the bottom we'll have to place static lines—"

Sharpe broke in like he hadn't heard a thing. "Funny, isn't it?" he said. "You offering me the ship. You gotta love the irony."

Sonny clacked his teeth together so fast it was audible. Everything he had just said was pure speculation, but it served to get some ideas on the table. There wasn't time here to screw around. *What is this asshole thinking?*

"For me, Sonny, this is a fucking wet dream," said Sharpe.

"Sharpe, listen to me. If we don't move soon, today, now . . . we will have a catastrophe on our hands that'll make the Fukushima Power Plant explosions look like a weenie roast."

"We?"

"Okay, then. Me! *I* will have a catastrophe on *my* hands. How does that sound?"

"It sounds wonderful, Sonny." Sharpe began to chuckle. "It sounds so wonderful that I'm not going to bail you out." He laughed harder, putting his right hand to his eyes to wipe away the tears. "A fucking wet dream!" he shouted. "Pardon the damn pun!"

Sonny ran his eyes around the conference room, exchanging looks with everyone. During the past few minutes, some of Frank Brooks' crew had wandered in, curious to know what was going on. They stood against three walls, listening, aghast. Sonny turned back to the screen. "Sharpe, don't be stupid. This is bigger than you, bigger than your hatred for what happened years ago. People will die, man. Lots of people. And God knows what else—"

"Are you fucking *kidding*? You want *me* to throw *you* a lifeline? After what you did to me?" Fury burned through the monitor. Sharpe's face was so close to his camera the image was distorted, his cheeks swollen, his round double chin receding into a blur. Cigar smoke layered his head. "The bankruptcy! The shame! The blame!" He backed away. A hiss escaped his lips. "You destroyed my company, you fuck. You destroyed Dutch Harbor, hell, the entire state of Alaska! All those millions of dollars you cost me, all those millions of gallons you spilled—"

"Fuck this!" shouted Captain Frank Brooks from across the room. He was on his feet in a flash, stepping around to the computer and pushing Sonny out of the way. He stuck his face into the camera lens. "It wasn't him, Sharpe. It was me!"

Dead silence.

On the screen Sharpe's grin froze. He turned his head to the right, then left, looking for phantoms in his darkened office. The cigar disappeared. "What the—"

CHAPTER 59

"You heard me," said Brooks. "Sonny gave me the wheel that night so he could go out on the tender and drop a couple radar reflectors. But he'd been training me for months. Technically he was the salvage captain, the captain of *Skeleton* when it was *your* boat, not the master of that big-ass oiler. He'd relinquished that job to me, even before that night. I was the man on the helm and the captain of record. Sonny was doing his job, a mile away."

When Mary looked over, Sonny turned his face away.

Brooks lowered his voice. "Sonny saw the ship go off course from way out there. He tried to get back. When he finally ran into the wheelhouse and took charge it was too late." Brooks closed his eyes and opened them again. His face stiffened. "The spill was all my fault, Dal. All of it. But Sonny took the blame anyway. Then I falsified the records by myself. There's no evidence he even knew about that part until weeks later, after the inquiry."

"Bullshit!" said Sharpe. "Why would he do—?"

"Because I was engaged to his daughter." Brooks looked across at Mary, standing at the table stunned. He had no words to convey his feelings, and they wouldn't be appropriate now anyway. He turned his attention back to the screen. "Sonny knew the spill would destroy my career and our future. So, instead, he let it destroy his."

By now, inside the conference room, everybody was standing,

looking at one another, unable to interrupt the monologue. Matt backed himself into a corner. Tick was unabashedly crying. Cowboy and Manny stared at the top of the table, unable to put their separate thoughts into words. Brooks' crewmen began to depart one at a time, melting away to their quarters. Their captain had just admitted to crimes on the high seas. Only Mary was strong enough to look her father in the eye. When he locked eyes with her and blinked back the tears, she ran to him and wrapped her arms around him. She began to sob.

Nothing like this was supposed to happen.

Outside, the sky was beginning to lighten. The electricity in the upper atmosphere was dissipating and in the northeast, the glow from the upper lip of a ragged sun threatened to peek over the top of the world. All over Dutch Harbor people were going to work. At the Coast Guard station it was time for the shift change. Winds were light. It was the calm before the storm.

In Sharpe's office the blinds were drawn. He removed a handkerchief from somewhere and wiped his face. His hired captain, Frank Brooks, was still peering out from the screen, a look of determination on his face. Sharpe addressed him as if he were the only one listening. His voice was conspiratorial. "You fucking idiot!" he hissed. "Do you realize what you're saying?!"

"Yeah." Quiet reigned as Brooks reached down on the console and picked up the handset to one of the boat's VHF radios. "Yeah, Dal, I do. And I'll go it one better." He pushed the transmit button. "Breaker one six, breaker one six, this is Captain Frank Brooks at the salvage vessel *Sharpe-Shooter*." He repeated himself, then rattled off the U.S. documentation number, along with the gross tonnage, net tonnage, and length. "Let it be known I was the one responsible for the *Knock Nevis* spill that devastated the shoreline three years ago," he said into the mike. Then he repeated the admission. He wasn't finished, though, and continued to incriminate himself with his story of betrayal.

At the gas station in Dutch Harbor, the aged owner had just entered his office after filling a pickup with diesel and taking the driver's credit card. He slipped his rubber boots off and placed them in front of the little space heater, then he reached across and turned the VHF volume up and lowered the squelch feature so he could understand the words more clearly. This was the first time he'd heard anything like this.

"...all you folks that have been on Sonny Wade's case, I'm here to set the record straight..."

Inside the big grocery store next door, Dean Martin had been singing *Volare* on the stereo. Suddenly the music stopped and Frank Brooks' voice rang out over the heads of the early morning shoppers.

"...and I was the captain of record that night. I'm going to repeat that, I was..."

At Willy's Tavern there were only three men at the bar, all of them drinking tomato juice laced with beer. The bartender took a minute away from his mop duties to turn the radio up.

"*As it happened, Sonny Wade was not on board at the time of the...*"

And all over Dutch Harbor and the surrounding area, people tuned in to listen to the admission of guilt by the captain of the largest and newest salvager in the Pacific.

Except at the little whorehouse, where the radio was off. Early morning was for sleeping.

But at the Coast Guard station, the announcement had created a stir in the Morning Room, so much so that the commander's aide had made sure the recorders were on and functioning before he went to wake his boss. This was evidence. He didn't need any screw-ups.

Brooks finished his speech. "So there it is, I was at the wheel. This is Captain Frank Brooks of the Salvager *Sharpe-Shooter*, out."

Frank Brooks replaced the mike, took a breath, and exhaled.

"You have no idea what you have just done," said Sharpe.

"Yeah I do," said Frank. "I only wish I would've done it sooner."

Sharpe curled his lip. "You're relieved of command, Brooks," he said. "Put it in the log. Where's Bacon? Put him on the screen. He'll be bringing *Sharpe-Shooter* in. All the way here, to Anchorage. I suggest he get on it now. You've got my ship sitting next to a time bomb. I'm not coming near that nuclear—"

"Bacon has quit. We'll bring you your boat. Adios, asshole." Frank turned the screen off.

During the ensuing pause, Sonny put his hand on the disgraced man's shoulder. "Thanks, Frank."

"You kidding me?" Brooks turned to Mary. "He made me swear to it. It's been killing me ever since. You gotta forgive me."

Mary was less than impressed. So much had gone over the bridge. The destruction of her family, her life, her father's life, everything had been based on a lie. She said, "Forgive? Check with me in a few years. But I'll never forget."

"Fair enough."

Sonny backed himself away from Mary and scanned the room. For a minute he didn't know what to say. Too much emotion at the wrong time. Then he decided that as long as most of them were here, it was a good time to take stock. "This meeting is still on, guys. It's just that Sharpe has canceled out."

Cowboy was the first to step up. "Sonny, man, I didn't know—"

"That was the whole idea."

"Are you okay? I mean, the fight, you know. Sorry about what happened back there. I really—"

"No apologies necessary." He turned to Manny and Tick. "From anybody. But I could use your help. Like I said, this isn't just about us. That thing's getting hotter all the time. And whether you think so or not, I can't pull a rabbit out of my hat. I'll need a crew." He locked eyes with Brooks. "I could use help from *all* of you."

"Cap'n Wade, we'd follow you to the ends of the earth."

"Good. Because that might just be where we wind up."

CHAPTER 60

As Sonny, Mary, Matt, Cowboy, Manny, and Tick climbed into the Whaler for the return trip, a shelf cloud to end all shelf clouds blotted out the daylight. At once the temperature dropped and a wild, counterclockwise vortex of wind slammed into the side of *Sharpe-Shooter* and heeled her over fifteen degrees, almost sinking the crew in their little boat tied up at the stern.

Brooks had been in his wheelhouse, but he saw what had happened and ordered three of his crew into *Sharpe-Shooter*'s Zodiac to keep a protective eye on the Whaler and to offer their services for the task at hand, services that Sonny was happy to accept. With Cowboy at the wheel, the Whaler clawed its way back across to *Skeleton*, the Zodiac right behind. In the midst of the tumult, thick drops of frozen rain shot sideways into Mary and the men and pinged off the steel combings of *Skeleton*, making a frozen slush on the decks and biting angrily at any exposed skin. The world was suddenly a different, more violent place.

They crowded into the wardroom, shivering with cold and anticipation. The leading edge of the storm system had arrived, and they could only hope that it would settle into itself soon and the wind would pick a velocity, choose a direction, and clock to the south like Sonny predicted.

He stood at the head of the scarred old table, feet apart, a mug of coffee in his hand. His crew settled in around him, restored mostly to their former places. The three men from *Sharpe-Shooter* stood against the rear bulkhead awaiting orders. "The shit has officially hit the fan, folks," he said. "In a couple hours, three at the most, the wind will be blowing in the opposite direction from its heading these past few days. And when it comes around, we better be ready because that's gonna be our only chance to bust our girl loose."

"Let's get it on," said Cowboy, clapping his hands together and rubbing them.

"Okay, huddle up, here we go. Cowboy, the other anchor is deployed and stuck hard into the bottom. I'll need you to put Tick and these new guys up on the bow of *Bennkah* and go over the procedure with them. Manny and I will bring *Skeleton* up under the bow and winch you guys the end of the hawser. It's six-inch and it's heavy, three hundred yards on the spool, and if we get *Bennkah* moving we'll have to put out even more. You'll be attaching your end to the hardware up there, then Cowboy, you'll be leaving them on their own. Give Tick a big maul to knock the dog away from the anchor windlass when the time comes, and give him a good radio with a charged battery." He addressed Tick. "Tick, when I give you the word, you knock that dog out. And duck, because there will be thousands of tons of pressure on that thing. There will be pressure on everything up there. Don't stand behind the hawser when I've got tension on it, either. It'll cut your head off if it goes."

"I'm all over it," said Tick. "I don't need a head, anyway."

Sonny pulled his own handheld from its clip and keyed the mike twice. "Frank, you there?"

"I'm here, Skip."

"Captain Brooks, the wind is starting to howl pretty good. But it's coming around already, and it'll be coming around more pretty soon, so *Bennkah* isn't pushing herself up on the bank anymore. "You willing to use *Sharpe-Shooter*?"

"You kidding? Yeah, man. This ride has thirty-thousand horses if you count the generators and pumps."

"I know it, man. So put all your fenders out over that big beautiful bow of yours. When I get set up on *Skeleton*, you're gonna push the nose of our Goliath around to three-hundred-and-twenty degrees and point her back in her track. Position yourself south of the bow about two hundred feet. You're gonna gallop some—we've got some seas—but it's gotta be done."

Sonny sheathed his radio as Matt stood to say something. "The core, Sonny, it might—"

"That's your baby," said Sonny. "I want you to take a temp gauge with a remote readout and sit on that fucking thing. And don't let it get any hotter without you telling me."

"What do *I* do," said Mary, "cook and clean, for Christ's sake?"

"You've got the voice, Mar. You're calling the Navy and telling them we've got a situation. But don't tell them what it is on any kind of open line. It's gotta be a higher-up thing. Ask to speak on a secure frequency with the biggest big shot admiral you can find. Explain who you are and what we've found, and insist they get their asses in gear. Everything you say will be recorded, so do it by the book. And don't mispronounce the word 'nuclear.' I hate when people do that."

CHAPTER 61

OUTSIDE IT WAS raining buckets. The edge of the front had come and gone and the wind had settled into a steady thirty knots, gusting to forty out of the east. A low ceiling of clouds whipped across the sky, gray and forbidding. The seas were growing by the minute, but soon, when the wind clocked around, they'd be coming off the bank to the south, which would help to keep them manageable. Visibility was down to a few hundred yards. The pelicans that had taken up station on *Bennkah* had decided to abandon ship. Even the seagulls were gone.

Mary sat at the big radio in *Skeleton's* galley, her body moving with the pitch and yaw of the hull. She gripped the table with her left hand, and the knuckles went white when the G-forces threatened to throw her body against the bulkhead. The *Skeleton's* anchor was up, and Sonny was at the helm, positioning the boat under the bow of the great ship.

"This is recovery vessel *Skeleton*, FRN 7193007311," said Mary into the ugly green phone. Her annunciation was crisp and clear when she repeated herself twice. *By the book*, she thought. "This is the *Skeleton* calling the United States Coast Guard Unalaska..."

On the back deck, Manny controlled the hydraulic levers that worked the giant spool of hawser cable. The end of the complicated, multi-plied wire and rope affair had been sent to the top of *Bennkah* with the help of a triple block and the cherry picker. Part of it had been connected to *Bennkah*'s towing bollards while a secondary loop had been shackled to a bridle that Cowboy and Tick, along with the borrowed contingent of crewmen from *Sharpe-Shooter*, rigged up on the spot. Working with such heavy equipment took skill and patience. And extra hands. The seas were getting bigger all the time. And the wind was coming around.

As *Skeleton* motored away from *Bennkah*, she pulled out more and more of the hawser, which created a larger and larger catenary, the homogeneous curve that formed when tension was put on a cable's opposite endpoints. The middle of the sag dipped into the sea and emerged with each wave. Sonny, working *Skeleton*'s throttle, put uniform tension on the assembly, and as the spool ran out, the tethered end-loop dropped over *Skeleton*'s horizontal, triple-bracketed king post, an engineering feature that Sonny had designed himself.

The wind came around another two points.

Sonny got on the radio and told Brooks it was time. Brooks had been busy, oiling up his big engines, airing up, deploying his heavy-duty fenders over the square bow and pulling the anchor. A few minutes after the call the *Sharpe-Shooter*, all two hundred feet of her, took her place athwart and two-hundred feet aft of *Bennkah*'s bow. She pushed on the hull only hard enough to maintain her position while they waited for the wind to clock another ten degrees. It would only take a few more minutes.

Meanwhile, Matt had gathered a knapsack of supplies and made his way down the now familiar middle stairwell into the bowels of *Bennkah*. The heat increased as he descended, and the corridor at the bottom level was almost unbearable, even before he got to the little platform with the window. He was already drenched with sweat. Rummaging in his backpack, he found the thermal sensor and stuck the magnetic sliding bracket onto the outside of the hot bulkhead. The gauge had a digital readout and was equipped with a remote unit with a lanyard attached. Matt checked that the remote was working and pocketed it. The temperature was so high he had trouble focusing his eyes. The corridor felt like an out-of-control sauna. The gauge on the bulkhead read 145 Fahrenheit.

The wind clocked around another ten degrees.

In *Skeleton's* wheelhouse, Sonny had been monitoring the operation and listening to the men work the radio. He checked his anemometer for wind speed and direction and decided it was time. *It's now or never.* He picked up his handset. He'd lived his entire life for these next few minutes. Good or bad, it had been his chosen field. Now it was time once again to test his mettle. He pushed the talk button and asked his people, "You guys know what a Swine Harp is?"

Brooks clicked his mike but didn't answer. Tick did the same, followed by Cowboy. Matt said, "I'll bite."

Sonny smiled into the forward ports, now awash with foaming seas breaking sideways over the starboard rail. "According to my father, a Swine Harp is a horse hair tied across a pig's ass. And we got Swine Harp tension, guys. I can hear the music. Corner time. Let's go!"

Sonny pushed both throttles forward into their corner seats and *Skeleton* leaped forward, water exploding out from under the lifting stern, black smoke pouring out her stacks. In no time Sonny had taken up the slack in nine-hundred feet of tow line. The trick was to pull to forty or so degrees off the bow, and as the hawser tightened and the bridle began to pull more from the starboard side, turn the *Skeleton* further north and bring her power to bear at a less than acute angle while *Sharpe-Shooter* nudged the bow out of the trough she'd made. At the same time Sonny was doing his thing, Brooks put the pedal to the metal on *Sharpe-Shooter* and huge gouts of water boiled out from under her as all that horsepower came to bear. At *Sharpe-Shooter's* bow, the grinding, tensile sound of steel being compressed put the Swine Harp analogy to the test. The rain had begun to pound again, sideways from the south-southeast, and the sky looked like the bearded black underbelly of hell. In the galley, Mary began to speak louder, her voice barely keeping up with the roar from *Skeleton*'s engine room. "Good evening, Coast Guard. This is *Skeleton*."

"This *is* the United States Coast Guard Unalaska. We have you loud and clear. Go ahead, *Skeleton*."

"We need a patch to the U.S. Navy. No, there is no oil in the water. Not yet, anyway. Patch me over, fellas. Now. It's urgent."

CHAPTER 62

Deep inside *Bennkah*, a roasting, sweat-soaked Matt felt the surge as the mighty ship absorbed the power exerted on her hull. The deck rolled to port three or four degrees, and he shot a hand out to steady himself. He pulled it away fast, the steel too hot to touch. He squinted into the gauge on the wall and watched as the needle slowly climbed above one-fifty. He waited a moment to see if it would go back down, but it did the opposite. Over the next few minutes he watched it climb. One fifty-five, then one sixty. He fumbled for his VHF.

"Sonny, this is Matt. Do you copy?"

"Go ahead, Matt."

"Sonny, this thing is getting hotter. You can't even touch the bulkhead with gloves anymore. I got a thermostat reading of one hundred sixty degrees where I'm standing,"

"Aw, hell. You listening, Frank?"

Frank Brooks and everyone else had heard Matt. "Yeah," he said. "I'm powering down. Half throttle."

Sonny pulled his own controls back to twelve hundred RPM. His cable slackened as he pressed his autopilot into duty. It was after midafternoon and the darkened sky was only going to get darker as the storm settled in for the long night to come. Somehow the day had come and gone, and now whatever they would have to do, they would have to do it in more severe conditions and no light. The rain was still coming down, with no chance of a letup, and the wind had clocked another ten degrees. If it came around too much more it would begin a westerly drift and put more pressure on them to get *Bennkah* moving.

Matt's voice came over the air. "The sea suction must have silted up completely with the surge. We went over a few degrees down here. She must have leaned into the mud."

Sonny keyed his mike. "Okay, Matt, you've done your job. Now stand down, get outta there. "You listening in, Cowboy? Where are you?"

"I climbed down the Jacob's ropes and jumped on *Sharpe-Shooter*'s bow. It wasn't that far. This is a big boat. What'cha need?"

On *Skeleton*, Mary had come up from the galley to find out what was going on. She sat at the rear bench behind her father, listening.

Sonny exchanged looks with her as he answered Cowboy. "You still got that big-ass Hawaiian spear gun?"

"My Whale Slayer? Hell yeah. It's here with my stuff."

"Get it for me, will you. I'm sending Manny over in the Whaler to pick you up."

Sonny called Manny and told him what he needed. Then he put the mike down for a minute and paced the wheelhouse, thinking. He knew where the sea suction was from the schematics Matt had found. He wished there was time to go over everything again, but there wasn't, and he'd have to deal with the situation as it was. It wasn't known among his crew or even his own daughter, Mary, but due to his SEAL training eons ago, Sonny's diving skills were excellent. When he was deep under the surface and his mind began to calculate any deep-sea calamity, nobody was more qualified for the job than he was. He would never consider sending someone else down in a situation like this. He retrieved the mike. "Come in, Frank."

There was a pause. Then, "I'm here."

"We'll need some stuff from your explosives locker."

Mary put her hand to her face.

"Cowboy is gonna put a small charge of C-4 around a spear shaft with a detonator and five minutes of primer cord. Get your engineer to find you a bilge magnet. You guys tape it to the point. Then replace the spear tether with the primer cord."

"You got it," said Brooks.

Sonny clicked the overhead light on inside the wheelhouse and turned to Mary. She had stood and was now leaning against the companionway hatch and holding onto the handholds. *Skeleton's* stern was pointed almost into the weather now, but the sea state was still uncomfortable and the bow was going up and down. "Mar, I'm gonna need a couple underwater flares and a striker."

"Dad—"

"And go get my dive gear ready. Two tanks."

On the radio, Brooks spoke. "Sonny, you can't be thinking what I think you're thinking."

Mary closed her eyes then opened them. A tear coursed down her cheek as she turned and left the room.

Sonny allowed a minute to pass. He keyed his mike once more. "Gotta blow that sea suction clear, guys. We don't have time for complicated solutions. There's only one way to do this. Old school."

Deep underwater, *Bennkah's* hull moved. Silt and mud roiled up from under her belly. The sounds of tensioned steel vibrated through the water.

Cowboy said, "It's almost full dark, Sonny. We got big seas, sleet, wind to forty knots. That's not old school, it's suicide."

"Maybe, but if we don't cool those rods down, we're all dead."

CHAPTER 63

MATT HAD TRIED to listen to every word broadcast over the radio, but he'd spent too long on *Bennkah*'s lowest deck playing chicken with the heat. Now he was paying the price. He was confused, and some of Sonny's words ran together in his mind. His fingers wouldn't work when he tried to manipulate the little spotlight he was carrying, and he was beginning to lose his sense of balance.

He was seeing shadows in the corners of the dark, also. He saw Mary, smiling at him from the swirling depths. She looked terrific in her jeans and sweatshirt. What a girl, he thought. *A vision.* He blinked. She faced him, displaying her strong shoulders and small breasts, the graceful neck tilting up at the line of her jaw to construct a perfect cambered cameo. Blue eyes that looked almost aquamarine. She laughed and her lips parted as she dissolved into shimmering waves of heat. *I'm going nuts*, he thought, *but what a way to go.* Mary Wade was everything that drove a man crazy, and she didn't even know it. He shook his head. *She's been hanging around all those roughnecks too long.*

The sweat on his body had dried up, and when he vomited onto the deck he thought about cleaning it up, then began to laugh as he realized how absurd that was. *My body temperature is going up*, he decided. *Ha ha, what a riot. I need to rest.* He sat down hard on the landing. Precious minutes went by while he tried to get his thoughts in order. He found his satchel beside him, but couldn't remember how it got there. Finally he reached inside for a bottle of water, then struggled with the screw-top for long minutes before he gave up and used his teeth to get it open. He took a long drink and replaced the cap. He checked his pocket for the thermal gauge, squinting at the readout before looping the lanyard onto his belt loop, another operation that took too much time. Then he read the dial on the bulkhead to confirm what he'd seen on the remote. They both read 180 degrees. *I'm at the center of the earth. Or I will be soon.* He turned and began the trek up the corridor. *One foot in front of the other. It's time to go.* Soon he made the stairwell and began to climb, each riser cooler than the one before.

* * *

Up in the northern sky, the Aurora Borealis was a no-show. The night was dark as pitch, the rain slogging down in icy sheets that cut the visibility to zero. Brooks had repositioned the *Sharpe-Shooter* to the port side, further aft, and used his engines to take some of the list out of *Bennkah*. Also on the port side of the ship, only marginally protected from the worst of the waves by tons of steel, Cowboy put the Whaler amidships and gave Sonny, sitting on the small boat's rail, the thumbs-up. With a nod, Sonny grabbed his mask with his left hand and somersaulted backwards into the cold, tumultuous seas. At once he was catapulted into chaos. In full dive gear, with a tool belt, a halogen spotlight in his right fist, and Cowboy's big-game spear gun strapped to his back, Sonny was at the mercy of *Sharpe-Shooter*'s wheel wash, which had created a curling vortex of water two hundred yards in both directions along the black hull. As the currents tumbled him in random directions, Sonny struggled to adjust his buoyancy compensator, finally managing to dump air and begin his descent. Cowboy watched as the glow of Sonny's light disappeared into the darkness.

At roughly fifty feet the turbulence subsided and a perfect calm ensued. Sonny had made it under the fury. He dumped more air and descended along the side of the ship. At eighty feet he felt the bilge strake, then the weld at the chine. He paused to take stock. The eerie noises emanating from the ship were twice as loud as they were on the surface. He swam aft for only a few yards before he saw it, a small torrent of mud and gas bubbles rolling up from the underside. He tipped his body up and kicked hard, trying to avoid bumping his breathing apparatus as he swam into the complete darkness under the ship. Between the hull knuckle and the muddy bottom there was only five feet of water, becoming less and less as he went further in. He would be swimming into a two-dimensional space where up and down were unavailable to him. He kept his spotlight focused on the bubbles, which shimmered in the artificial light as they followed the slight curve of the hull. After fifteen feet he had to start talking to himself. Swimming with something over your head takes practice. It has panicked more than one experienced diver. And the gap he was swimming in had shrunk to four feet. *Nice and easy*, he told himself. *Just keep calm.*

At thirty feet into the gap, the distance between the hull and the mud was only three feet, mere inches over his tanks. He began to wonder if he had read the schematics wrong. Surely he would have found the ship's raw-water suction by now. They wouldn't put it in by the keel. It would have to be toward the outside of the hull so that in shallow water or in the event of a less than catastrophic grounding, the pumps wouldn't starve and foul their impellers.

At forty feet from the side of the ship, with less than three feet of room, he was swallowed up by a wide cavity—almost like a sump— full of silt and debris, emitting bubbles, leaking mud. He let out an audible sigh into his regulator and did a three-sixty, slamming an elbow into one of the directional fins on the front side of the chamber. *Watch yourself, old man. You're getting moved around. There's current in here.* He thought about it. There had to be a tiny bit of suction still in the forward pipe. Otherwise the core would have blown by now. He shined his spotlight around the enclosure.

Then his spotlight went out.

CHAPTER 64

WHEN MATT MADE it up to the first landing he considered it a victory. He'd never felt this tired in his life. The temperature had gone down precipitously, though, and his balance had begun to assert itself, even though the weakness that had taken hold of his body had not let up. He stopped and drank the last of his water. He tossed the bottle aside as he began to climb again. Soon he was on the next landing. In the well of darkness all around he tried to concentrate on the feel of the steel risers under his feet. His spotlight had been fast losing power, so he'd had to turn it off and put it in his satchel for emergencies. *Can't see, anyway. A fireworks show behind my eyes.* All around him steel was expanding and contracting, groaning with the strains put on the ship. *One foot, then the next.* The dry heat that had surrounded him had turned into chills and flop sweat. He had to keep climbing. He had to cool his body. This was a lousy way to die.

* * *

Inside the raw water sump Sonny took stock. He'd tried to get his spotlight working, but either the battery had died or the element had burned out. Now he was stuck in the dark with a hell of a job to do. The blackness surrounding his mask was all encompassing. He held his hands to his face and wiggled his fingers in the silt.

Nothing. No fingers. Black. *Keep cool. You've got your flares.* He bent his head back and stretched his body, trying not to let claustrophobia creep in. *Breathe easy. In and out like you're in a swimming pool.* He reached his hands out and found the sides of the cavity, then he pulled himself hand over hand to the furthest forward intake on the keel side, the intake he'd seen briefly with the light. It was as big around as his body. According to the drawings, this was the only suction pipe that didn't go to the engine room. It just ended abruptly without an explanation. It had to be the one he was looking for. And the mouth was full of trash and silt. He began shoveling the larger pieces of debris out. Ten inches into the opening he felt the screen, a bronze contraption, quarter-inch welded wire that was hinged on the forward side and clipped into the intake with a pin on the aft side. The holes in the screen were mostly clogged with mud. He found a pair of slip-joint pliers in his tool belt and used his hands to position them onto the pin. He pulled it free. The screen swung down and he caught it before it could hit his head. He pushed it as far forward as it would go.

When he could wave his arms up into the cavity, he felt the dogleg, a ninety-degree elbow that angled up into the ship. He would have to get his spear gun up as far as the elbow. He took the gun in hand and held it aloft. He wiggled his arms into the pipe until his shoulders were just past the horizontal bracket for the pin he'd just pulled, and his forearms were almost at the turn. His tanks wouldn't let him go any further. He shoved the gun as far as he could reach into the pipe, then he brought it back and held it over his head, the stock hard against the back wall of the pipe. When he pulled the trigger the spear fired up through the muck, into the nether reaches of the inlet where no doubt the mud was packed hard against a heat exchanger coupling. It stuck. The magnet had done its job. Very carefully he backed himself out of the suction, fighting against the slight draw of the current.

With the primer cord fuse still on his reel, he pulled a flare from his tool belt and tried to position it so that he could light it and touch it to the primer cord in one movement. But holding on to the spear gun and the flare together proved to be impossible. Before he could reposition his hands, the flare spun away into the darkness, unlit. *Damn.*

He'd made his first bad mistake, one he couldn't afford to make again.

He retrieved his other flare from his tool belt, gripping it as if his life depended on it. *My life depends on a flare. Concentrate.* This time he held the spear gun under his armpit, pushing against the side of the cavity. He positioned the clicker with his right hand and struck it against the top of the flare. Nothing. He tried again. Nothing. On the third attempt, the flare burst to life and the sudden shock of light in his eyes blinded him and almost made him let go again. He recovered, but not before he singed his fingers snatching at the phosphorous with both thinly gloved hands. The spear gun was still under his arm. He took the spool and held it to his eyes. He needed to light the very end of the primer cord because he would need all of the five minutes before detonation to get his ass out from under the hull.

* * *

Matt had reached the fourth landing, almost to the first big watertight hatch that had been left open. He was getting dizzy again, and his vision wouldn't clear, even though there was now a ghost of gray shapes above him. He was as tired as he'd ever been, so tired that he tried to put his foot on the next step up and missed. He stumbled and fell to his knees.

Then all hell broke loose. When he tried to get up, he placed a foot down and gripped the waist-high rail with hands covered in oily soot. The slick sole of his boot lost traction and for a moment he was suspended between the rail and the diamond plate steel. His hands let go, he rolled to his side. There was nothing to stop him. Suddenly he was tumbling upside down into the void, screaming as he fell, his body slamming into outcrops of handholds and equipment. He snatched at air, he tried to hook a railing, he banged into the side of the next landing down, but he was weak and his hands were clumsy. When he went by an abandoned fire hose, a piece of dysfunctional gear that had been laced side to side over an empty fire extinguisher bracket, the end loop snatched Matt's leg and took a turn, coiling around his ankle and coming taut. He screamed again and passed out.

* * *

Sonny was ready. He touched the flare to the primer cord and watched the progress of the burning fuse as it completed a loop and started up into the pipe. *Okay, let's get outta here.*

Then things started to go awry. He tried to turn around, but his tanks were in the way and he got stuck. He tossed Cowboy's spear gun aside. The current was pulling on his hoses, bending them out of shape over his head, threatening to snag the screen bracket. *Breathe easy. Quit gulping air.* He began backing out of the muddy hole as the lit primer cord disappeared up inside the inlet. His knees bent awkwardly, and the ends of his fins curled up as they were made to push backwards out of the hole. *Follow the bubbles. No time to fool around.* But then the muddy bottom came up to greet Sonny as once again he tried to turn around in a limited amount of space, and could not.

* * *

I know my eyes are open. I can feel the heat and there's a glow of some kind, but where am I?

Matt pulled himself upright, using every bit of strength he could muster, wrapping his arms around the flat hose. The fog began to clear and his vision improved as he hung upright in the darkness trying to catch his breath. His heart was hammering. His head was reeling. Directly under him there was at least thirty feet of nothing before he hit bottom. If he landed wrong, he was dead. Even if he landed upright his legs would be broken and he'd lay there and boil in his own juices. He steeled himself and took a second wrap around the hose with his left hand. His right found his radio. He put it to his lips and depressed the button. *I need some help.*

"Mary," he said into the transmitter. His voice sounded like it was coming from another person. "You got your ears on?" He mouthed a silent prayer someone could hear him. With his body well underneath the waterline and surrounded by so much steel, he might not be broadcasting at all, or his signal would be so weak that a receiver had to be within a few hundred yards to pick up anything.

* * *

When Matt's voice skipped over the VHF radio, Mary had been tending *Skeleton*'s wheel, monitoring the autopilot and watching the weather. The rain had not abated, but the wind had come around another five degrees. It was almost due south now. But it wouldn't last. She reached out for the handset and turned down the squelch. The voice was weak, hardly recognizable.

"This is Mary. What's up, Matt? I can barely hear you."

"I'm in trouble, Mary. I need help." His voice swooped in and out like he was a hundred miles away.

"I think I got that. You're in trouble. I'm at the wheel, Matt, and we're outta guys. What happened?"

"I slipped and—No—" His voice clicked off.

"Matt?"

There was no response. Nothing.

"Matt? Matt!"

But Matt had dropped his radio.

*   *   *

He listened to it fall, bouncing off occasional obstacles on its way to the bottom landing and the bilge.

Now he was on his own. He had no choice but to try and climb hand-over-hand up the hose.

CHAPTER 65

Sonny was in trouble. He'd been able to turn around okay, finally, but he'd ripped the shoulder of his neoprene suit on a bolt that he hadn't seen until it was too late. He figured there must be an unused mounting bracket for hull zincs inside the sump. Then, as he was turning up under the corner of the hull and escaping the clutches of both the current and most of the mud, his weight belt caught on another zinc bolt, and he was pinned between the hull and the bottom, unable to get his hands around and unhook himself. *I need to be better. To be smarter. I'm goddamn scared.*

Deep inside the raw water inlet the primer cord burned closer and closer to the C-4 at the end of the spear. The charge was going to be powerful, about the same as three sticks of dynamite. And the pipe would funnel the charge fore and aft, up into the heat exchanger and down into the sump. There were only a couple minutes left.

* * *

Matt took his right hand and wrapped the wrist one time around the hose. He gripped the wrist with the left and pulled up, getting a few inches. He'd reclaimed most of what he'd lost in the fall, and was only a few feet from the deck and salvation. He was beginning to feel a little better. The sensation of roasting alive was dissipating. He looked up into the gloom, daring to believe he could make it . . .

... and saw the shape of a man silhouetted against the smoky pall.

He couldn't be sure, but he thought it was O'Connell. It looked like O'Connell. *What the hell? I'm dying and I see O'Connell?* And he reached up ...

... and lost his grip, falling through the dark, the big hose reestablishing itself and coming tight around his ankle once more, this time without any cushioning effect caused by the hose friction as it whipped away from its mount on the rear bulkhead. With the abrupt stop his knee felt like it had ripped apart. His hip rotated and the socket refused to expand, sending spikes of fire to his brain. His heart beat fast, blood pounding down and sheeting his face. He felt his forehead pulsing and felt blood pouring from his nose, the capillaries in his eyes exploding. He screamed, the pain taking control of his life. *There's someone down here and it looks like O'Connell, the only guy in the world who wants to kill me.* He passed out again.

* * *

Sonny ticked the seconds off in his mind. He had one minute, no more. He tried frantically to free his weight belt from the bolt, but the harder he struggled, the more the belt seemed to twist.

Fifty seconds. *I'm not good at this! My fingers aren't good at this!*

He went to his waist with his left hand and felt around for the latch, but it was an old-fashioned rig with pouches for the weights, and the latch was nothing more than an old buckle. Cowboy had tied it in a square knot to keep it on.

Thirty seconds. *My head is exploding. My ears are ringing. Stop the fucking gasping!*

He worked his fingers, trying to loosen the ends, pushing the webbing, trying to create a loop. But the current was making his body act as an underwater sail, putting tension on his hands, seating the knot.

Fifteen seconds. *I need to feel. I need to feel something fast.*

He ripped his gloves off, first the right, then the left. His wedding ring flew off his finger and fell away. Inside the pipe, the primer cord was only a foot from the explosive charge.

Ten . . . *My ring. I lost my fucking ring!*

Sonny had a dive knife on his calf. He reached down for it, but was unable to twist his body around. *Stuck. So you're stuck. Calm down!* He tried again, wrenching around painfully and losing one of his fins.

Five . . . *My fingers are working.*

He grabbed the handle of the knife.

The primer cord licked at the C-4.

. . . three . . . *Please*

. . . two . . . *just*

. . . one . . . *Do it!*

. . . and it blew, just as Sonny cut the belt loose and sprinted for the edge of the hull. He might have made three feet before the shock wave grabbed him and twisted him around. A payload of rocks and silt hit him head-on with such force that his mask shattered, filling with blood and knocking him unconscious.

Silence. *Too dark . . .*

Yet amid the roiling debris, his body twisted and his tanks clanged against the underside of the ship, pushing upwards, trying to equalize its new specific gravity without the weights. And his body followed the exploding gas bubbles to the edge of the ship and up, past his nitrogen stop, into the maelstrom at fifty feet, twisting away from the currents created by *Sharpe-Shooter*'s wheel water.

And up toward the surface.

* * *

In the Whaler, Cowboy sat in the chop and the rain waiting for Sonny to appear. He'd heard the explosion, like a small depth charge, except his captain was supposed to have been ahead of all that. Then he saw something floating twenty yards away and it didn't look good. He put the outboard in gear and sidled up to Sonny, slumped backwards over his tanks, his regulator destroyed, his vest in tatters, and his neoprene suit ripped, no gloves, one flipper. Cowboy leaned over the gunwale and grabbed Sonny by one of his armpits. As he held on, he stripped the tanks from Sonny and let them drift down. He put his other hand under his boss' torso and heaved. When he got him in the boat he turned him on his back. Sonny's shattered mask was full of blood, so he ripped it away and started CPR compressions as fast as he could. One minute went by. Then two and three. Cowboy began to feel the familiar anger that had dogged him all his life. He raged. He slapped his captain. He took Sonny by the shoulders and began to shake him as he screamed:

"Oh no you don't—no you fucking don't! Don't you fucking die on me!"

Sonny's eyes finally fluttered open. He tried to focus, but all he could see amid the sun spots was Cowboy's often-broken nose three inches from his face. His ears were ringing. His body felt like he had rolled down a mountain naked.

"Sonofabitch, you're ugly," he said, regurgitating water into Cowboy's face.

CHAPTER 66

INSIDE THE GREAT ship, O'Connell grunted as he retrieved another foot of fire hose. He reached down and took a fistful and dragged yet more of the hose up onto the landing, putting a wrap on the rail so he wouldn't lose anything. Over and over he repeated the process, keeping an eye on Matt's form as he slowly materialized from out of the gloom. When Matt's boot appeared over the lip of the steel decking, O'Connell reached down and grabbed him by the seat of his pants. He ignored the screams as he wrestled him onto the landing. For three minutes neither of them moved or said a word.

Finally, when the pounding in his head began to subside, Matt groaned and began to take in great lungfuls of air.

"You alright?" O'Connell said.

"Yeah," said Matt. "Except my nose hemorrhaged, my ass is killing me, my knee's gonna need reconstruction, and my foot is blue from the fire hose. Other than that I'm just dandy. What are you doing here?"

"Mary was scared. She sent me over to find you. Nobody else would have known where to look." O'Connell tried to smile. He wrapped his hand around a VHF radio he'd clipped to his belt, slipped it from its sheath, and handed it over to Matt. "You ought to call her and let her know you're okay. You are okay, aren't you?"

Suddenly the VHF crackled on. Sonny's voice echoed from the speaker. "Matt, you there?"

"I'm here now, Sonny. What you need?"

"The sea suction is clear, we think. Is that core cooling down?"

Matt fumbled in his pocket for a minute before remembering that he'd tied the remote sensor to a belt loop. He examined the readout and smiled. He pushed the talk button. "It's cooling, sir. Uh, Sonny. We're back down to one-fifty."

Sonny's voice sounded relieved. "Okay, then. You and O'Connell jump in the *Sharpe-Shooter*'s Zode and get your asses back here. We need all hands."

O'Connell and Matt exchanged looks. For a week there had been no love lost between the two, yet now, maybe because of Mary, O'Connell had saved Matt's bacon. Somehow they were tied together—reluctant partners. So what should Matt expect in the next few minutes?

Does O'Connell want forgiveness? If he does, he's come to the wrong place.

CHAPTER 67

TEN MINUTES LATER, O'Connell and Matt stepped onto the last riser and emerged from the shadows onto *Bennkah*'s deck. Matt was limping badly. They would have to climb over the rail, go down the Jacob's ladder, and jump into the Zodiac that O'Connell had tied up earlier. The wind had not decreased—if anything, it was stronger—and the rain was still coming down in furious waves. Matt's internal thermostat was out of sync, but the water actually felt warmer than it did a few hours ago. There was less ice. The front from Japan had taken control now and even though the winds were howling, the temperatures seemed to be moderating a bit.

Matt wiped the rain from his face and took a few steps toward the rail. He turned around and squinted into the falling water. O'Connell wasn't there. He turned back and yelled over the drum-roll noises emanating from the steel deck. He found O'Connell gazing out at the rain-shrouded ocean as if he could see something. He was standing at the lip of the massive hole they'd just crawled out of, leaning against a loading davit that *Bennkah*'s crew must have once used to load and unload equipment down into the depths.

Matt stepped up to within a few feet of the man and planted his feet. The noise of the rain was deafening. He spread his arms in a questioning gesture. "Let's go, man."

"Y'know," shouted O'Connell over the rain, "my wife, she's a big ol' gal." He seemed to grope for the next sentence. "And she ain't the prettiest thing in the world. Got some bulldog in her. But she's the only one who ever cared for me. For that, I love her through and through."

Matt cleared his throat. *What is he doing this for? To me? I'm the guy he hates.*

O'Connell had to raise his voice even higher to be heard over the rain. "Tell her I said so," he exclaimed.

"Tell her yourself," Matt said. He turned to go. Again, O'Connell didn't follow. Matt turned around. "What are you doing? And get away from that hole, man," he bellowed.

O'Connell continued, as if he knew Matt would come back and listen to his words. "Tell Sonny my real name is Cobb. Terry Cobb. I'm wanted in Texas for DUI manslaughter." He squinted into the pelting rain. "I was drunk. Ran down a cop. You think I'm an ass-hole now, you should have seen me back then." O'Connell's attempt at confession fell flat. "So anyway, Dal Sharpe knows cops. Does favors for them. He sniffed around and dug up my sheet. After that he wouldn't let me alone." O'Connell reached into his pocket and retrieved a cell phone. He tossed it to Matt. "Give that to Sonny. There's some text messages. He'll know what to do with 'em."

Matt looked at the phone in his hand. He wiped it off and stuck it into his pants pocket, then he nodded to O'Connell. He didn't know what to say.

"You're okay, kid. You know that?" said O'Connell.

Matt stood there before the man who had just saved his life, rain pouring down his body. "You say that now."

"Aw, hell. I don't expect you to forgive me. I don't expect anyone to. There's no forgiving what I done. I kept thinking if I could get something out of this, you know? A few bucks somehow, I could gather my old lady and we could disappear." He paused, wiped the rain from his face with his left hand. His eyes were closed. The timbre of his voice fell and the volume dropped to nothing. "There's no forgiving what I done, though. That's the truth."

"Guess you're just gonna have to live with it."

O'Connell raised his head and opened his eyes. "That's just it. I don't think I can."

Then he smiled with his lips open wide—a sad display meant for no one, the rain pouring into his mouth and eyes, parting his ginger hair and turning it into slick ringlets, water running down his chest and stomach, pouring off him in cataracts. "So long, kid." And then the darkness reached out and collected him as his feet pushed off backwards, sending him plummeting headlong into the abyss, a vertical corridor of steel and depth and nothing, plummeting headlong, an escape from the shame, from his wife's disappointment, from the world. No more Dal Sharpe, no more looking over his shoulder, no more fear, falling into a reward of sorts for all his failings. And a fall that released him from the disgrace of Sonny's forgiveness . . .

. . . or the crew's understanding.

Matt shouted as he groped for O'Connell at the edge of the drop, before his hands made contact with the rail. He stared into the dark hole. He heard no sounds, no shouts, no scream, nothing but the wind and the rain. All he could feel was shock. Then anger: "Fuck!"

The rain fell sideways. Rivers of water ran over the deck. Matt leaned down, trying not to bend his bad knee, and retrieved O'Connell's hat. He went to the edge of the ship and sailed it out over the ocean, then he climbed over the rail and down the ropes to the Zodiac.

CHAPTER 68

MARY'S HANDS GRIPPED the wheel as she watched two small blips on *Skeleton*'s radar. They were barely discernible amid the clutter of rain and seas, but she knew that Cowboy and her dad were coming in the Whaler, and Matt was piloting the Zode. It was now or never, but she didn't want to put the pedal to the medal until they climbed aboard. With all the wheel water the engines would generate, she could drown them. She hit the toggle on the deck intercom.

"Manny, you still on the rear deck?"

"Yeah, Mar. I'm headed back down into the engine room now."

"Wait a second, just long enough to let me know when my dad and his company are aboard."

"Will do. I think I see them through the rain. They're less than a hundred yards away."

"Are they both sitting up?"

"Yeah."

A minute later Sonny and Matt both climbed aboard. While Cowboy motored away in the Whaler, Manny gave Mary the word. She spoke into the VHF handset with a ragged voice that displayed the tension she was feeling. Her voice had somehow gone hoarse during her father's dive.

"Let's go, boys. Mush time. Kick those dogs, as my dad would say." Then she took both controls and pushed them all the way forward. *Skeleton*'s stern sank down a foot as she got purchase, then she leaped ahead and the towing hawser slowly came tight once more, lifting the stern as the five-bladed, six-foot screws dug in.

At *Bennkah*, Brooks put all of *Sharpe-Shooter*'s thirty thousand horses on the table again, pushing at *Bennkah*'s starboard bow. The wind had steadied out at due south, the perfect angle to unseat the hull, providing they could put enough power to bear.

Skeleton's port side wheelhouse door swung open and Sonny and Matt rushed in, Sonny still in his neoprene, Matt limping badly. They were both soaking wet. "I got this," Sonny said, and grabbed the wheel and the throttles from Mary's hands.

"About time," she said. "I thought you guys ran out on me."

In the Whaler, Cowboy had dropped back to do engineer duty, inspecting the towing assembly and the anchor chain from under *Bennkah*'s bow. Galloping over the white water, he put his boat in position and looked up into the rain, wiping away the water from his eyes. The chain had been tight when *Skeleton* began her charge a minute ago, but now there was an obvious sag. The opposite was true of the hawser. He pulled the Whaler ahead fifty yards and looked back and up. In the gloom he could see a trio of figures taking up the slack on the chain using the walk-around capstan. Tick was doing his job.

Suddenly Sonny broke through on the VHF. "Cowboy, get your ass on one of the tugs. Get away from that hawser. Who's on the *Bennkah*'s bow?"

Tick answered before Cowboy could get to his radio. "That's me, Boss. I'm still here. And we're getting some slack on this big ol' chain. We're walking it up as we speak, praise Jah." At his feet in the alcove beside the anchor room, a nine-pound maul lay ready. He would grab it on command and knock the huge locking pin free, scuttling the anchor chain and freeing *Bennkah* to follow her tow. "Say the word, the dog is done," he said.

"Okay, Tick. Praise Jah," said Sonny. "Whatever that means."

"All the help you can get," said Mary, standing in the darkness beside her dad. "And how do you like that wind now?"

Sonny turned and grinned at her and Matt, who was standing behind both of them. "I think we figured it right," he said. "I'm on a heading of about three hundred degrees and Frank is pushing the bow around at two seventy. Between us, *Bennkah* should come free."

Over the radio he said, "Okay, folks, we're all tight. Let's move this ship. Frank, don't let up even for a second. I need all you got. Put the children overboard and make 'em kick if you have to."

Mary tapped her dad on the shoulder. "I'm going aft to see how Manny's doing."

"Stay away from that cable, kid. If she parts anywhere near us, her weight won't be enough to slow her. She'll ride this train across the deck and take out everything in her path."

"I know, Pop."

"Just so you do."

Lightning rent the sky and thunder roared over the Goliath tanker. Rain came down in blinding layers and wind gusting to forty and forty-five turned the seas white. The world was sideways, with the ship's stacks black-smoking and sparking, metal groaning with the strain of the hawser and of *Sharpe-Shooter's* push-pit bow digging into high steel sides. But still, *Bennkah* refused to be shoved from her trough.

"I got nothing!" shouted Brooks into his mike. "Nothing but water!"

"Keep 'em digging, goddamnit."

"I got nothing, Sonny!"

"It's now or never, Frank," bellowed Sonny. "Keep—those—wheels—digging!"

* * *

Deep under the water, just aft of midships, the gash in the ship's hull began to cavitate. Mud boiled up from under her bottom . . .

. . . and still she didn't budge.

CHAPTER 69

WATER-SOAKED, MARY SLOSHED up the port rail and took the stairs up to the wheelhouse landing. She opened the door and stuck her head inside. "Manny's in the engine room. Cowboy's on the stern, Dad," she reported. "He says the king post is starting to bend. And, oh yeah, the Whaler is awash back there."

"Speak up, child," shouted Sonny. "I can't hear you."

She pushed her way inside and slammed the door. "I said . . . the Whaler's awash in our wheel water and the towing steel is about to rip up the deck and take it all south. Not to worry, though, Dad. The Navy's on the way. Be here in two shakes, or maybe days!"

"Shut up, Daughter."

In a minute Cowboy stumbled up into the wheelhouse. He'd come through the galley, leaving a trail of water. "Hey, kids." He scanned the gauges on the wheel bench. "Don't look now, but those Cats are at two hundred degrees and rising."

"Maybe you go down and piss on 'em, cowpoke," said Sonny. "But we're firing 'til they blow. The black smoke has turned to white, so I'm thinkin' they're getting used to the load. Engines are funny that way."

The VHF sputtered and popped. "Still not moving, Sonny," growled Brooks. "We need more horses."

Sonny flipped the intercom switch to the engine room. Down

below, in front of Manny, a strobe light flashed on the forward bulkhead and he took his ear protectors off in time to hear, "Yank those governors, Manny!"

"Aw, Skip—"

Cowboy exchanged looks with Matt and Mary.

"Do it, Manny! Yank 'em now! And don't give me any of that 'Ahab' crap!"

Manny began to whistle as he put his ear protectors back on. An old superstition says that only the captain is allowed to whistle on a vessel at sea. Otherwise you could whistle up the wind. But Manny didn't see it that way. It was already blowing a gale, and no one could hear a thing in the engine room, anyway. By the time he finished the first chorus of *Rancho Grande* he'd removed both shims from in front of the breathers mounted on top of the engines. He shouted into the intercom, "Go for it, Skipper. I'll start going through the inventory for engine parts."

Everyone standing in the wheelhouse held their breaths as Sonny pushed the throttles past their stops. They could hear the RPMs ramping up. The turbo chargers began to screech.

"Oh damn," said Cowboy, "I don't know, Sonny—"

Sonny interrupted. "Yeah, well, I do." His jaw was set, his eyes straight ahead. A joke was okay sometimes, but not as a condition of failure. This was on him. This was his *real* make or break time; not that underwater stuff. It might be his swan song, too, but maybe not. Maybe he would win one. He looked down at his ring finger. The white skin where his wedding ring had been was crinkled from being immersed. *You gotta keep trying.* Because if failure was going to be his legacy, he wasn't going down without trying everything in the book. *I've been too damn easy on everything and everybody, and maybe just a little too hard on myself.*

Sonny blinked. The engines were screaming, but still *Bennkah* balked. *Get your game on!* Then he noticed something. The rain seemed to be letting up. There was a break in the cloud cover, just enough for him to see something in the distance that wasn't supposed to be there...

... but there it was again, off to his starboard, pitching up and down, side to side, a set of running lights that looked an awful lot like *Bones'* configuration. He knew the pattern well. Every captain knew his own boat at night. And on *Bones*, on top of the A-frame, there was a mast light and the glass lens had broken a year or so ago, the last time Tick had changed the bulb. He'd climbed down off the rig and run into the galley, and found an amber jar by the coffeepot. It was full of powdered creamer, but Tick had dumped it out and soon the jar had replaced the broken lens.

And there, three hundred yards away, was *Bones*, amber Cremora jar still glowing, steaming toward them as hard as she could go.

Sonny put his big spotlight on the intruder.

The VHF boomed. "Hey, Sonny, it's me! Jimmy! Jimmy Reston! What'chu need, Big Dog? A little help?"

Jimmy Reston? Jimmy with the wife and kids in the pickup truck and the fishing boat covered in mud at the wharf? Jimmy Reston, who only had two thousand dollars until spring?

Sonny grinned from ear to ear, never happier to hear someone in his whole life. "Understatement of the year, my man. And, Jimmy, have I told you lately that I love you?"

"Just last week, in your own sweet way. Now, where do you want this old nasty boat of yours?"

"Careful, now, Jimmy. *Bones* has feelings," said Sonny.

CHAPTER 70

"BUT PUT HER on the bow of this big ship you're looking at, Jimmy, shoulder to shoulder with *Sharpe-Shooter*. Now. And don't be shy when you use the throttle. Hit her hard, give it everything you got."

"Roger that."

Brooks broke in. "My engines are getting hot, Sonny."

"Keep those things walking, Frank. We're almost there."

Jimmy turned *Bones* to port and followed the tow line almost all the way to *Bennkah* before he made a wide circle and brought her up next to the bigger tug. He stuck *Bones'* bow fenders into the side of *Bennkah*. "I'm on 'er, Sonny," he said.

Sonny clicked his mike. "Attaboy, Jimmy. Now let those horses loose!"

Bones was only a single-screw, but her engine could develop eight hundred horsepower in a pinch. Jimmy slammed the throttle full forward and held his ears.

Now three boats gave it everything. *Bennkah* sat mired in the mud for five, then eight, then ten long minutes, props churning, water foaming, wind from the south at forty knots, everything conspiring to make something happen.

"C'mon, *Skelly*," Sonny whispered to his boat, "you can do it." He sneaked a look at the framed photo of his ex. She was still smiling out at him through the scotch-taped glass. *You should be here,*

*right here, so you could hear the engines hammering and see the water
churning and feel the power, and maybe understand a few things
about effort, about how hard I worked for you. For Mary. For us.*

But you're not here.

You'll never be here.

He checked his gauges. The steel under his feet was beginning to
vibrate with a harmonic resonance unsettling. His boat was beginning to fall apart with the strain.

*   *   *

Mary stood at Sonny's shoulder, watching the gauges climb, refusing to say anything, no complaining, no bitching. She turned back
and gave Matt a strained smile that never climbed past the tip of
her nose.

*   *   *

Cowboy, too, was listening, watching the gauges, feeling the strain,
praying for a break. He started to say something, but was cut short
by Manny on the back deck intercom:

"Hey! Hey! Hey! We're—"

*   *   *

And with a monumental lurch the Bennkah *rises, her huge bow ten,
twenty, then forty feet past her waterline, water cascading down the
sides as tons and tons of steel climb up and glide off the bottom in a
surreal, slow-motion pantomime that releases several million pounds
of torque and energy into the boundless sea as . . .*

. . . the Skeleton's *stern is lifted fully out of the water and the hawser*

comes apart, both ends whipsawing in fatal arcs, one sharded end across the stern of Skeleton, *the other over the bow of the Goliath of the sea.*

* * *

And as the huge steel-and-poly hawser came from out of the mists, right at the quartet of men on *Bennkah's* bow, one of them, Tick, ignored the danger and grabbed his hammer. He had been waiting for this moment. "Yes, Jah," he said to himself. He gripped the handle with both hands and reared back and swung with everything he had. The nine-pound maul went around in a wide arc and connected perfectly with its target . . .

* * *

. . . and the crews on *Sharpe-Shooter* and on *Bones*, and the guys all the way out on *Skeleton* could hear Tick's bloodcurdling scream as the hawser slashed across and the dog was dispatched and the anchor chain fell into the sea.

PART V

CHAPTER 71

Near Dutch Harbor
DECEMBER 1, MORNING

THE CLOUDS OVERHEAD scattered to the four corners just after dawn, when a fluid sun appeared three points north of east, peeking over the snow-clad mountains of mainland Alaska. The wind had abated, the seas were calm. To the west, gulls squabbled and another trio of pelicans skimmed the water in front of a peach and lavender sky.

Sonny was at *Skeleton*'s wheel, giving instructions on the radio. Behind him, in tow, was the largest ship ever built, escorted by *Sharpe-Shooter* and *Bones*, whose captains and crews had decided to help bring the monster in.

If Sonny cast his eyes ahead a few miles, he could discern the silhouette of Dutch Harbor, with the white church steeple poking up over the rest of the town and the red and white range-finder tower on the high bluff, marking the channel from the sea buoy in. A group of small boats, maybe fifty or so, floated in the waters north of the harbor—a greeting committee lining up to welcome Sonny and his crew with *Bennkah*.

Squatting among them was a U.S. Navy warship, just now deploying its launch.

Sonny had only been at the wheel for an hour. Mary and Matt and Cowboy had let him sleep until such time as he was needed. Exhausted, Sonny had gone to bed at midnight.

When Mary woke him, he lurched to a sitting position. His face was crisscrossed with sweat and the pillow he'd been lying on was soaked. He sat on the edge of the bed for a time, clearing the cobwebs. He got up and dressed and stepped lightly to the wheelhouse. "Coffee, Mary. I need coffee."

An hour later Sonny had forgotten all about the bad dreams he'd experienced through the night. It looked like the whole town had come out in boats. And in the cozy wheelhouse, Mary, Matt, and Cowboy stood by to help him enjoy the moment.

"How'd you know to use a jump line, Dad?" said Mary.

"Everybody knows," he said. "It's common sense. Put the heat on the main cable with the bridle, let the jump line grab what's left." He turned and looked at Matt. "Right, Matt?"

Matt shrugged. "Uh, yeah. Of course." He smiled at Mary and winked.

Cowboy rolled his eyes and barked like a dog.

"How's Tick doing?" said Sonny.

"He lost a finger," said Cowboy. "One lousy finger. Two hundred feet of six-inch hawser bulldogged over his head and our resident klepto Rastafarian ducked and pounded the anchor dog with his hammer, and the recoil took his pinkie."

"You gotta love irony. Where's Manny?"

Matt answered. "Working on the Whaler now, cleaning the salt out of her engine. Earlier he took a couple guys and pulled O'Connell out. They shut the hatches to that area. When we got to deep water they flooded it. *Bennkah* is riding below eighty feet again, but the nuclear box is cool."

"The Lucky Diamond tug crew said they collected more than thirty bodies from the Inuit guys," said Sonny. "They never got an actual count. The corpses were too burnt up. Just bones and rags."

"It's sad, Pop. But not our affair. Especially now," said Mary.

"They never even knew they were an atomic pile surrounded by oil. They probably just thought it was a job like any other."

"Another sea story," said Cowboy.

Sonny took a deep breath. Exhaled, decompressing. For the first time in a while, he was starting to feel okay about things. "That's just . . . really good," he said, smiling to his companions. He looked down at the photo of his ex-wife. Mary followed his eyes and sidled up to him. She rubbed his back tenderly.

"Question," she said.

"Shoot."

Mary hesitated for a moment. "Did Mom know you weren't to blame?"

A long beat passed.

"Yes."

"And still she bailed," said Mary. It wasn't a question. Sonny looked at her. Mary stumbled and turned away. She seemed like she wanted to say something, to rant and rave. But instead she turned back and smiled and went down the companionway to the galley. Cowboy followed her, too uncomfortable to remain in the wheelhouse.

Sonny stood with Matt, face forward, silent, watching the U.S. Navy launch get closer and closer. They both looked like they'd gone twelve rounds with Mike Tyson. Sonny picked up the photo of Judy. He looked at her picture one last time, before he opened the door and sailed it like a Frisbee out into the water. It skipped like a flat stone a few times, then sank to the bottom forever.

The cabin was quiet for a minute. "Guess that's why they call you Skipper," said Matt.

"Good one, kid."

"Nah." Matt reached into his shirt and retrieved something, tossed it to Sonny, who caught it in his right hand.

"But this is. A memento . . . for a job well done."

A big smile spread across Sonny's face as he stared down at a scarred-but-operative Vladimir Putin bobble-head doll. He set it on the wheel bench where the framed photo of his wife used to be.

He looked up and out. Nothing more needed to be said.

CHAPTER 72

TWO HOURS LATER *Skeleton* and the other boats finally finished what they'd started with *Bennkah*. She'd had no anchor so they positioned her with the help of some town boats and tied *Sharpe-Shooter* to her port side amidships. When Brooks sank his boat's spud anchors into the bottom, the giant tanker was temporarily stationary. A lot of oil was going to be pumped off in the next few days, so a more permanent anchor rig would have to be found.

Skeleton and *Bones* were also moored to the side of the great ship, ready to accept company from the U. S. Navy. The launch came alongside and tied off on her rail. Admiral Harry Stinson, Commander of the Pacific Fleet, was first to board. He found Sonny among the crew, smiled broadly, took Sonny's hand and shook it.

"Sonny Wade, you sonofabitch, how the hell are you?"

The warm greeting relieved Sonny. "I'm fine, sir. Surprised you remembered me."

"How could I forget? If you'd learned to roll with the punches, you'd be commanding the SEALS by now. It's a damn shame you left the Navy, son."

"I didn't leave the Navy, Admiral. It left me."

Stinson regarded Sonny for a moment, measuring his words. Finally, "I wouldn't touch that remark with a ten-foot pole," he said with a hint of a grin and mischievous glint in his eye.

By now everybody had gathered in the wardroom to hear what Admiral Harry Stinson had to say. He was a large man with a squashed nose that had seen more than one bar fight in more than one bar. And he wasn't the kind of man to stand on ceremony. "You guys sure did bite the shit sandwich, didn't you?" he began. "Goddamn but that was a ballsy job. Might get dinner at the White House for that one."

Tick scratched himself. "I'll have to buy some underwear."

"Shut up, Tick," said Mary.

The admiral accepted a cup of coffee from Matt, two sugars, and one jigger. He sat in the proffered chair at the foot of the table. "So here's what's going on," he said. "There's a bunch of angry idiots in Congress that want my guys to tow this thing back to Russia, drop it on their doorstep. Someone, maybe you, Captain Wade, if they call you up, will have to tell them that in addition to the oil, all this Russian steel is technically the property of Skeleton Salvage." He took a sip of his coffee, grimaced appreciatively, and smiled. "The UN has issued one of those worthless censures they do, which should please you to no end. When you talk to the press, though, it should make your nads curl up and hide. He shot everyone in the room a look of warning that said, *Watch yourself with those guys. They're experts at getting you to say things you don't mean.*

"And oh yeah, there's supposed to be a meeting of the big boys at The Hague this week. No doubt Russia will call us all liars and you guys will be *agents provocateurs*. So steer clear of Moscow or anywhere that serves borscht for that matter if you're planning a little R & R in the next few weeks."

Sonny removed his hat and gingerly wiped his bruised face. "I think we'll beg off on all that stuff, if you don't mind, Admiral. Our dance card is punched out. And we've got to watch some oil being pumped, and I'll have to supervise the re-ballasting so that you can do what you're gonna do with the radioactive stuff. I'd also like to get these guys some rest."

"I can imagine. We'll take it from here, then. I've got ground tackle and a spud barge coming. We'll anchor *Bennkah* right here for the time being." He sipped his coffee again and set the cup on the table.

"Good deal," said Cowboy. "*Sharpe-Shooter*'s our temporary anchor. She has to get going."

"I've talked to my engineers. We'll put a pump on that heat exchanger this afternoon. Then you can organize your oil pumpers. When you get some real rest, Captain Wade, you'll have to be debriefed. The witness to the suicide will be available, I take it. And someone with badges and guns will want any other facts about this case. The feds are upset with everyone but you, by the way. They could have been assholes about things and found something to fuss with you about, but the press is already calling you the savior of the Pacific Ocean, so a little bird from the Pentagon told them to lay off. The Atomic Energy Commission is sending a quartet of bureaucrats to display outrage for Fox News."

"Dutch Harbor's a friendly place," said Sonny. "But it's fixing to get pretty cold around here, so the press won't hang around long. Our only motel has twelve units."

"We can set up cots and a soup line in the fish house," said Manny.

"Think warm thoughts," counseled Tick. His t-shirt said *Can you take the Big Bamboo*?

CHAPTER 73

ALMOST TWENTY-FOUR HOURS later, Sonny sat across from Frank Brooks on *Sharpe-Shooter* to thank him for his help. The big salvager would be heading out within the hour, so they were alone in the modern, beautifully appointed galley, a bottle of Haitian rum and two glasses on the table in front of them.

Sonny said, "Your life is about to go belly-up for a while, Frank. You know that, right?"

"That's alright." He lifted one of the glasses to his lips and drank. "I could use a change of scenery. I'm sure Sharpe has found a replacement for me already."

Sonny sipped his rum. "I wouldn't worry too much about that. The FBI has taken an interest in some phone records. Don't be surprised if the U. S. Marshal tags this big ol' girl of yours when you get her to Anchorage. They might want to know what you know. They might want to make a deal."

Brooks said, "Do you know Sharpe's story? Do you know how he got all this stuff?"

"I never paid much attention," said Sonny.

"As a kid he was nobody. Lived in a tin-roofed, plywood house on a gravel road outside of Seattle. Then he joined the Navy. Sixteen years later he gets his Honorable and gets himself involved in some shit. There's some old federal documents, I saw the copies. They explain he was busted in a scheme to steal sixty tons of copper from the naval docks down in Portland. But instead of going to jail, he became a federal witness and ratted out all his people, and also all the naval personnel that were going to let it happen. It was a big scandal. His reward for being such a pillar of righteousness was they cleaned up his record and let him keep all the money he'd accrued as a supply officer in the Navy. I don't think they know, but it was over six hundred thousand dollars. So our pal Dal Sharpe knows something about being a weasel. Don't underestimate him."

* * *

A few hundred miles away, on the top floor of Sharpe Salvage Inc., Dal Sharpe was busy feeding the paper shredder in his office. He wasn't looking out his big window when six FBI agents drove up, parked, got out of their black sedans, and entered the building with guns drawn. Earlier, during their initial briefing, the agents had been told that the man they were going to arrest might be armed. They were told he could be dangerous. They were told to secure the top floor until it could be searched for evidence. They were told that he had been a government snitch in the past, so was a consummate liar and all around sneaky bastard.

CHAPTER 74

"But I don't want to go," said Sonny.

"You have to go. The party's for you," said Mary, pulling on her dad's arm. "So get dressed. And wear a shirt with a collar. The governor is out there, and the mayor, and the commander of the Coasties, and a bunch of people from town, along with some reporters who'll take your picture with all those bruises on your face. You need a haircut."

Sonny got to his feet and began to dress. "I didn't sign up for this."

"Yes you did, actually. The day you had me call Maggie."

Fifteen minutes later Sonny stood on the dock, embarrassed, as a crowd of cheering fans welcomed him into their bosom. The governor gave a speech, the mayor gave him the keys to the city, Larry Punkin Johns finally shook his hand, and the Coast Guard commander slapped him on the back. His crew offered him drinks.

Sonny was polite yet unimpressed, until the crowd parted and Maggie materialized, smiling, beautiful, her auburn hair flying away with the breeze. *She looks good. Real good.*

"Hi, Mags."

"Shut up, sailor," she said, putting her arms around him, kissing him on the lips.

Sonny turned red. *I'm outta my league.*

Then they kissed again. And the crowd cheered their approval.

* * *

Behind them Matt and Mary stood together, grinning. Matt looked at Mary and arched his eyebrows.

"Don't get any ideas, bub," she said.

Matt squinted and turned away. He started to back up.

"I'm kidding, I'm kidding!" Then Mary Wade reached out and grabbed Matt's shoulders.

"Uh—"

"Shhhh," she said now, her lips and inch from his. Then her lips connected with Matt's. She leaned into him and suddenly the gulf between them fell away. When their lips parted, she brought her mouth to his ear and said, "Thank you. For everything."

When they separated she said, "Did I ever tell you you've got nice eyes? Even when they're bruised as hell."

CHAPTER 75

THAT EVENING MARY was sitting at home, unwinding with a larg-er-than-usual glass of Pinot, waiting for Matt to pick her up in his beat-to-hell Ford F-150. They were headed to the local pizza parlor for their first date and although she might never admit it, she was as excited as a schoolgirl. Suddenly her cell phone rang. She rec-ognized the Seattle area code and frowned. She let it ring a while, thinking. Finally she picked it up and put it to her ear. "Hello?"

A hesitant voice said, "Hello, Mary."

When Mary didn't respond, the voice said, "Are you going to say hi? This is your mother, Mary. I've missed you."

There was a long, pregnant pause. Mary took a breath, then clicked the phone off and put it back down on the kitchen counter. Gently but firmly.

* * *

Maggie awoke to the sonorous eight bells that signified the time. Eight o'clock in the morning. She hadn't slept that long since God-knows-when. She rubbed her eyes and looked across the little room and found the brass chronometer on the wall. It was old, but some-body, probably Sonny, had polished it. It was German. "Schatz" was printed on the face. Directly underneath was an old barometer, also polished. There was a steamer trunk on the floor, recently varnished by someone, probably Sonny. She felt the hum of the generator. And there was the rich smell of brewing coffee wafting down the companionway. She sat up and the blanket fell away and the memories of last night came flooding in. Good memories. Not love. Not yet. But maybe.

He's a good guy. A great guy, actually. A keeper. And here I am in his bunk, naked, unashamed. And I haven't been with a man in so long, especially one that understands a woman with a career. And the wall next to my head is gray steel and no, it's not the Four Seasons or the Ritz-Carlton, but I love it.

A girl could get used to this.

And there's a port in this gray steel wall and look, it's actually snowing outside. The little bar across the wharf has lights around the window. Christmas lights? Already? Of course.

Maggie stood and dressed and went down the companionway to the galley to behold a bare-chested Sonny, standing at the stove in his Levis and boat shoes trying to separate bacon slices for the frying pan. A carton of eggs was on the counter. He'd pulled a toaster from one of the lockers, but hadn't plugged it in yet.

"The coffee smells heavenly."

"One hundred percent Kona. I've been saving it for a special occasion. I'd say this qualifies," he said. His hands appeared thick-fingered and clumsy as he fumbled with the bacon. It was clear he was not used to cooking.

"Maybe you should let me do that," she said.

He turned around, smiled, and shrugged. "I was hoping you'd say that."

"Really? Then kiss me," she said, "so I know you really mean it."

And he did.

When they parted, he said, "Maggie, I don't really know what to say—"

"Then let's not say anything. Let's just eat. And go back to bed."

* * *

Hours later, Sonny was helping her with her bags and driving her to the airstrip, where the Lloyd's Lear jet was waiting. On the gravel runway, she hugged him one last time.

She said, "I feel awful. But I gotta run. You know the drill." He nodded and dug his hands deep in his pockets. He was hoping for more somehow. "The upside, though, is now you have an excuse to visit the Bay Area." She winked and he smiled.

"I would love that. Swan Oyster Depot still packing them in?"

"Every day but Sunday."

"Gee, what do we do on Sunday?" he asked, eyes twinkling.

She snorted.

"Okay, count me in," he said.

Just then her cell pinged. Another text message had arrived. She read it. Then studied Sonny's face. "Quick question, Sonny. How do you feel about Morocco?"

"You kidding? Marrakesh? Casablanca? I had a goat tagine in Fez that I still dream about. I'm ready when you are."

"Think your crew will feel the same way?"

"My crew goes where I go. 'Sides, it might be a while before we get paid from this last fiasco. You know how the feds are." He tilted his head, curious. "Why? You got a gig for us, Maggie?"

She smiled. "Stay tuned, Sonny," she said, pointing at her text message. "The world is an enigma. I might need you."

"I'm here, Maggie. Call any time. I'm here for you."

She kissed him again. When they parted, she put her hands to his face tenderly, turned, and climbed into the jet.

CPSIA information can be obtained
at www.ICGtesting.com
Printed in the USA
BVOW08*0333220217
476804BV00001B/1/P

603-8444

1